A
DEADLY
BONE
TO PICK

**PEGGY
ROTHSCHILD**

BERKLEY PRIME CRIME

New York

BERKLEY PRIME CRIME
Published by Berkley
An imprint of Penguin Random House LLC
penguinrandomhouse.com

ISBN: 9780593437100

The Library of Congress has cataloged the
Berkley Prime Crime hardcover edition of this book as follows:

Names: Rothschild, Peggy, author.
Title: A deadly bone to pick / Peggy Rothschild.
Description: New York: Berkley Prime Crime, [2022] | Series:
A Molly Madison mystery; 1
Identifiers: LCCN 2021031209 (print) | LCCN 2021031210 (ebook) |
ISBN 9780593437087 (hardcover) | ISBN 9780593437094 (ebook)
Subjects: LCGFT: Detective and mystery fiction. | Cozy mysteries. | Novels.
Classification: LCC PS3618.O86874 D43 2022 (print) |
LCC PS3618.O86874 (ebook) | DDC 813/.6—dc23
LC record available at https://lccn.loc.gov/2021031209
LC ebook record available at https://lccn.loc.gov/2021031210

Berkley Prime Crime hardcover edition / February 2022
Berkley Prime Crime trade paperback edition / January 2023

Printed in the United States of America
1st Printing

Book design by George Towne

PRAISE FOR *A DEADLY BONE TO PICK*

"Flawless and descriptive writing frames an enviable beach community where ex-cop Molly Madison is determined to start a new life."

—*New York Times* bestselling author Krista Davis

"Mystery fans and animal lovers alike will delight in this caper about a straight-shooting ex-cop turned dog-wrangling sleuth. With Rothschild's deft plotting, a sweeping cast of quirky characters, and an endearing canine duo, this is a book worth barking about."

—Tessa Wegert, author of *Death in the Family*

"*A Deadly Bone to Pick* is a smart, solid mystery that fans of Sue Grafton's Kinsey Millhone will enjoy."

—Olivia Blacke, author of *Killer Content*

"A delightful beachy mystery that's gone to the dogs! Peggy Rothschild's debut is a tight and twisty tale featuring my favorite kind of support team: an adorable duo on four paws that gives the phrase 'a nose for crime' new meaning."

—Victoria Schade, author of *Who Rescued Who*

"Smart. Fun. Furry! Murder abounds and clues are buried deep in this whodunit. . . . It's doggone good!"

—Abby Collette, author of *Body and Soul Food*

"Readers won't have any bones to pick with Peggy Rothschild's debut mystery, *A Deadly Bone to Pick*, which delivers a delicious puzzle while also providing a wealth of dog-training tricks."

—Lauren Baratz-Logsted and Jackie Logsted,
authors of *Joint Custody*

"Rothschild's twisty mystery, filled with adorable canines and abundant clues, is plain paw-some."

—Jennifer J. Chow, author of *Mimi Lee Cracks the Code*

For Richard,
who never wants to know how the story ends,
but brings unending support and enthusiasm to the journey

CHAPTER 1

"Please be careful with that." I winced as the two muscle-bound men, dressed in matching navy-blue uniforms, wrestled the antique ship captain's desk through the front door. "It was my great-grandfather's." In reality, it had belonged to something like my great-great-great-great-grandfather. But why would they care? Nor would they care that Mom insisted I take the desk—part of a misguided effort to show she believed I'd move back to Massachusetts one day.

My golden retriever, Harlow, tail waving, practically vibrated with her desire to meet these potential new friends.

"Stay." As much as I expected every person to love my dog, this was not the time. Ever obedient, she settled onto the travertine tile.

"Where do you want it?" Muscle Man Number One said.

"On the second floor. Here, I'll show you." The front door stood wide open. I looked back at Harlow and told her to stay again, then led the way up the broad staircase. I hoped my few possessions all made it safely inside. But, even if they didn't, nothing here was irreplaceable.

I wanted this move to work out. No, not wanted. Needed. I needed this move to work out. My gaze blurred. I wiped my eyes and hustled to the landing.

When I reached the hall, I hesitated. Was I sure I wanted to use the ocean-facing room for my office? The alley-facing room to the left would offer morning light. Shaking my head, I entered the first door on the right side of the hall. It didn't matter where I put the antique desk. My work life was effectively over.

Ruined. Destroyed. Finito. Just like my personal life.

Shaking off a fresh wave of sadness, I entered the smallest of the three upstairs bedrooms. "Right there." I pointed at the bare wall under the west-facing window.

As the movers unwrapped the desk, I trotted back downstairs. Harlow stood and smiled, tail still wagging. I knelt next to her and scratched the spot below her ears. "You are such a good girl. I move you all the way across the country and you roll with it." I buried my face in the ruff along the back of her neck. As soon as my eyes closed, Stefan's face shimmered before me. I took a deep breath and looked into Harlow's warm eyes. "We may not be lucky, but we've got each other, right?"

Harlow thumped her tail.

"Helloooo?"

Startled, I raised my gaze to the vision filling my open front door. Standing at least five feet ten, not counting the cobalt-blue stilettos, the bottle blonde in an emerald tank and black leggings gave a finger wave. "Hi."

Before I could scramble to my feet, she strutted inside. "Sorry to intrude. Are you the new neighbor?"

"That's me. Molly Madison." I extended my hand. "And you are?"

"Seville Chambers." We shook, then she gave a mock bow. "At your service. Since you're new, I figured I should tell you to keep your doors shut. Always."

The moving men tromped down the stairs. Faced with two people who dwarfed her—at least in bulk—Seville stepped past me into the great room. "Sorry to pop in this way when you're not even settled. But I saw the open door and thought you should be warned."

That didn't sound good. "Warned about what?"

"Frankendoodle."

I couldn't imagine anything called Frankendoodle being a cause for concern. But the crease between Seville's eyes seemed to indicate she was serious. Not wanting to be labeled the neighborhood grouch, I kept my expression interested. "I'm sorry, but who—or what—is a Frankendoodle?"

Seville pointed at the doorway. An ivory and mocha monster filled the opening, upturned tail swinging like a metronome. "That's the Frankendoodle."

"Good lord." The dog had to weigh close to two hundred pounds. I checked Harlow. She was still sitting, but her nose twitched, obviously eager for the go-ahead to meet a new play-mate. I neared the door, holding out my hand to the dog. "Hey, there."

He nudged my palm. "So, you want some pets, huh?" Seeing Harlow bristle, I called her closer and told her to sit. Keeping my body between the two dogs, I reached one hand out to stroke the Golden while running the other along our visitor's curly coat. "You're a sweet fella, aren't you?"

"Excuse us." The movers approached the front porch with my sofa.

I urged the humongous dog inside and out of their path. He gave a deep woof as the men entered. "It's okay." I rubbed his head and soft brown ears, then turned my focus to the moving men. "That goes over there." I pointed at the great room before glancing up at Seville. "I'm guessing he's a Saint Berdoodle? Half poodle, half Saint Bernard?"

"No clue. Don't get me wrong, he's friendly enough, but if you leave your door open, he'll walk right in and drool all over everything. Six months ago he absolutely ruined one of my silk blouses."

The ropey skein hanging from his mouth backed up Seville's drool claim. "Where does he live?"

"Just down the street. At Dr. Joe Handsome's."

"Dr. Joe Handsome?"

"Okay, his last name is Johannson. But he really is a doctor. Once you get a look at him, you'll call him Joe Handsome, too."

"You actually call him that?"

"Not to his face. Besides, the man barely speaks to me anymore. Not since the Silk Blouse Summit."

Not sure whether to pursue this detail, I dried my hand on my jeans and straightened. "And which house is yours?"

"I'm right across the street. The tan Mediterranean. If you need help getting to know where anything is in town, just ask." She pulled out her cell. "Give me your number and I'll send you mine."

"Sure."

We exchanged digits. I checked on the movers while keeping one eye on the dogs. The men were still unwinding the plastic from my sofa. After patting Harlow, I ran my fingers through the Saint Berdoodle's fur and found his tags. Who engraved their dog's name on a tag but didn't include a contact number or license? Goofball. "So Frankendoodle's a nickname."

"It's appropriate."

I looked back at my retriever. "Harlow, come." My dog bounded over to meet the Saint Berdoodle. "Meet Noodle." Both dogs sniffed each other, tails wagging. I grabbed a thick piece of knotted hemp from the toy basket and tossed it to them. Harlow bit down on one end and shook it. Noodle pranced, then snatched the other end and pulled. "Smart dog."

"I couldn't help noticing the moving van's almost empty."

Since the truck was blocking a large section of the alley, I was sure all my new neighbors were counting down the minutes until it left. "They'll be out of the way soon."

Seville shook her head. "Don't worry about that. I just mentioned it because your furnishings seem sort of sparse."

I looked around, trying to see the ground floor through Seville's eyes: no entry room table, no stools lining the kitchen bar, no dining table, no pictures on the walls, no tchotchkes or mementos of the past anywhere in sight.

"Is another truck coming with the rest of your things?"

"Nope. This is it. For now."

"Is this some sort of feng shui thing?"

No way was I going to explain how I'd sold or given away nearly everything Stefan had bought for our house in Duxbury. "Most of my old stuff wouldn't look right here, so I got rid of it." I checked to be sure the dogs were still getting along before turning back to Seville.

"If you want tips on great places to buy furniture locally, just let me know. There are definitely places you want to avoid. And I've got a terrific decorator if you want to hire one." Her tone and expression said an emergency call to said decorator was warranted ASAP.

The movers gave me a pretext to dodge her offer of assistance. "Excuse me. They have the sofa facing the wrong way."

"Sure."

To my surprise, instead of leaving, she sat on the stairs. When the sofa was situated where I wanted it, I returned to the entry. The dogs were still playing tug-of-war and Seville was examining her manicure. "Sorry I don't have any coffee or tea to offer. Haven't gotten that stuff unpacked yet."

"No problem." She gave me a lazy smile, as if she had nothing better to do all day than sit on my staircase. "So, what brings you to Pier Point? From your accent, I'm guessing you're not a California native."

"No. Massachusetts."

"Makes sense. I moved from there, too."

"Really? What part?"

"The Vineyard."

"Year-round?"

"Yes." She gave a faux shudder. "But I couldn't stand the cold. My folks owned a real estate firm that handled sales and seasonal rentals. Plus they had a couple rentals down in Tisbury. I had the 'fun' of cleaning them between tenants. What part of the state are you from?"

"Duxbury."

"A South Shore girl. Lifelong?"

"The past dozen years. What brought you to California?"

"College. I only applied to West Coast schools. It was so fricking frigid on the island. Of course, we didn't get snow like you on the mainland. But the sun hardly ever came out. Except during the summer. I wanted to move somewhere with lots of sunshine. How about you? Did you move here for work?"

Moved to get away from work was more like it, but I wasn't going to dive into that tangled mess. Instead I pointed at Noodle. "Does the doctor just let his dog run free all day? On these narrow streets?"

"Not exactly. Frankendoodle's an escape artist. A giant, drooling escape artist." She pointed at the splotches of saliva dotting the tile entryway.

"I should probably take him home."

"Good luck with that. Joe Handsome is an emergency room doctor. He's rarely home."

"Oh. Well, I can't let the dog run around outside. He could get hit by a car."

Seville shrugged, then stood. "I guess that means you're dog sitting." Before leaving she gave another finger wave.

"Nice meeting you." When she moved out of view, I turned to watch the cavorting dogs. Even though I had boxes to unpack, I couldn't help but smile. "Looks like you've made a new friend, Harlow."

Over the next fifteen minutes, the movers carried and positioned items while I provided direction and the dogs continued playing. When they ran out of steam, Noodle investigated Harlow's crate in the great room while my Golden went to her large fuzzy pillow and began to circle. Noodle cocked his head, seeming to look for a bed of his own. After rubbing his ears, I told him to give me a minute. I trotted up the stairs, grabbed Harlow's other sleeping pillow, and toted it back to the first level. Setting it a half-foot away from where Harlow was curled up and watching beneath heavy lids, I patted the soft fabric. "Bed, Noodle."

The huge dog sniffed the pillow. It seemed to meet his approval and he sprawled across it, hind legs partway on the floor. I picked up the rope toy and quickly shifted my grip to the less drool-drenched end. After dropping it back into the basket, I wiped my hand on my jeans.

"Where do you want this?" Muscle Man Number Two held my coffee table aloft.

"In there." I pointed toward the great room. "In front of the sofa."

While the dogs slept, I accompanied the movers up and down the stairs as they brought in the last few items, pointing out where things should go. When the men deposited their final load and handed over the paperwork, I gave them a generous tip, then poured myself a glass of wine and climbed to the rooftop deck. I hadn't yet bought furniture for this area, so I leaned against the railing, staring along the curve of road that gave me a coveted ocean view.

Our two-story in Duxbury had also been near the water, though we couldn't see it from the house. A colonial saltbox with narrow, double-hung windows and a sharply pitched roof in back, it always made me feel like I was about to bang into something. My new home was masonry and wood with huge windows that let in the light along with peekaboo ocean views. The place felt airy, spacious, and unburdened by betrayal.

My stomach grumbled. I checked the time. Seven-fifteen. I hadn't realized it was so late. The quality of light here was different. It being summer, of course the sun was still up, but even so . . . it was more than that. Pier Point would take some getting used to.

Also, it was time to take Noodle home.

Returning downstairs, I realized Seville never actually told me which house was Dr. Johannson's. She'd only waved toward the street. I grabbed my cell and did a quick Google search, but without the doctor's first name, my quest for an address and phone number fizzled.

I looked at the dozing canines. "At least it's not a big street."

Even calling it a street was an exaggeration. My garage and front door—along with those of my neighbors—faced a narrow alley that I'd been told beachgoers used as a shortcut. "Harlow, Noodle. Come." I jingled my Golden's leash. She stood and shook herself, then charged to my side, pressing her cold, damp nose against my leg. I attached the leash and patted her flank. "You don't mind if I let your new friend use your old leash, do you?"

She swung her plume of a tail, which I took as approval.

Noodle remained on the pillow. "Has no one trained you, boy?" I pulled two treats from my pocket. After telling Harlow to sit, I offered a biscuit and she gobbled it. "Noodle." I held out the second treat. "Come." The giant sniffed the air, then wandered to my side. The biscuit disappeared from my palm, a small pool of drool left in its place. "Wow. No way to train you out of that."

I hooked the other leash to the large beast's collar. "Hope someone's at least taught you to walk on a lead. Otherwise this could get ugly. I'm pretty sure you outweigh me by eighty pounds." Mouth hanging open, the Saint Berdoodle waved his curly tail. "All right, let's go."

When I opened the front door, the massive dog lunged. I pulled up on his leash. Knowing Harlow wouldn't bolt, I dropped her lead and used both hands to keep Noodle in check. "Heel." Noodle continued straining against the leather strap. "Harlow, heel." My Golden moved beside me. "Noodle, heel." I held out a second treat.

Noodle stopped pulling but didn't move to my side. "Come." I tightened my grip on the leash and crouched to his eye level.

He shuffled over and hoovered up the snack. "Good boy." I picked up Harlow's leash, holding both in one hand while I rubbed the massive dog's curly head. "Let's find your home. Can you show me where it is?"

The sky turned peach as we wandered from one end of the alley to the other and back again. I shook my head at the Saint Berdoodle. "Not willing to take me to your leader, huh? Okay. We'll do this the hard way." I guided both dogs to the house next door. Most of the structures on my street were two stories, though the styles varied. This one looked like something from an English countryside fantasy, with river rock facing on the first level, smooth plaster on the top story, and a faux thatched roof. Noodle gave a mighty woof, then settled on his haunches. "Is this place familiar?"

As if in answer, he gazed up at me with big eyes and drooled on the concrete path.

I rang the bell and waited. After ringing it again and getting no response, I moved on to the next home. This one had a beachy appearance: gray paint with sparkling white trim, a life preserver hanging from an exterior wall, and a "This way to the water" sign. Unable to find the doorbell, I knocked. A few moments later, the door swung open.

A sinewy man dressed in black bicycle shorts and a char-treuse jersey stood on the other side of the threshold. His face told me he had to be in his seventies, but his body swore he was a couple decades younger.

I was well on my way to forty. Maybe I should take up cy-cling? I was going to have to do something with all the spare time looming ahead of me. I shook off that disturbing idea. "Hi. My name's Molly and I just moved in down the street. I'm—"

"You bought the white house with sage trim?"

Wow. Truly a small town. And street. "That's the one. I'm still unpacking, but this gentle giant dropped by today."

"Frankendoodle." He nodded at the Saint Berdoodle.

"You know Noodle?"

The man gave a broad smile. "Everyone on this street knows that dog. If you leave your door open, you're likely to find him on your sofa or bed." He shook his head. "Don't get me wrong, I like dogs, but the drool . . ."

"I've noticed. Do you know where he lives?"

"Sure thing." He stepped past me to the path and pointed at a tan and brown three-story located a couple doors down on the opposite side of the alley.

Trailing after him, I studied the six-foot-high fence running along the blacktop. "Wow. The dog really is an escape artist."

"I respect the dog's initiative but have no desire to deal with the saliva." He held out his hand. "Excuse my bad manners. I'm Hank Foster. Welcome to the neighborhood."

"Thanks." I shook his hand. "Nice to meet you. And thanks for the clue to this dog's home."

"No problem. Have yourself a nice night."

"You, too."

I'd walked the dogs past the tallest house on the block twice and Noodle had yet to show any signs of recognition. "Have you been playing me, big guy?" Noodle wagged his tail and drooled onto the asphalt. "Don't know whether that's a yes or a no, but let's go see if your person's home."

We crossed the narrow alley. The horizontal planks of the wood fence ended at the garage, hiding the home's first story from view. As I paralleled the fence, security lights clicked on. One of them shone down on the gate set into the fence and on the doorbell. I pressed the button and waited.

A tinny voice said, "Yes?"

I looked around but didn't see the intercom. "Is this Dr. Johannson's house?"

"Yes."

For a doctor, he didn't seem eager to show off his vocabulary. "I have your dog, Noodle."

A loud click. Then the disembodied voice said, "Gate's unlocked. Bring him in and I'll meet you in the courtyard."

I pushed the gate open. Noodle practically pulled me off my feet as he charged inside. "Heel." The dog kept pulling. The poor fellow needed some serious training. Especially at his size. No matter how sweet-tempered the animal, many owners lost patience when a dog tipped the scales north of one hundred fifty pounds and didn't understand the rules.

Though Noodle continued to ignore my command, Harlow sat gazing up at me. I shut the gate behind us and studied our surroundings.

Strings of warm lights crisscrossed above the patio. A long rectangular fire pit was to my left, flanked by wicker chairs. A stainless steel barbecue and granite-topped bar sat directly ahead. The French doors facing the patio swung open. A tall man dressed in shorts and a sweat-marked T-shirt crossed toward me.

Seville was right. Joe Handsome described this guy perfectly. Though with a last name like Johannson, I'd expected someone who looked more Swedish than Latino.

He held out his hand.

At first I thought the doctor wanted to shake hands, but quickly realized he was wordlessly asking for the leash. The leash I'd loaned to Noodle. I passed it to him. "You can return this whenever it's convenient."

The doctor bent down and uncoupled the leather strap and handed it back. He didn't pet or talk to the dog. Noodle leaned against his leg, but the doctor seemed oblivious.

The poor dog was obviously starved for affection.

Though it was none of my business, I couldn't keep my mouth shut. "You know, with a dog this size, getting him some training could be beneficial. It'll make him easier to walk and easier to deal with inside the house. I'd be happy to—"

Dr. Johannson brushed past me and opened the patio door. "Thanks for bringing him back."

Wow. Abrupt and weird. Maybe I'd made him feel judged? "Bye, Noodle." The giant canine smiled. "Come on, Harlow."

The door snapped shut behind us. I looked down at my Golden and bent to kiss her forehead. "That poor dog, right?"

Fog rolled in as we walked home. Once back inside, I mixed Harlow's dinner of wet and dry food. While she gobbled it, I checked the time. It was after 11:00 p.m. on the East Coast. Too late to call Mom as I'd promised. Instead, I texted, letting her know the furniture had arrived safely and that Harlow and I were getting settled. After ordering a pizza, I popped into the shower. Within minutes of drying off and pulling on shorts and a sweatshirt, the food arrived.

I ate two slices standing at the kitchen sink as Harlow scavenged for crumbs around my feet. Thoroughly exhausted and still feeling out of sync with my new time zone, I worried Harlow might be feeling a little lost, too. I grabbed the crate and one of the dog pillows, turned off the lights, and carried them upstairs. "Harlow. Bed." Nails clicking on the wood stairs, she trotted after me.

I set the crate next to my bed and placed the pillow inside. Harlow gave it a thorough sniff before she circled and settled. I stared around the room. The cedar chest and armoire were from our home in Duxbury. The bed, blanket, sheets, and pillows were new. I hadn't wanted to bring anything with me that would remind me of Stefan. Or how he died.

For all my planning, once I climbed into bed, all I could think about was my dead husband.

CHAPTER 2

The sun streamed through the bedroom window, waking me. I cursed and shielded my eyes. Buying drapes or blinds moved to the top of my to-do list. Harlow's crate rattled. I rolled onto my side and looked down at her. The Golden nosed the latch again. No more sleep for me. I sat up and gazed at the dog. "I'm awake, girl. Give me a minute to pull myself together, okay?"

The retriever sighed and lowered her chin onto her front paws.

Opening the armoire, I sorted through the meager collection of unpacked clothes. I chose shorts and a sweatshirt. A few minutes later, I headed downstairs, Harlow two steps ahead of me. She reached the kitchen first and sat beside her empty bowl, giving me sad eyes. "Outside first." I opened the slider to the backyard. "Do your business."

I plugged in the coffeemaker, then mixed a batch of dry and wet food. While the heady coffee scent filled the kitchen, I set the device's digital clock and rinsed my face in the sink. Harlow raced back inside and buried her muzzle in the bowl. "You poor, hungry girl."

Before the coffee finished brewing, Harlow's bowl was empty again. She padded over and sat at my feet.

"You win. A walk before coffee." I slipped into a pair of cross-trainers, then snapped on her leash. Today would be the retriever's first time exploring the local beach. After a jaw-cracking yawn, I opened the front door.

Noodle stood on the concrete path, tail wagging.

"Hello there." I thought back to the six-foot-high wall surrounding the doctor's house and shook my head. Impressive. "Harlow, stay." I retreated inside and grabbed a couple pockets-ful of treats and the spare leash for the Saint Berdoodle. While I was at it, I found a rag to handle his drool. Crouching by the big dog's side, I wiped his flews and ran my hand through his curly coat. "You truly are an escape artist." I hooked the lead to his collar and straightened.

The beach was only eight houses away, but even over that short distance, it felt like Noodle was trying to wrench my shoulder from the socket. We reached the sand without actual injury, and I stared at the churning ocean. The Pacific smelled fresher than the Atlantic—or was that my imagination?

I led the dogs to the hard-packed sand by the water's edge and set off at a brisk pace.

An Airedale lollopped by off leash, chasing seagulls. His person smiled at me and the dogs. "I know the sign says to keep them on a leash, but at this hour, no one complains. If they're good with other dogs, you can let yours run free."

"I don't know about this big guy, but my Golden would love that." I unhooked Harlow while holding on to Noodle. The re-triever raced along the beach, letting every shorebird she encountered know who was in charge. Noodle wagged his tail but gave no indication he also longed to run. While poodles were slow but steady runners, his staying put jived with what I knew about Saint Bernards. We wandered on, with him occasionally pulling me off-balance and me working the "heel" command and rewarding him with a biscuit. If he was going to keep visiting, I'd need to stock up on dog treats—he'd gobbled at least ten as I tried to train him.

When we reached an empty stretch of sand, I finally felt it was safe to set him free. Unlike Harlow, he didn't bolt. Nose down, he meandered across the sand. No longer worried he might go after a smaller dog, I pulled off my shoes and waded into the ocean, relishing the cold water lapping against my feet and calves.

Morning sun scattered jewels of light across the ocean. About thirty feet out, dark fins broke the surface. A dolphin arced out of the water, launching itself at least five feet in the air, sleek body gleaming. Another dolphin leapt, followed by another and another. "Wow."

I glanced at the people farther down the beach. They all looked as enthralled as I felt.

Harlow trotted to my side, coat damp. "Did you see that, girl?" She shook herself, spraying me with sand and water. A minute later Noodle galumphed over to join us.

"What have you got there, big guy?" The Saint Berdoodle turned away, putting his body between me and the newfound treasure gripped in his mouth. I hoped he hadn't found a dead bird. "Drop it."

The dog ignored me. After snapping on his leash, I turned Noodle's head to face me.

"Oh no." The familiar spike of adrenaline hit. My mouth

went dry and my heart began to race. Jerking up, I pulled my cell from my pocket and tapped in 9-1-1.

"What's your emergency?"

"My dog found a hand."

"You want Animal Control. Their number is—"

"No. I'm not calling about my dog. I'm calling about the hand."

"All types of dogs—including hounds—are handled by Animal Control."

Was the sound of the ocean muffling my voice? "Not a hound. A hand. A human hand. H-A-N-D."

"Oh. A hand? Not a body?"

"Just the hand."

"What's your location?"

I told the dispatcher where we were and then added, "It's not actually my dog and I haven't been able to get him to drop it. He doesn't look like he's going to eat it, but . . . Please hurry." Not waiting for her response, I disconnected and crouched in front of the Saint Berdoodle. Avoiding the pale fingers protruding from his drool-laced jaw, I ran my hand along his neck, hoping I could get him to open his mouth and release his trophy.

The hand looked wet. Drool? Or had Noodle found it in the water? Four of the five fingertips were missing. Didn't look like the work of a knife. Eaten by fish or critters? Unable to turn the big dog's head, I shifted position to see the other end of his grisly prize. The hand was severed at the wrist, and the cut was slightly jagged. Not a surgical removal. Maybe a boat propeller?

Even though I'd been off the job for more than a year, I could still detach myself and see this combination of bone and flesh as evidence, not part of a person.

Another treat finally got Noodle to drop his prize. The arrival of two cop cars in the nearby cul-de-sac on the other side of the seawall set the half-dozen people on the beach scurrying to leash their pets. When the officers reached us on foot, Harlow began to bark while Noodle growled and drooled. The trailing saliva added a note of menace to the Saint Berdoodle's appearance.

The shorter officer stepped back and pulled what looked like a canister of capsicum from his duty belt. "Get your dogs under control."

Turning my back on him, I stepped between the cop and the dogs. "Come, Harlow. Noodle." I urged them farther away and soothed the Golden. Since I hadn't appreciated the cop's hostile tone, I let Noodle growl a bit longer. Once sure the message had been received, I held out a treat for the big dog. "Sit." I lifted the biscuit above his head. As he raised his chin, I pressed down on his hindquarters. When they touched the sand, I let him have the treat. "Good dog."

Seeming to feel they had adequately protected me, both dogs settled on the warm sand but kept their focus on the newcomers. I, too, turned my attention to the officers, directing my words to the cop who hadn't threatened the dogs. He looked about twenty-five, his mocha-toned skin wrinkle free. With long lashes most women would kill for and the full lips dermatologists tried to recreate with injections, his strong jaw and nose kept him from sliding into "pretty man" territory. "It took a while, but I got him to drop the hand. It's under that empty poop bag." I pointed at the piece of green plastic. "Figured I should cover it in case any kids came by."

Using a pen to lift an edge of the bag, he looked up. "Did you touch it?"

"No."

"Looks wet. The dog find this in the water?"

"Maybe. I didn't see where he got it. But he drools a lot."

The cop stood, duty belt creaking. After speaking to his partner, voice low, he stepped toward me. He smelled of Old Spice and shoe polish. Noodle growled again. "Okay if I approach your dogs?"

"Should be all right. The big one belongs to a neighbor, but he's been gentle with me." I crouched and extended an arm out on either side, stroking the fur along each dog's back. Both tails wagged. "It's okay."

The young cop drew near and held out a large hand to the Golden. "What's his name?"

"Her name's Harlow."

"Hey, beautiful." The dog belly-crawled closer until he patted her head. He turned to the Saint Berdoodle and offered his other hand. "And this one is?"

"Noodle."

"Hi, Noodle."

Mollified by this gesture, Noodle rested his huge head on his front paws. The cop straightened and stepped back. "While Officer Willis is calling this in, I need to get your name, address, and contact info."

"Sure." I gave him the requested information.

He glanced back where the hand lay. "Since you live up the street, go ahead and take the dogs home. You can wait for the detectives there."

"Really?"

He gave an awkward shrug. "Willis is afraid of dogs."

"Ah. Okay." That explained the pepper spray. "Any idea how long it'll be before a detective comes by?"

"I suggest staying available for at least the next two hours."

"Got it. Thank you. Officer . . . ?"

"Gregory." His wide smile moved him firmly into the handsome category.

The dogs looked disappointed as I guided them away from the water but perked up when we neared home. Rather than keep them inside, I took them to the modest backyard. I rubbed the Golden's fur with a towel and brushed her coat. The temperature had jumped. Spending time outside would soon dry Harlow the rest of the way and get rid of the wet dog smell. I patted both dogs' flanks.

Would Noodle still be here by the time the detective came and questioned me? The wall around my yard was at least a foot shorter than the one at the doctor's. With all the toys scattered about and his new pal to play with, at least the Saint Berdoodle shouldn't take off due to boredom.

I went inside and sprawled on the sofa. Checking the time, I pulled out my cell and called my mom at work. I caught her up on the move and told her about Noodle, while omitting the fact that he'd found a severed hand.

"So, you like it there?" She couldn't disguise the worry in her voice.

"Yep. The house is nice and so's the neighborhood. It's an adjustment, but you can't beat the weather."

"Maybe not. But in a few months, you'll miss having a real autumn."

"Entirely possible. But come springtime, I won't miss mud season."

"Touché."

After we hung up, I filled the time waiting for the detectives to arrive by unpacking more boxes and wondering about Noodle's find. Was the hand from a boating accident or something more sinister? I was setting plates inside a cupboard when the doorbell rang. In the yard, both dogs began to bark.

I walked to the screen. "Good dogs. I'm okay." They settled down and I headed for the front door.

Two men stood on the stoop. The good-looking one of the pair wore a tailored gray suit with a red power tie. The other was dressed in a wrinkled khaki jacket that looked a size too small, and navy trousers. Both were obviously cops. Power Tie looked to be in his forties, his partner maybe a decade older. With his disheveled clothes and hair, the older guy probably wasn't aiming higher than his current position in the department.

Power Tie took the lead. "Ms. Madison?"

"That's me. And you are?"

"I'm Detective Vasquez and this is Detective Wright. May we come in?"

It wasn't really a request, but I played along. "Of course."

Detective Wright moved past me, bringing the scent of stale coffee and sweat. He pointed at an open packing box sitting near the base of the stairs. "You going somewhere?"

"Arriving, not leaving. Moved in yesterday."

"Welcome to the neighborhood." Vasquez gave a heart-melting grin, then walked into the great room and sat on the sofa. Detective Wright joined him.

I bit back the urge to say, "Make yourselves at home," as I settled on the fireplace hearth.

Vasquez held up his phone. "I'll be recording this. Hope you don't mind."

I nodded, knowing this also wasn't a request.

"At approximately what time would you say you found the hand?"

I pulled out my cell and checked the log for the time of my 9-1-1 call. "The dog brought it to me at about eight." I cleared my throat. "I noticed most of the fingertips were gone. Will you be able to get prints off the remaining one?"

Vasquez raised his eyebrows. "That part's up to the techs."

"What about the tattoo?"

"What tattoo?"

I bit back a sigh. This guy pretending ignorance made no sense. He knew I'd seen the hand. "The one between her index finger and thumb. Looked like a daisy or maybe a marigold."

"Why do you say 'her'?"

"The hand and fingers were slim. Dainty, even. Didn't look like a man's."

This time Vasquez's eyebrows drew closer together. "I'm surprised you noticed all that detail. Most people would be too squeamish to look closely."

Since it wasn't a question, I waited.

Detective Wright leaned forward. "About the dog, do you think it might have eaten some of the evidence?"

"He wasn't out of my sight very long. But I've seen him vacuum up food, so who knows? That said, he wasn't wet. If the hand came from the ocean, he didn't pick it up until it washed ashore."

"Good observation," Vasquez said. He and Wright exchanged a look.

I didn't like that look. "As I told the officer at the beach, the dog who found the hand isn't mine."

"We're gonna want to speak to the owner."

"Sure." Outside, Harlow resumed barking. "Excuse me." I checked on her. A squirrel sat on top of the back wall while Harlow paced below. The sound of the slider opening was enough to drive my dog's tormenter away. Closing the door, I returned to my guests.

"Everything okay out there?" Wright's tone didn't hold much genuine concern.

"Yeah." I resettled on the hearth. "I don't know the address for Noodle's house, but it's the only three-story on the block. The guy's an ER doctor. I've been told he's not home until late most days."

"You know if he's a surgeon?"

"You mean does the doctor bring home spare body parts for his dog to play with? I think I would've noticed if Noodle had showed up here with a hand in his mouth."

Wright rested his forearms on his knees. "How long have you been the doctor's dog walker? And what time did he drop him off today?"

Did he not hear me say I'd just moved here? "I'm not his dog walker. And I barely know the owner. Noodle's an escape artist and I don't like the idea of him wandering these narrow streets. He could get hurt." In response to Wright's raised eyebrows, I added, "That's why I've taken him in the last two days." I leaned forward. "Has this happened before? I mean, is there some sort of current that brings the remains of boating victims to this beach?"

Vasquez cocked his head, seeming to study me. "No."

"So, you're saying the odds that the rest of the DB will wash ashore here are slim?"

"DB?"

I opened and closed my mouth, wishing I could hit rewind.

Vasquez exchanged another look with his partner. "You work in law enforcement?"

"Used to. Back in Massachusetts."

"Uniform or detective?"

"Uni."

"Explains a lot." Vasquez tucked his phone inside his jacket. "I think we've covered everything." He stood. "Thank you for your help. We'll be in touch if we have more questions."

"Of course." I walked the men to the door, grateful my admitting to once being in uniform had put the brakes on their questions about my career in law enforcement. After the detectives left, I loaded both dogs into my old Honda 4Runner and drove them to Hillside Park. My real estate agent—another dog lover— had told me it would be a great place to hike with Harlow. The dogs kept their noses out the back windows for the entire drive.

I pulled into a spot and climbed out. The two pranced in anticipation while I stowed my purse in the cargo area, grabbed my knapsack, and stuffed a fresh water bottle inside. Located four miles inland, Hillside Park was warmer than the beach. I peeled off my sweatshirt before opening the back door. I grabbed Noodle's leash first. "Come." He hopped down and I urged Harlow out.

The park was huge. Beyond the edges of the bowl-like grassy area, trails carved their way through chaparral-covered hills. Finches and swallows flitted among the trees dotting the basin, their chirps a pleasant soundtrack as we headed for the closest path. The ascent was sharp but something I knew Harlow could handle. I studied the Saint Berdoodle's hips and stride as we climbed. He moved effortlessly, if not quickly. After ten minutes of seeing no other dogs or hikers on or near the dirt path, I let Harlow off her lead. The Golden ran ahead, tags jingling and ears flopping, exploring the scrub and barking at birds. Noodle and I followed at a more sedate pace. When Harlow flushed several quail, Noodle barked in support.

I watched the Saint Berdoodle to see what types of things he liked to explore. The scrub held little interest for him, but a hole in the ground next to the path sent him into digging mode. After several attempts and two more treats, I got him to heel again.

So, Noodle was a digger. I wondered if he'd dug up the hand.

After thirty minutes, the Saint Berdoodle slowed. "Getting tired, boy?" I whistled for my dog. The retriever trotted back to me. I pulled the collapsible bowl from my knapsack and filled it with water. While the dogs took turns drinking, I snapped on Harlow's leash. When both had lapped their fill, I shook out the bowl, stowing it and the bottle in my pack. Then the three of us headed back down the hill.

Noodle stopped to nose a gopher hole. "Heel." The big dog returned to my side. "Good boy."

I shook my head. I'd moved cross-country to give myself a peaceful new start. In only two days, I'd managed to become a large drooling dog's trainer. And find a severed body part.

Looked like peace and quiet were going to be harder to find than I'd hoped.

CHAPTER 3

After our walk, the dogs and I were lounging in the great room when the doorbell rang. Noodle started barking and Harlow joined in.

"What now?" I herded them into the backyard, then hurried to the door. My neighbor Seville stood on the stoop, dressed in tan leggings and a leopard-print tank top. She again wore four-inch heels. My feet ached on her behalf.

She grabbed my hand. In spite of the warm day, her fingers felt icy. "I heard about the head. It's all over town that you found some poor person's head on the beach."

"It was a hand. Noodle found it and brought it to me."

"Oh." Lips pursed, she dropped my hand. "Well, that's still bad. You must be in shock. Seeing that in Frankendoodle's mouth . . . I don't know if I'll ever be able to pet that dog again."

In our one previous encounter, I'd not gotten the impression Seville longed to touch or even get close to Noodle. The poor dog had a bad reputation on the street already; serious damage control was needed. "Upsetting as it was, it's not the dog's fault. Noodle didn't hurt anyone. If anything, he may help someone find closure."

After an awkward silence, Seville raised her hand and covered her eyes. "You're right. I get that. The damn dog was acting on instinct."

"Exactly. As far as Noodle's concerned, he found something new and smelly. Dog noses are amazing. Way more sensitive than ours. But they appreciate scent in a totally different way than we do." I touched Seville's shoulder to draw her attention back to me. "One time, I watched this gorgeous, beautifully groomed sheepdog shoulder-roll into a pile of fresh cow manure. His owner was appalled, but the dog was ecstatic."

She nodded. "And you're right about closure. Someone's either dead or severely injured. We need the police to figure out who it is."

"They're working on it."

"Is Frankendoodle—I mean Noodle—okay?"

"Yeah. He and Harlow are playing out back. He's got no idea the ruckus his find has caused."

"I get that. But why was he with you at the beach? Or here now?"

"He escaped again."

"And you're dog sitting."

I touched the tip of my nose. "Got it in one."

"You're a way better person than me." Seville glanced over her shoulder at the narrow alley. "I mean, I get it. The hand thing isn't Noodle's fault. But the dog's still a drool factory." She gave a mock shudder. "Kudos to you for letting that saliva fountain into your home. Anyway, I've got to get back to work. Glad to know you're all right."

After Seville left, I organized the kitchen. Once that was done, I turned my attention to the office, pulling files from one of the boxes and organizing them in the bottom desk drawer. At six thirty, I took the dogs out for a short walk. It was past Harlow's normal mealtime when we returned. I didn't want to feed her in front of Noodle, or possibly annoy Dr. Johannson by giving his dog dinner. I compromised by giving them each a small serving of kibble. When seven thirty rolled around, I figured it was late enough to bring Noodle home. If the doctor wasn't back from work, I'd keep the big dog with me for the night.

I snapped the leash onto the Saint Berdoodle's collar. My Golden trotted up. "Sorry, Harlow. You need to stay. If the doctor's in, I've got to talk to him. And you're so cute I won't be able to focus if you're with me. I'll be back in a few." I kissed her forehead, then led Noodle out the front door.

Fingers of sunlight still streaked the sky as we headed down the alley. Though it was mid-June, fog rolled in from the water. I shivered and wished I'd grabbed a jacket. Nose up, Noodle woofed at the seagulls flapping away.

We crossed to the other side and approached the tallest house on the tiny street. The harsh security lights clicked on. Shielding my eyes, I rang the bell and waited for the disembodied voice to respond.

"Ms. Madison. I see you have my dog again."

I looked up. Of course the guy had a camera along with the lights. "Yep."

The lock clicked. "Come in. I'll be right out."

The strings of amber lights crisscrossing overhead gave the

empty patio a festive air—as if a party was due to break out any minute. Several lavender plants flowered near the house, and the air was rich with their sweet scent.

While waiting for the doctor to appear, I offered Noodle another treat and gave him the "sit" command. He settled his haunches on the Saltillo tile, eyes fixed on me. "Good boy."

The French doors swung open and Dr. Johannson strode outside. Tonight he was dressed in suit pants and an untucked white button-down shirt. As he had on the previous night, he wordlessly reached for the leash.

I held onto the leather strap. "Something happened today that you need to know about."

The doctor raised his eyebrows but didn't speak.

"Noodle found a severed hand at the beach."

"What!" Eyes wide, he seemed to see me for the first time. "Sorry. I didn't mean to shout. Especially when all you've done is bring back the dog." He retreated a step and stared at Noodle. "Excuse my bad manners. I'm Santiago Johannson. 'Sandy' for short." He gestured toward the bar. "It sounds like you have a story to tell. Perhaps you'll join me for a drink as you share it? I have beer, wine, Scotch . . . or maybe you'd prefer a tequila?"

"A glass of white wine would be great—if you have it."

"Of course. Excuse me a moment. I have a bottle inside."

He disappeared into the dark house.

Apparently, all it took to get this guy to play nice was to tell him a gruesome tale. I strolled to one of the wrought iron bar-stools and climbed up. The granite counter felt cool beneath my forearms. I moved my hands to my lap. Noodle gave a mighty woof and settled at the base of my chair.

A few minutes later, Sandy emerged, wine glass and snifter in one hand, a bottle of chardonnay in the other. After filling my glass, he pulled a bottle of tequila from behind the bar and gave himself a heavy pour as well. "I'm hoping my dog isn't a crime suspect."

I snort-laughed and raised my glass. "I'm pretty sure if you get Noodle a good lawyer, he'll never spend a day behind bars."

On that note, we clinked glasses. The wine was buttery with a hint of pear and helped warm me. The bottle probably cost more than I spent on alcohol in a year. Whatever his faults, the doc was a generous host. As we sipped, I unfolded the tale of his dog's find. "I take it the detectives haven't contacted you yet?"

"No. Why would they?"

I shrugged. "I'm not in the loop. All I know is, they said they were going to."

The doctor held his snifter to the light, seeming to study the tequila's tawny hue. "Do these detectives think the dog has some sort of insight about the hand that he'll only share with me?"

I snorted again. This time fine wine burned my nasal passages. Once I recovered, I looked at my host. "There's no nice way to say this, but they probably want you to study Noodle's . . . output over the next day or so. In case he ate anything not fully digestible related to the crime."

"Ah. They want me to dig for 'treasure,' as it were."

"Yep."

His expression darkened. "I apologize for behaving badly yesterday. You were good enough to take care of and return the dog." He sighed, head dropping toward his chest, dark hair flopping across his forehead. "I told Jessica not to buy him. That a dog his size wouldn't fit our lifestyle. She made a point of mocking that word. Lifestyle." The doctor straightened. "But with my schedule, there was no way I'd have time to spend with him, not the amount of time a big young dog needs. Plus, I knew she'd grow bored with him and never properly discipline him. And now she doesn't even visit the dog."

I glanced down at the gold ring on his left hand. "I take it you're separated?"

"Divorced. Well, EBTP."

"What?"

"Everything but the paperwork. Jessica refuses to sign the agreement. Keeps making new demands. Last week she wanted some embroidered pillowcases my great-aunt gave us for a wedding present. The week before that, she wanted a sterling bud vase. I had to tear the place apart to find it. That's why I can't get attached to Noodle."

"I don't follow."

"If Jessica hears I've bonded with the dog—and believe me, she will . . . The woman has spies in the neighborhood who tell her everything I do. Someone's probably calling her right now to let her know the new neighbor is talking to her soon-to-be-ex." A deep furrow formed above the bridge of his nose.

"I'm missing something. Why does this mean you can't get attached to Noodle?"

"Right." He shook his head as if shedding a bad memory. "If Jessica finds out I've grown close to the dog, she'll demand I give him to her. And that woman will never care for him. He'll be a sad trophy who never gets what he actually needs. I don't dare hand him over to an adoption or a rescue agency until the divorce is final. The minute the dog is gone, my ex will add possession of him to the settlement." He stared at his drink again. "I feel bad for Noodle. I do. But . . . my dog Tiger died of kidney disease a month before Jessica brought Noodle home. I can't get close to him. I can't stand to lose another one. Not right now."

"Let me help."

"How?" Sandy gave a wry smile. "Know someone willing to rub out my ex?"

Time seemed to slow as fear stabbed my gut. Had the doctor checked into my past? His expression appeared free of ill intent. I released the breath I was holding. "I can help with Noodle. I have a lot of experience working with and training dogs. I can help him become more adoptable for when your divorce is final. Plus, the Saint Bernard part of him is very social. They don't like to be left alone. He can hang with Harlow and me during the day. The dogs can play and I'll work on his training."

"I can't ask you to do that."

"You didn't. I'm volunteering. And I'm not doing it for you. I'm doing it for Noodle."

"I can live with that."

We worked out the details of the Noodle Training Plan, and then Sandy went inside to find a spare key to the courtyard door. He rejoined me at the bar, the key still warm from his hand.

He spun slowly, seeming to see the patio for the first time. "Of course, the dog might not be here when you come for him tomorrow." Hands on hips, he nodded at the wood fence fronting the yard. "I know he's big, but Noodle's no leaper. That said, I've got no idea how he keeps getting out."

I studied the space. One end of the six-foot-high fence abutted the garage; the other, a masonry wall. Creeping fig climbed the surface, cloaking large swaths of stucco with glossy green leaves. I rose and walked the perimeter. Noodle moved to my side, staying close as I stopped in front of a five-by-three-foot deck box sitting next to the wood portion of the fence. "What's this for?"

"We—I mean, I—store the cushions in there. For the chairs. To protect them from the salt air."

I pointed at the metal structure rising beside the bin. "And this is?"

"Bike shed. Jessica's SUV took up too much space in the garage. We didn't have enough room for our bicycles. We got that to store them."

I nodded and climbed on top of the wood bin. "Oh, sorry. You mind me being on this?"

"Go ahead."

The big dog stared at me, upright tail wagging. "I'll be right back, Noodle."

From the box I climbed onto the bicycle shed. The metal roof bowed slightly. I froze. The surface held. I took a tentative step, then crossed to the concrete wall. Shaking my head, I chuckled and turned back to face the doctor. "You've got yourself one smart dog. He's hopping onto the deck box, using that to reach the top of the bike shed. From there, he can jump the wall and land on your neighbor's trash enclosure. It's about a foot below the wall. They've built some sort of lean-to on one side. I'm betting Noodle's using it like a ramp. Once he's in their side yard, he only has to jump a tiny three-foot fence and he's free."

"No. He's not that clever. Is he?"

"There's one way to know for sure." I climbed down and told Noodle to stay.

Together Sandy and I moved the deck box to the side of the garage. The bike shed was a more awkward proposition, but we only needed to shift it five feet over.

When the task was done, the doctor dusted his hands. "Think that'll do it?"

"Yep. I doubt Noodle can jump on top of the bike shed without a leg up from the deck box. And, even if he does make it to the top of the shed, he won't be able to leap to the wall." I moved toward the door. "Thanks for the wine, but I better get home. I've got a hungry dog waiting for me."

"Sure. And thanks for your help."

"No problem." I crouched to pet Noodle. "See you tomorrow, big guy."

The next morning the sun woke me again. I needed to get back on track and buy some window coverings.

After feeding Harlow, I hooked on her leash and we walked to Noodle's house. The big dog woofed as soon as I inserted the key into the patio door. "Hey, Noodle. It's us."

When I pushed the door open, he jumped up, front paws landing on my shoulders. "Oof." I rubbed behind his mocha-toned ears. "Careful, there. You nearly knocked me down. Now sit."

He complied, body twitching with excitement.

I'd left the spare leash here last night and snapped it onto the Saint Berdoodle's collar. "Let's go."

The three of us walked to the beach. Like the day before, a half-dozen dogs ran off leash while their people hurled balls into the waves and across the sand. I set Harlow free and the retriever bit several frothing waves before tearing after a group of sandpipers. When we were well away from the other dogs, I dropped Noodle's leash. Once again, I watched his behavior. I was sure the cops had checked the beach for other body parts, but still . . .

Noodle had found that hand somewhere.

CHAPTER 4

For the second morning in a row, Harlow and I picked up Noodle. When we reached the beach, fog hung on the horizon though clear sky arched overhead. The cries of gulls foraging for food punctuated the ocean's roar. Within minutes of reaching the sand, Harlow was soaked. Noodle remained beside me on dry land. I grinned at him. "Smart dog."

Though I waved at a few of the people out with their dogs, I kept far enough away to discourage conversation. I suspected the leading topic would be Noodle's discovery of the severed hand. While Harlow attacked the foaming water and chased birds, the Saint Berdoodle spent his time nose to the ground following a series of scent trails. Each time he began snuffling along in a new direction, my shoulders tensed. But fortunately, no new body parts turned up.

By the time we returned from our walk, the fog had burned away and the day was growing warm. I toweled off Harlow and brushed her coat, then left both dogs in the backyard. After a

quick shower and change, I checked online for drapery companies. A store in neighboring Ventura had the best reviews. I
went outside to kiss the dogs and hopped in my 4Runner. The
GPS instructions and light traffic got me to the shop in ten
minutes. Four other cars were in the lot. I cut the engine, then
remembered I hadn't brushed my hair. Finger-combing it, I
climbed out and checked my reflection in the sideview mirror.
Presentable. I strolled across the blacktop.

As I entered the shop, a bell tinkled.

"Can I help you?"

In spite of the cars parked outside, the only person I spied
was a slender man with short hair and a close-trimmed beard. He
stood halfway across the store behind a chest-high counter.

Rather than shout back, I closed the distance between us
before answering. "Hi. I need to get some sort of window covers."

"You have a style in mind?"

"No."

An eye-glazing description of the available options followed.
When he paused for breath, I interrupted. "Roller shades. I'll go
with those. The ones with the canisters sound perfect."

Looking slightly miffed at being cut off, he came out from
behind the counter. "I recommend blackout shades for the bedrooms." He guided me to a large island piled with huge sample
books. "These are all the manufacturers we work with." He
picked up the thickest binder and thumped it onto a clear patch
of counter. "As you'll see, there are a variety of materials, fin-
ishes, and colors to choose from." Flipping halfway through the
book, he pointed at the swatches on the left page. "These are
the blackout varieties." He shifted another book free from the
pile and turned the sample-laden pages. "And here are shades
that will allow you to look out, but not let people look in."

"Perfect. I'll browse through these." Worried he'd stay and supervise, I pulled the sample books closer. "I'll let you know if I find something."

Looking like a kicked dog, he walked back to the counter. Had my tone been too sharp? The fact that I asked the question told me I needed to interact with people more often.

After studying a variety of textures and patterns, I decided on a blackout shade with a faux weave motif. I turned my attention to the available colors. I'd never seen so many names for what was essentially beige. A half-hour later, I lugged the pertinent sample book to the counter and waited for the clerk to finish a phone call.

"Find the one you want?"

"Yep." I pointed to the fabric swatch. "This is the winner."

He flipped the piece over. "Sand. That's one of our most popular colors." He noted the item number on a quote sheet. "Before I can give you an estimate, we'll need to have someone come out and measure all the windows you want done."

"Sure." I gave him my address and contact information.

He turned to his computer screen. "Hmmm." A sharp V inserted itself between his eyebrows. "The first available appointment we have is in ten days. On Monday the twenty-second. In the afternoon."

"Nothing sooner? I'm flexible. It can be any time."

"Sorry."

"Okay. I'll take the Monday. But if anyone cancels before that, please let me know."

He tapped away at the keyboard. "I'm making a note of that."

I could expect more early mornings until the shades were installed. Reality clicked in: if the sun didn't wake me early,

Harlow would. Even though I planned to move her sleeping crate to the great room at night, one bark from her and I'd be up. And bark she would. Harlow took her bathroom breaks and breakfast very seriously.

On the drive home, cyclists outnumbered cars on the road. I paused at the entrance to the alley and hit the turn signal. A cyclist dressed in black-and-tan Lycra signaled for me to go first. I recognized my neighbor, Hank, and waved hello. He gave a jaunty salute in return.

I parked in the driveway and entered the house through the front door. After dropping my purse on the kitchen counter, I opened the slider to the yard. Harlow and Noodle bounded toward me, each jumping with excitement, as if I'd been gone for months, not hours. "You kooks. You sure know how to make a person feel welcome. Let me change and we can play catch."

Once I'd run the dogs around the yard for thirty minutes, I poured fresh water into their bowls. They splashed as much as they drank. When they were done, I began working on Noodle's training. A smart dog, he was already responding to sit, stay, come, and heel commands. As I worked the Saint Berdoodle, Harlow followed along, happy to get treats for actions she regularly performed.

Still unsure when the doctor gave Noodle his dinner, I fed him along with Harlow at six thirty, then walked him home. I hadn't seen Sandy since he gave me his patio key. After unlocking the door, I bent down and rubbed the dog's thick coat. "I'm glad you get to spend the days with us. You must've been so lonely here." Noodle grinned and drooled. I kissed his forehead. Before leaving, I used the outdoor spigot to top off his water bowl and wash the drool from my hand. "See you tomorrow, big guy."

Home early enough to enjoy the sunset, I poured myself a

glass of chardonnay and climbed the stairs to the rooftop deck. I chided myself for neglecting to buy a chair and leaned against the rail, watching the sky transition from blue to gold and salmon.

The week streamed by. Each day I felt more settled. The dogs were a big part of that.

On day five, I found the perfect spot to hang Harlow's agility rosettes and plaques. After buffing the trophy she won at the GRCA's National Specialty Event in Agility last year, I waffled about where to put it. Ten minutes of shifting the heavy thing from place to place and I was still undecided. I left it on the nightstand.

On day six, I shelved my signed first edition Sue Grafton mysteries and took my first foray to Pier Point's small commercial center in search of furniture. I cruised the town's one-street business sector, but all the parking spaces were filled. Widening my search, I found a spot on a residential street two blocks away, then made my way back to the main drag.

Folks dressed in shorts, T-shirts, and bathing suits strolled and window-shopped. The majority of stores on the street's north side focused on food and beverages: frozen yogurt, tacos, Thai food, coffee, cookies, and a brewhouse. On the south side, Sweet Johnny's sat closest to the water. A peek inside revealed the place sold beachwear and surfboards. Next door, Gilda's Gifts proudly displayed ocean-themed tchotchkes and souvenir ballcaps in its front window. At the used bookstore, Flipping Pages, I allowed myself to be sidetracked and went inside. I breathed in the sweet, musty scent of old books and began to explore. Forty happy minutes later, I left with six new-to-me paperbacks and stepped out onto the sundrenched sidewalk.

A real estate company and an insurance agent occupied the next two office spaces. At the last shop before the corner liquor store, "Home Stretch" was painted in gold script on the front window. The name sounded promising.

A quick glance told me the store's inventory focused more on home décor than furniture. But it wouldn't hurt to look around. Tall glass shelves on the right displayed candles, as well as ceramic, brass, and glass candleholders. Large decorative pillows in a rainbow of colors filled another rack. I wandered past a table stocked with molded-glass sea stars and urchins, picking up a glass conch shell to examine closely. Setting it down again, I spied a ceramic urn behind two antique milk cans, about thirty-six inches tall and glazed a soft teal. The surface of its rounded center had been incised with swirling abstract lines. It would look perfect beside the great room hearth. I hefted it. Not as heavy as I would've preferred. Maybe I could pour some sand inside and make it less likely to topple if a dog bumped it. I checked the price tag and carried it to the counter.

A sixty-something man dressed in a lavender dress shirt, gray vest, and blue jeans pushed his glasses on top of his silver hair and smiled. "Good choice. If I had an inch more space in my house, I would've bought it myself. Are you familiar with Sterla's work?"

"No. I just like the way it looks."

"He's a local ceramist and quite talented. Bit of a recluse. No web presence. Doesn't like to attend openings—even for his own work. That sort of behavior might be common for people my age, but this guy's in his thirties."

Made total sense. Of course I'd been drawn to the work of an antisocial artist.

When had this isolationist attitude become part of me?

Once upon a time I'd enjoyed people. And I couldn't blame this on my husband's death. Well, not all of it.

The clerk removed the price tag, then pulled two sheets of brown paper from a drawer below the counter and began wrapping the vase. "All right if I put this in a box? I don't think we have a big enough bag and it'll protect the piece better."

"Sure."

"I have a pretty good memory for faces and I don't think I've seen you before."

"I just moved to Pier Point. This is my first time exploring the shops. I was actually hoping to find some high stools for my kitchen counter. And maybe an armchair."

"Maybe?"

"An extra place to sit would be nice, but I'm kind of liking the empty floor space."

He slid the padded ceramic piece into a box and sealed the top with packing tape. "You should stop by the surf shop."

"Really?"

"I know—totally counterintuitive. But there's a young man who does lovely woodwork. The owner lets him display a few pieces there. They handle any sales and pass the money on to him."

"Thanks for the tip." Carrying the big box and bag of books, I retraced my steps to Sweet Johnny's, as recommended. Brightly patterned shirts, shorts, and T-shirts were on display near the front. An array of surfboards filled the center of the store. I assumed the differing lengths followed the same principle as snow skis—longer for speed, shorter for maneuverability. The colors and painted designs were gorgeous.

At the back of the shop, I found a small area with an eclectic mix of wood furniture. Three charming outdoor chairs with surfboard backs tempted me. I set down my box and bag and sat. Comfy. There was also a simple but elegant wood bench, a pair of end tables with mosaic tops and matching coasters, a console table—with what looked like an inlay of turquoise—and four wood barstools with swivel tops. I hopped onto one of the stools. Wow. Talk about perfect. And the right height.

After I retrieved my car, the clerk manning the register helped me load the two stools I'd bought into the back seat. Though everyone I interacted with had been pleasant and welcoming, I headed home, eager to hang out with the dogs.

CHAPTER 5

When the sun woke me the next day, I stretched and smiled. No more boxes were left to unpack.

After quickly washing my face and brushing my hair, I fed Harlow and snapped on her leash. Together we walked to Noodle's. To my surprise, Sandy waved at us from inside the house and opened the French door.

"Hi. What's up?"

"Nothing." He wiped his hands on a dish towel. "Since I haven't been here when you've picked up and dropped off the dog, I just wanted to check in. Everything going okay?" His dark hair curled damply above his shirt collar.

"Yep. We're getting on fine. Noodle's training is really coming along."

"Glad to hear it. And thanks for the help. Sorry to rush off, but I've got to get to the hospital."

"No problem."

He waved again before retreating into the home's dark interior and shutting the door.

I urged the dogs out of the patio and the three of us headed for the beach again. Hank the cyclist was saddling up for his ride when we passed his house. I waved.

"Gorgeous day, isn't it?"

"That it is. Have a good ride."

"Always do." He grinned and pedaled off.

Today the ocean looked more green than blue. The breeze off the water carried the scent of salt and seaweed. To the south, past the breakwater, a handful of sailboats cut across the chop. Seagulls wheeled above and several dogs ran free across the sand. I spied Marge, the Boston terrier, her thin legs a blur under her wiry body as she chased a seagull foolhardy enough to land near the sand. GiGi and JoJo, the black labs, raced back to their owner, the larger of the two gripping a tennis ball in his mouth. I waved at their people.

While the Golden charged after shorebirds, the Saint Berdoodle sniffed his way to a clump of beach grass and started digging. Curious, I followed. When the hole was six inches deep, I moved closer. Something briefly shone through the grains of sand. My pulse rate spiked. "Noodle. Leave it."

The dog lifted his sand-covered nose.

I backed up several steps. "Come." After a moment's hesitation, he trotted to my side. "Good boy. Sit." I offered him a treat. The dog vacuumed it up.

"Stay." Once I was sure he wasn't going to follow, I moved to the hole and peered inside, but spied nothing sparkly. Had the quartz fragments in the sand caught the sun and fooled me into thinking I'd seen a flash of gold? I knelt, then thought better of it, and returned to the dog. Grabbing an unused poop bag from his leash, I slipped it over my hand and sifted through the loose grains at the bottom of the hole. My fingers wrapped around something smooth and round.

I extracted it from the sand. A ring. The heavy gold band was engraved with a vine-and-leaf pattern. I turned to the Saint Berdoodle. "Is this from the hand?"

Noodle looked at me and drooled.

"Good job, boy. But no finders keepers." I pulled out my cell and took a quick picture, then did a search for the police department's business line. The phone rang three times before a husky voice answered. "Pier Point Police Department."

"Hi. I'd like to speak with Detective Vasquez."

By the time the detectives rolled into the cul-de-sac, I had Harlow back on her leash and both dogs were napping on the sand. Detective Vasquez moved toward the water's edge while Wright remained beside the car. I raised one hand to catch Vasquez's eye. Changing course, he strode toward me. Today he was dressed in tan slacks, a golf shirt, and a brown leather jacket. His polished tan oxfords looked incongruous on the beach.

"Ms. Madison."

Detective Wright huffed his way from the car and arrived at our sides, scowling.

"Not a big beach fan?"

Wright's frown deepened. Grinning, Vasquez turned away. Maybe I had an ally after all. When he'd composed himself, I pointed at the hole and the gold ring sitting on the plastic bag beside it. "Noodle dug that up."

"You touched it." Wright sounded like he'd gargled with gravel.

"I used the bag when I picked it up. Like a glove."

"You should've left it where it was."

I did my best to keep my tone level. "I didn't know if it was anything. I glimpsed something shiny, but for all I knew, it was a piece of quartz."

"But you took the precaution of putting a bag on your hand?" Disbelief laced Wright's voice.

I glanced at Vasquez. Eyes shielded behind dark glasses, his expression remained neutral. Even so, he still seemed the friendlier of the two. I directed my words toward him. "Noodle found a hand here five days ago. I was being cautious."

Wright shook his head. "And the dog just strolled across the sand and dug this up?"

"No. He seemed to be tracking a scent."

"Uh-huh." He pointed at me. "Stay."

Heat rushed up my face. I took a deep breath of the salty air. Wright was showing me who was boss, as I did with the dogs. I didn't like it, but there was nothing I could do about it.

He walked to the bag and glared down, then strode past it. After mashing a button on his cell, Wright murmured into his phone.

Vasquez edged closer. "You think the dog actually tracked a scent to a ring buried in the sand?"

"Yep."

"Impressive."

A few minutes later, Wright lumbered back. "Techs should be here shortly. In the meantime, let's start at the beginning." He nodded at his partner. Apparently, Wright was showing Vasquez who was boss, too.

The younger detective pulled out his cell. "I'll be recording this for our report. What time did you arrive at the beach?"

"About eight."

"What happened when you arrived?"

I uncrossed my arms. "When we got clear of the other dogs, I let Harlow run while I followed Noodle. He had his nose down and seemed to be tracking something."

"Then what?"

"He went to that clump of beach grass and started digging."

Wright harrumphed. "And the dog stopped when he found the ring?"

I tamped down another wave of irritation. "No. Like I said before, I thought I saw something sparkly, so I called him away."

"And started digging yourself." Wright smirked.

A fresh flash of anger warmed my cheeks. "More like sifted through the sand."

"Sure."

"And then I called Detective Vasquez."

"Which we appreciate." Vasquez lowered his sunglasses and eyed his partner. Wright's color rose, but he kept his mouth shut. Vasquez returned his attention to me. "Why's the dog with you? I thought he belonged to Dr. Johannson."

"I'm helping with his training."

Wright gave an unamused chuckle. "Guess this means you're the guy's dog walker after all?"

"Call it what you want."

Vasquez turned off the recording app on his cell and tucked the phone inside his jacket pocket. As soon as he pulled his hand free, the phoned burred. Extracting it again, he glanced at the screen and excused himself, answering only after he'd moved out of earshot.

Wright hunkered down and studied the ring. "Thought

you'd be interested to know I checked you out." He squinted up at me. "Called Boston PD. They said you never worked there."

Ah. The official interview was over. This was where things would get ugly. Or rather, uglier. "Didn't say I had."

He rose, wobbling as the sand shifted underfoot. "Found out you worked for the police department in some dinky beach town called Duck Berry."

I didn't correct him.

"You were their K-9 officer until you quit eighteen months ago."

"Yep." It still hurt that the department hadn't let my six-year-old partner retire and leave with me. "And why'd you check out my background?"

"Because you didn't volunteer the fact that you used to be a cop."

"So?" I looked across the beach at Vasquez. He appeared engrossed in conversation.

"In my experience, most ex-cops can't wait to tell an active-duty officer about how they were once on the job, too. The ones who aren't eager to share usually didn't leave the force by choice."

"I did."

The wind ruffled the detective's thinning hair. He flattened it over his bald patch. "Any particular reason?"

"Yep."

"What was it?"

I closed my eyes. This whole conversation felt inevitable and I knew how it would end. "I was pregnant and my husband wanted me to quit. Over the years, I'd miscarried three times and he was convinced the job had something to do with it.

When I got pregnant again, he was frantic for me to turn in my badge."

"And you did?"

"Yep."

"Then you became a private eye?"

"That way I could at least use some of my training."

"But you didn't start your business until three months later. With your law enforcement background, you could've been licensed in two to six weeks. I checked Massachusetts's licensing laws." He gave me a triumphant look.

I didn't bite.

"Why the delay?"

I was sure the bastard already knew the reason. "I started my business after I miscarried again."

"You quit a job you loved and lost the baby anyway. Is that when you decided to kill your husband?"

I clenched my fists and clamped my lips shut.

"I can't believe you got away with it. Did you do it for the insurance or because you were pissed he'd made you change your life?" He waved away his question. "Not important. But it is kind of genius. Hiring one of your own clients to kill the husband who was cheating on you with that client's wife. Twisted."

Tears stung my eyes and I blinked them back. I'd gotten far worse grillings from my former colleagues. Grillings I felt I'd deserved. I hadn't pulled the trigger, but I'd stupidly unleashed the weapon. "I was never charged."

"That could still change."

Vasquez returned, a look of disgust traveling across his handsome face. When he reached us, he spoke to the older man. "You need to call the commander."

Wright's gaze stayed lasered on me. "You may've moved all the way across the country, but you know damn well there's no statute of limitation for murder."

Vasquez waggled his phone in front of the other detective's face. "Now."

Wright sneered at his partner. "Like you're some great judge of character where women are concerned." Looking like he wanted to say more, he swore and stomped all the way back to the car.

Vasquez sighed. "Caught the tail end of that. Hope he wasn't giving you too hard a time."

Was this the good cop/bad cop routine? "I'm okay."

"I know I shouldn't say anything, but the guy's going through a rough patch."

I raised my eyebrows.

"Ugly divorce. He's not been on his best behavior lately. Especially with attractive women." He stepped toward the dogs. "Mind if I pet them?"

Warmth spread across my face. The handsome detective thought I was attractive? "Go ahead."

Once the techs arrived, Vasquez gave the dogs a final pat and told me I could leave. I kept my gaze forward as I walked past Wright, dogs at my side, eager to get home.

When the doorbell rang a half hour later, I was sprawled on the sofa with Harlow by my feet and Noodle on the floor beside the coffee table. Both sat up and barked. The mild headache that had started after my run-in with Wright still lingered. I groaned, then stood. After leading the dogs to the backyard, I trudged through the great room to the front door.

Today Seville wore scarlet leggings and a sheer white top

revealing a baby-blue bra and matching stiletto heels. Was this a special Flag Day ensemble? "Hi."

"Hi yourself. I heard through the grapevine you're training Noodle."

Wow. The doctor and I had only made our arrangement five days ago and I'd yet to see Seville when I was out walking the Saint Berdoodle. Maybe the doctor's ex really did have spies on the street. "Where'd you hear that?"

"What? It's not true?" The breeze lifted her hair and she shook it back into place.

"No, it is. I'm just wondering how you know."

She shrugged. "Came up in conversation—I don't remember with who. How's it going?"

"Pretty good. He's a smart dog. Just needs some direction."

"You have a lot of experience doing that sort of thing?"

"Fair amount."

A huge grin split Seville's face. "I thought so." She held out a small white box. "The way you handled that giant drooly dog when we met . . . I would've bet money you knew what you were doing." She waggled the cardboard container. "This is for you."

Uneasy, I took it. "What is it?"

"Open it and find out."

I lifted the lid. "Are these business cards?"

Seville nodded. "I have a promo company. Impressions, but with IMPRESS in all caps. We print messages on mugs, banners, sticky notes, key chains. The works. Including business cards. I made these up for you. Go ahead, pull one out."

The box was tightly packed, but I managed to ease a card free. I stared at the gold ink on ivory cardstock: Molly Madison, Dog Wrangler.

"It's cute, right? Dog wrangler? When I heard you were training Noodle, I just had to make you some cards. Believe me, tons of folks in Pier Point need help getting their dogs under control. And when I asked you about work the other day, you ignored the question. Which makes me think you're not a nine-to-fiver like me. But even if you do have some sort of paying gig, I figure you can still make time to train a few dogs. A little extra moolah never hurts, right? Maybe help you buy some new furniture. Fill up the bare spots." She gestured at the empty foyer.

I tried to smile. My phone number was on the cards.

"I also printed some flyers. And put a few up around the neighborhood."

"Like where?" Maybe I could run around and take them back down again.

"Let's see." She seemed to study the cloudless sky. "The liquor store. Bookshop. Laundromat. Ooh, I put one up at the studio where I take yoga. A couple women there were interested."

I opened, then closed my mouth. Though I didn't like the idea of strangers having my phone number, it was a sweet gesture. And in spite of my semi-empty house, I didn't need the income. The sale of our home in Massachusetts plus the savings we'd banked due to Stefan's lucrative career had been more than matched by his generous life insurance policy. Money was one thing I didn't need to worry about. But Seville was right. It wasn't as if I had some other gainful employment to fill my days. "Thank you. It's very thoughtful. And the cards are cute."

Seville gave a finger wave and spun on her heel. I closed the door and stared at the card still gripped in my hand. Training other people's dogs might be a fun way to fill my time. But if Wright spread the word about my husband's murder—along with the suspicions that continued to swirl around me—the venture was unlikely to succeed. I tucked the card back in the box.

Only a crazy person would hire a murder suspect as their dog wrangler.

CHAPTER 6

Harlow and I picked up Noodle the next morning and the three of us headed for the beach. I was pretty sure doing this every day for a week meant we'd created a morning routine. Already Noodle had come a long way, no longer pulling as we crossed the sand. My shoulder gave thanks.

Cool air blew off the water. I scanned the beach. Fewer people and dogs were here today. The site of Noodle's latest discovery wasn't marked by yellow crime scene tape, but perhaps cops showing up here twice had made folks leery?

I had to admit, this gorgeous sun-drenched slice of coast did feel sullied.

Yesterday Detective Vasquez had ignored my questions, but common sense said the Saint Berdoodle finding a hand and what looked like a wedding band on the same beach must be related. Still, the logistics made no sense. If both washed ashore from a boating accident, how did the ring wind up buried in the sand?

And how in the world did Noodle find them? Locating the

hand could be written off as luck. But digging up a ring that once encircled its finger? If it indeed had. As I'd told Seville, dogs had amazing noses. Could Noodle's be that good?

If it was, maybe he'd enjoy scent work. I needed to do more research on Saint Bernard–poodle mixes.

After our walk, I put the dogs in the backyard and sat on the sofa with my laptop. I was reading up on Saint Berdoodles when a series of sharp raps came from the front door. Noodle and Harlow woofed through the screen as I went to answer.

A child wearing a gingham sundress stood on my stoop, coppery braids tied with matching blue-and-white ribbon, a sheet of yellow paper clutched in her small hand. "How much do you charge?"

"I'm sorry?"

She held out the wrinkled sheet: a flyer sporting the silhouette of a dog with the banner headline "Molly Madison, Dog Wrangler."

Oh God. Seville had put my home address on the flyer. Was she out of her mind? I shifted my gaze back to the young girl. Dealing with Seville's poor decision would have to wait. "You having a problem with your dog?"

She gave a curt nod. "Butterscotch chewed up one of Rick's Ferragamo loafers. He's really mad. He says we may have to get rid of her."

Whoa. Talk about an overreaction. "Who's Rick?"

"My father."

Odd. "How old is Butterscotch? And how old are you? And does Rick—or your mother—know where you are?"

"I'm eight and one-quarter years old. Butterscotch is four months old."

"And your parents know where you are?"

"Rick's at work. Jemma's meditating. I'm not supposed to bother her when she meditates."

"Is Jemma your mother?"

She nodded.

What eight-year-old called her parents by their first names? Or had "wrangler" in her vocabulary? "Why aren't you in school?"

"I'm homeschooled. Jemma says the regular school system doesn't adequately meet my needs."

Eight seemed about right for the child's height and general size, but her vocabulary and bearing made her seem older. "You live nearby?"

"Five houses from here. The terracotta two-story with white trim."

"Terracotta?"

"That's a shade of red. Kind of like a brick."

An eight-year-old knew the word "terracotta"? "That it is. What's your name?"

"Ava Greenwood."

"And what breed of dog is Butterscotch?"

"Rick calls her a Heinz 57 dog." She frowned. "But that's not a real breed."

I tried to hide my amusement over her indignant tone. "You're right. But it paints a picture. At four months, Butterscotch is still teething. Chewing helps her sore gums feel better. That's going to be an ongoing issue. At least for a while. The best thing to do is make changes to her environment. Make sure things she shouldn't chew are out of reach."

The girl nodded. "How much will it cost for you to train her?"

Detective Wright's veiled threats ran through my brain. I didn't want to promise this girl something I couldn't deliver.

"I should talk to your mom or dad first. They may not want a stranger in their home."

She crossed her spindly arms over her chest. "You're not really a dog wrangler, are you?"

I decided to embrace the title. "I am. But I don't think we should set up any training arrangements without the approval of at least one of your parents."

Ava pulled an iPhone from the pocket of her sundress. "Jemma should be done meditating in ten minutes. We can talk to her then."

"Okay. Wait right here while I get something." It felt rude leaving her on the porch, but any parent—even one who was okay with a child calling them by their first name—would freak about a stranger inviting their kid inside. I hurried to the kitchen and grabbed one of Harlow's Kong toys. Once back on the porch, I held up the sturdy beehive-shaped piece of rubber. "Something like this will help with Butterscotch's chewing and keep her engaged. Do you have one?"

"No."

"See the hole here? You put different kinds of food inside and the dog works to get it. It keeps both her mouth and mind busy. That's especially helpful when she's home alone."

"I don't think Rick will buy Butterscotch any treats or toys. He's livid with her."

First "terracotta" and now "livid"? The kid had a vocabulary. I held out the toy. "Take this one. We'll need to wash it in hot soapy water before we load it up. Are you allergic to peanut butter?"

"No."

"You have some at home?"

The girl shook her head, braids swinging.

"Don't worry. I've got some. When you put food in the toy, you'll need to seal the opening with peanut butter. Hang on." I retreated inside again, grabbed an unopened jar and a package of dog biscuits, and returned to the front door. "You can put a treat or two inside it each time and use the rest of these for training."

Her stormy expression faded and she smiled. Ava checked her iPhone again. "We can go now. Jemma should be done meditating by the time we get there."

Not sure what I was getting into, I locked the door and accompanied the girl along the narrow alley. We passed the faux English country house and Hank the cyclist's house, the white stucco with black trim, and the salmon-toned one with the arched front door. Dr. Johannson's three-story loomed on the opposite side of the street, shadowing its neighbor to its right. Ava's was on the same side of the street as mine. And terracotta-colored, just as she'd said. She led me along a flagstone path, through a wooden side gate, and around the house to the backyard. A russet-colored dog with short legs, long ears, and a low body raced across the postage-stamp lawn, upright tail wagging so hard she could barely keep her balance.

Butterscotch jumped about Ava's legs and the girl bent to meet her. The dog's paws were huge.

My best guess said the dog was a basset-retriever mix. "How big is she supposed to get?"

The girl looked up from hugging Butterscotch. "I don't know."

"Well, I think she's going to be good-sized. Somewhere between forty and seventy pounds. That's a common range for Basset-Retrievers." I crouched and offered my hand to the dog.

Butterscotch licked Ava's face one more time and then did the same to my fingers. "Does she spend most of the day out here?"

"Rick says she can't come inside until he's convinced he can trust her again."

"Oh."

A slender, fey-looking woman dressed in paisley leggings and a flowing pink top opened the sliding glass door and wandered onto the deck. About half of her dark hair had escaped its ponytail holder. The dog thumped her tail, then ran toward her. The woman froze.

Apparently, Jemma didn't care for Butterscotch any more than Rick did.

Ava's mother finally noticed me. I stood, wiped my hand against my jeans, and crossed the lawn to the deck. "Hi. I'm Molly Madison. I just moved in down the street."

"She's a dog wrangler." Ava trotted over to join us, holding out the crumpled yellow flyer. "Molly's going to help me train Butterscotch."

Her mother took the flyer but didn't introduce herself. "The dog does need it." She flinched as Butterscotch pressed against her calf. "All right, then. We can resume your lesson in a half hour." With that, she turned and walked back inside.

No one's family was completely normal, but these people seemed caught in a weird dynamic. Trying to shake off her mother's lack of concern about my credentials, I crouched again and offered my hand to the dog. Butterscotch leaned into me.

"You've got a lesson in thirty minutes?"

Ava nodded.

"What's the subject?"

"Life Science. I'm just starting to study algae and fungi." She looked up from petting Butterscotch. "Fungi includes things like yeast, mold, and mushrooms."

"Right."

"Did you know fungi don't make their own food like plants do?"

"Have to admit, I never gave it any thought."

"Plants use photosynthesis to make their food, but fungi break down stuff that used to be alive to get the necessary nutrients."

Photosynthesis? Geez, I probably didn't master that word until I was twelve. "You like Life Science?"

"Yeah. After that class I get a lunch break. Then I take Poetry and Ancient Civilizations."

"Your mom is able to teach all that?"

"The classes are online. Jemma checks to make sure I got the correct answers on the post-tests."

Didn't sound like mom was straining any brain cells on her kid's education. "You like studying that way?"

"It's okay. Jemma says it lets me advance at my own pace."

"How long have you been home-schooled?"

"Since first grade. Everyone was reading two grades behind me and a lot of them didn't know how to add or subtract—and I was already doing multiplication. I kept getting in trouble because I told Mrs. Friedermacher her lessons were dumb."

"So, does that mean you're a bit of a smarty-pants?"

Ava shrugged. "I'm not sure. Is that a good thing?"

Huh. She knows "photosynthesis" but not "smarty-pants"? "It can be. Being smart can make life easier. As long as you're nice about it."

"Jemma says I'm too smart for my own good."

"As long as you're nice about it, you'll be fine." Doing something that required patience—like training the dog—might be good for both Ava and Butterscotch. I ran my fingers through the Basset-Retriever's thick coat. "Since she's going to be a big girl, it's important for her to learn the rules now. While she's young."

"Okay."

"The ultimate goal is her being welcome inside again, right?"

"Right."

"Can you show me around the house? So I can get the lay of the land."

"Sure."

I gave Butterscotch a pat and stood. The dog settled on the wood deck.

Ava led the way, opening the slider to the family room. The distant rush of running water told me Jemma was taking a shower. "I guess meditating's hard work."

Ava turned to me, brow furrowed. "What?"

"Nothing." I walked deeper into the room. A warm brown leather sofa and recliner centered on a tan and chocolate rug seemed like a decorator's idea of masculine paradise. The cherry-wood coffee and end tables added to the mellow mood. Unfortunately, it looked like Rick was a bit of a slob. A pair of men's shoes had been abandoned in front of the recliner, navy socks lay on the sofa, a silk tie hung over the edge of the coffee table, and a lone cuff link glimmered between the fibers of the area rug. "Is it okay to show me the bedrooms?"

She shrugged again.

I was starting to think of this as her signature move. We climbed a flight of wood stairs to the second floor. A white button-down shirt hung from the newel post. Rick's clothes seemed to have a rough time finding their way to the hamper—

or his closet. We entered a room that was clearly Ava's. A poster of Jupiter and its four largest moons hung on the wall next to a framed photo of Marie Curie. On top of the desk sat a LEGO parrot that dwarfed the completed treehouse next to it. A Spirograph and a solved Rubik's cube were stacked on top of the packed bookshelf. On the shelves themselves, Natalie Babbitt was well-represented, as were J. K. Rowling, Suzanne Collins, and Pam Muñoz Ryan.

Ava was tidy and indeed a smarty-pants. "Lead on."

The next bedroom was used as a combination office and workout space. A small desk sat along one wall, while a stationary bike, rowing machine, and treadmill took up the majority of floor space. The types of abandoned items here changed to sweatpants, socks, and T-shirts. All men's. "Is it okay if we peek inside your parents' room?"

"Uh-huh."

The whoosh of the shower grew louder when we walked through the double doors to the master bedroom. Walnut side tables flanked a king-size bed. A pair of boxers lay on top of the one on the left. A colorful painting of a mermaid filled the wall above. The taller of the two dressers sat near the bathroom door; its wide, squat companion took up the wall opposite the window. The room confirmed my suspicion that Rick was no neat freak: shirts, ties, trousers, socks, and shoes were scattered on the carpet and lone chair, most items abandoned at heights even a short dog like Butterscotch could reach.

This might be tricky. It wasn't just the dog who needed training.

The sound of pounding water stopped. Ava and I exchanged a look, then scurried from the room and down the stairs. Once we were outside on the deck, a giggle escaped Ava, and I joined in laughing. Eager to be part of the fun, Butterscotch barreled over to us.

I bent and stroked her silky coat. "What does she know how to do?"

Ava shrugged. "Be nice to me?"

With no school friends and a disengaged mother, the girl had to be lonely. "That's important. Since we don't have a ton of time, let's work on a couple basic commands today: sit and stay."

"Okay."

I handed Ava a dog biscuit. "Hold the treat above her head. Close to her nose so she'll smell it and look up."

Ava held the biscuit aloft and the dog snagged it. "Uh-oh."

"No worries. Let's try again." I handed her another treat. "This time hold it a bit higher. Good. As she looks up, move the biscuit up—getting Butterscotch's nose to follow it. Good. Now that her nose is up, tell her to sit."

"Sit."

Nose up, the dog remained standing.

"This is still new to her, so we're going to need to push her butt down until she's seated." I did that for Ava as she continued holding the treat above Butterscotch's nose. "Okay. Give it to her along with lots of praise."

The dog inhaled the biscuit. Ava stroked the dog's head and back. "Good, Butterscotch."

"All right. Let's get her to move a bit. Why don't you throw her that ball?"

Ava retrieved a tennis ball from the lawn and tossed it toward the side wall. Butterscotch darted after it and ran in circles instead of returning it.

Duh. The dog hadn't been trained. Of course she wasn't going to bring the ball back. I handed Ava another biscuit. "Get her attention, then give the command."

"Butterscotch. Butterscotch." The dog stopped running. Nose twitching, she trotted to Ava. "Sit, Butterscotch."

This time I stood back and let Ava be fully in charge. Butterscotch dropped the ball. The dog needed another butt push to get her hindquarters all the way down. It took two tries, but Ava managed it. Butterscotch gobbled the treat.

"Great job. Both of you. Let's try 'stay' next." I slid another treat to Ava. "First you're going to ask Butterscotch to sit. When she does, you'll put the biscuit close to her nose and tell her to stay. Why don't you try that part first? Just don't give it to her yet."

"Okay." Once again Ava had to push the dog's butt down for the full sit but did it with more confidence this time.

"Now, tell her to stay, then take two or three steps away."

Ava did as instructed. The dog followed her and the treat. The girl frowned.

"Don't worry. Butterscotch is young. This is part of the process. Tell her 'no.'"

"No!"

"Good. But a stern tone can be more effective here than a loud one. Tell her to sit again . . . Great. Now show her the biscuit and give the 'stay' command. Try moving a few steps away again."

Ava nodded. "Stay." She backed up. This time Butterscotch didn't budge.

"Go ahead and give it to her along with some more praise."

The girl fussed over the dog and Butterscotch's tail went wild.

I checked my cell. Ava's half-hour break was almost over. "If you have some time after lunch and when your lessons are done for the day, try working those commands with her again, okay?"

"Okay." Ava beamed.

"I'm kind of surprised your mom let you get a dog. She doesn't seem all that fond of Butterscotch."

"She's afraid. The only dogs she likes are those little ones you can carry around in a purse." Ava rolled her eyes. "But I told Jemma a dog would help with my socialization."

"You did?"

"Uh-huh. And that a dog would give me someone to talk to and play with every day."

My throat tightened. "What about friends? I haven't been here long. Don't any other kids live on this street?"

Ava gave another eyeroll. "Jemma says she's abandoned the idea of setting up playdates for me. The children around here are so stupid."

"How so?"

"The last time Francine and Mahala came over, they wanted to play airplane. They spread their arms and ran around the yard making engine noises." Ava huffed. "Everyone knows you have to distribute an airplane's cargo evenly. I kept telling Francine she had to move either her bracelet or her watch. She was wearing them on the same wing. But she wouldn't listen."

"You were right. Obviously. But no one likes to be told they're wrong. Maybe next time you guys play airplane you can tell Francine what a good pilot she is."

Ava's hands planted themselves on her hips. "But she was doing it wrong."

"True, but she was flying anyway. She might hear what you're saying better if you congratulate her on her skill—since it's almost impossible to keep a plane level when the load is unevenly distributed."

Arms now hanging loose at her side, she nodded. "Got it."

Good God, this kid was way too smart. "That said, it's not always easy finding people we click with."

"I think you and I click okay."

"I think so, too." I bent down and stroked Butterscotch's flank. "She's got a few tangles. With this coat, she needs to be groomed regularly. Where's her brush?"

"She doesn't have one of her own. I share mine."

Tears stung my eyes. I blinked them back. "Tell you what, I'll bring a spare with me tomorrow. What sort of things does Butterscotch like to do?"

"Run. Dig in Jemma's flowers. And chew Rick's shoes."

I snort-laughed. "We're going to have to teach her some better behaviors. Her mix of basset and retriever means she's got a strong hunting instinct, so she's going to need lots of exercise." I walked to the table on the deck and picked up the Kong toy. "Let's go inside and wash this for her."

The kitchen was spacious, with cherry cabinets, a granite counter, and stainless steel appliances. Unlike the rest of the house, the surfaces and floors were immaculate. Ava opened the cupboard under the sink and pulled out a bottle of dish soap. "Will this work?"

"Perfect." I scrubbed the toy in hot water, then Ava dried it. "What does Butterscotch usually eat?"

"Puppy chow." Ava dragged a large bag out of the pantry. We loaded the toy with kibble and a couple dog treats.

"Some people like to spray bitter apple on stuff to keep dogs from chewing. But that doesn't always work. I prefer engaging the dog with healthier activities. Which is where the Kong toy comes in. It'll give her something tastier to chew than your dad's shoes."

Ava nodded.

I opened the jar of unsalted Jif and scooped a dollop across the toy's opening. "Why don't you finish sealing it?" I handed her the butter knife.

As Ava spread the peanut butter to seal the toy, the tip of her tongue protruded.

"Good job." I lowered my voice. "Here's the deal: training Butterscotch is going to be the easy part. The tough part— especially when your dad lets her inside again—is to make sure all the closet doors are shut so she can't get at anyone's shoes. And to check that clothes and things you don't want chewed are kept out of her reach."

Ava frowned. "Rick's not going to like that."

"I'll bet. But if you do catch her chewing something, you need to disrupt the action."

"Like grab it?"

"It's better if you can startle her with a loud noise. Butterscotch will probably drop whatever it is and you can put the item somewhere safe. If you try to grab it, she may think it's a game—like tug-of-war. Which won't be good for shoes or clothes. And don't chase her if she grabs a shoe and runs. She'll think that's a game, too. If you have to, you can offer her a treat so she'll drop whatever she's got in her mouth."

I paused for emphasis. "The main thing is to make sure Butterscotch gets plenty of physical and mental exercise."

"Okay."

"Before we give Butterscotch the toy, let's check with your mother to see if there's a good time I can come by regularly. I think we could work with Butterscotch together for a half hour every day to start. If we need to do more—or less—we'll figure that out. How's that sound?"

She ran to the foot of the staircase. "Jemma! When can Molly come back and play?"

I tried to hide my grin.

When no answer came, Ava returned and handed me the Kong toy. "I'll be right back." When she pounded her way back down the stairs, another smile lit her face. "Jemma says we can make my morning break a half hour from now on so we can train Butterscotch."

"Perfect." I handed the toy to her. "Let's see how she likes this."

The dog loved it, which earned me another smile from Ava.

"You both did great today. But some days are likely to be tougher than others. She's still very young."

Ava nodded.

"The thing to remember is: if the problem doesn't get better right away, we can try other strategies, okay? At no charge."

CHAPTER 7

The evening fog rolled in as I walked along the alley after returning Noodle. I hoped the doctor would get home soon and let the dog inside. The misty air hadn't yet sunk to street level, but when it did, the poor dog would get damp. Sure, he had a thick coat, but still . . .

My cell phone burred inside my pocket. When I pulled it out, the name on the screen sparked a smile. "Hey, Murph. How're you doing?"

"Feeling blessed. As always. The more important question is: How're you doing, sugar?" Though Murph had spent the past dozen years in Boston, her voice still carried a hint of Georgia.

"Pretty good. I'm not sure where I stashed most of my jeans or sweatpants, but at least everything's unpacked. And the kitchen's set up."

"Glad to know you won't starve."

"Like I'd let that happen. I've also organized my books." I turned down the front path to my house.

"Just what you need for company—dog-training manuals."

"Those aren't the only books I own."

"But they're the ones you read most often."

"Busted." I unlocked the front door. Harlow capered and barked with enthusiasm over my return. "I think there's a certain beautiful dog who'd like to say hello." I held out the cell. "Say 'Hi' to Murph." The Golden gave a mighty woof.

"Tell her I miss her, too."

"Will do."

"Seriously, though . . . I know it's early days, but have you talked to any actual humans since you moved? Those short transactional exchanges you favor don't count. I mean a real conversation."

"I have. With three different people."

"Sugar, California's changed you."

I sank onto the sofa. Harlow jumped up beside me. After circling, she rested her head on my thigh and I stroked her silky coat. "Actually, now that I think about it, one of the exchanges was pretty transactional. I'm training the dog of a too-busy-for-normal-life doctor."

"Of course you are. And the other human-to-human convos?"

"One's a neighbor who likes to drop by and insert herself into my life. She's nice. I'm not sure any of our interactions have been the sort that'd meet your high standards, but we're getting to know each other. And she did make me a set of business cards. That I didn't even ask for."

"Business cards for what?" Murph's voice reflected a note of caution.

"Dog training. She thinks I should use my spare time to help the people of Pier Point get their canines under control.

Not sure I'll get much business." Unbidden, a grin formed. "But I did meet someone who I really hit it off with. She likes her dog way more than she likes most people. And the girl speaks her mind."

"Sounds like you found your clone."

I ran my fingers along Harlow's flank. The Golden sighed and closed her eyes. "Well . . . she's also super-smart."

"So, she can teach you a thing or two."

"Funny. And she's eight years old."

Silence filled the line. "You still there?" I asked.

"I know you're socially lazy. But how in hell did you befriend an eight-year-old?"

"We bonded over dog-training woes."

"Maybe this move wasn't the right thing for you after all."

"Maybe not. But not because I don't have any grown-up friends yet." I told Murph about Noodle finding the severed hand.

"And the detectives on the case have already figured out you're an ex-cop?"

"Yep. And more."

"Should I expect a call?"

Murph had left the force when a bullet shattered her hip. Not content to sit at home collecting a pension, she'd opened an office for small owner-operated businesses, renting furnished spaces and providing front desk services to those who needed them. She'd been my work landlord for over a year and my best friend for ten. Though she couldn't see me do it, I shrugged. "I'm not in the loop and don't know for sure."

"But . . ."

"It's possible. The lead detective's already dug around in my past, which means there's a good chance he'll be in touch. I'm just hoping the story doesn't blow up. If it does, I'll be looking for a new place to land. Again."

"Oh, sugar."

After we ended the call, I shifted Harlow and retrieved my laptop. The Golden resettled her head against my thigh. While Harlow twitched in dreamland, I read up on Saint Berdoodles. After perusing several websites, I found an article on Saint Bernards in *Smithsonian* magazine. According to its author, this breed had a nose with an amazing pedigree. For two hundred years, monks had used them to locate lost travelers along a snow-filled pass in the western Alps. Impressive.

I opened a new search window and found out the poodle was no slouch either, an excellent tracking dog with a great nose. When the two were combined, you had the potential for a dog with an outstanding sense of smell.

If Noodle had that sort of gift, he needed encouragement and stimulation. I did a quick search for scent-training classes in Ventura County. An intro-level drop-in class was held Monday evenings at Playtime Academy for Dogs in Moorpark. I input the town's name and found it was only twenty-five miles away. Not bad. The same place offered a six-week course on Tuesday nights and Saturday afternoons during the summer.

I doubted the doctor would be willing to pay for any classes. Hell, he wasn't even paying me. But it would be fun for Noodle. Maybe Harlow would like it, too.

The next morning, I was in the midst of hooking Harlow's leash onto her collar when a loud series of raps came from the front door. I looked at my Golden. "Has your pal Noodle learned how to knock?"

The retriever wagged her tail.

I opened the door and my heart sank. "Detective Wright." I looked past the rumpled man to his partner. "Detective Vasquez." Today Vasquez sported tan trousers, a striped dress shirt, and a navy blazer. Once again his partner looked like he'd grabbed his ensemble from the hamper—or possibly the floor.

"May we come in?" Wright brushed past me before I had the chance to answer.

Tightness gripped my chest as I stared after him.

Turning left, he strode into the great room, rested his hands along his belt, and surveyed the surroundings.

Vasquez gave me an apologetic shrug, then followed the other detective. "Looks like you're more settled than the last time we were here."

"Yep."

Wright sat on the sofa without waiting for an invitation. After settling on the opposite end, Detective Vasquez spoke again. "We've got a few more questions for you."

"Figured as much. Give me a minute." I didn't wait for an answer and led Harlow into the kitchen, then opened the slider. Crouching, I kissed her forehead then unhooked her leash. "We'll walk later, girl. Promise."

Before returning to the great room, I took a deep breath. Rather than sitting, I positioned myself in front of the fireplace. The room had a new spicy smell. Either Vasquez or Wright had a heavy hand with his aftershave. "What do you need to know?"

Wright frowned up at me. "Pretty interesting timing on you finding that ring." He turned and nodded at Vasquez.

The younger man pulled out his phone and held it up. "I'll be recording this for our notes."

I nodded to Vasquez before turning to Wright. "What's so interesting about it?"

He waved me off. "We'll get to that. First, when did you leave Massachusetts?"

"Saturday, May 30."

"And when did you get to California?"

"Why?"

"Just answer the question."

In spite of my rising temper, I managed to keep my voice calm. "June 9."

He lifted his eyebrows.

The unspoken question of why the journey had taken so long hung between us. I caved first. "I took a lot of driving breaks for the dog. And we made a three-day stop along the way."

"You moved into this house on June 9?"

"No. We stayed in Oxnard the first night. At a pet-friendly hotel. The movers were scheduled to arrive with our stuff the next day, so we checked out Tuesday morning and waited here until they showed. Why?"

"And the three-day stop—were you visiting friends?"

"Kind of. Harlow competed in an AKC agility meet in Denver. The weekend before we arrived in California."

Wright frowned. "AKC?"

"American Kennel Club."

"What's an agility meet?"

"A competition. A few people I know had dogs taking part. Once our moving plans were set and I was sure we'd be able to get to Denver before the trials, I entered Harlow. I figured it'd break up the drive and be fun for us."

"Where in Denver was the competition?"

"At Schaefer Athletic Complex."

"Names? Of the people you knew there."

"Why?"

Wright leaned back and sighed. "Just answer the question."

I gave him the names of three people I'd spent time catching up with at the event.

"Phone numbers?"

I bit back another "why," then pulled out my cell and shared their information. My jaw began to ache. Great. I was grinding my teeth. I took another deep breath before speaking again. "What's this got to do with finding the ring? Noodle found it on June 10. A week ago. Why are you asking where I was the ten days before that?"

"That's not your concern. Yet."

Vasquez cleared his throat. "We're just gathering information. No need to be worried." Wright glowered at him.

I pretended not to notice the rising tension between the two men. "Have the techs determined if the ring came from the hand Noodle found? Or how many days—or hours—passed between when the hand was cut off and when Noodle found it? And whether the person was alive when it happened?"

Vasquez opened his mouth, but Wright cut him off. "You know how this works. We ask, you answer. Are you sticking with your story about the dog magically digging up that ring?"

"It's not a story. Saint Berdoodles have an amazing sense of smell."

"Right." He dragged out the word, disbelief dripping from each letter. "Let's talk about your husband."

And there it was. My stomach twisted. I'd hoped what happened to my husband wouldn't follow me all the way to California. I glanced at Vasquez. He kept his gaze pointed down at his hands. "You mean like, what were his hobbies? Interests? He was a huge Pats fan. And loved to fish. Played harmonica. Is that what you're looking for?"

Wright gave another sigh. "You know it's not. Tell me about his murder. I've already spoken with the lead detective on the case, which means there's no point in not giving the full story."

"So why ask me? Sounds like you know everything already."

"Ah. But that's just it. According to Detective Reilly of the Kingston Police Department, you've been holding out on your former colleagues. If you don't want to answer our questions here, we can go to the station."

My face grew hot. The way the cops back home had turned against me was almost understandable. The relentless accusations launched by Stefan's family had begun to tarnish the entire department. But this jackass coming after me because he was angry over his messy divorce? "Am I under arrest?"

He bared his teeth in a poor imitation of a smile. "You know better than that. If I arrest you, I gotta read you your rights. But if you want to be arrested, I'm willing."

I glanced at Vasquez. His expression looked pained. I was sure his partner was bluffing, but my lawyer was back in Massachusetts. It hadn't occurred to me that I'd need a defense attorney here.

"Ask your questions."

"Tell me about your involvement in your husband's murder."

I breathed through the fresh wave of anger at his use of the word "involvement." It wasn't wrong, but it was damn unfair. "As you must know, Wendall O'Malley, the man who killed my husband, is in jail awaiting trial. And yes, his killer hired me to find out if his wife was cheating. She'd started going out on Wednesday nights, claiming she had a Tai Chi class. He grew suspicious. Didn't tell me why. But when he dropped in on the class to see if Alice was there . . ." I spread my hands wide. "She wasn't."

Wright arched an eyebrow. My pulse ticked up another notch as I continued. "O'Malley told me he didn't care who his wife was cheating with. He just wanted to know if his suspicions were correct. The next Wednesday night, I followed Alice five miles to the Pilgrim Motel in Kingston, where she stayed for two hours. I didn't see the man and figured he'd arrived before her. Since my client hadn't hired me to determine the man's identity, I made no attempt to get information from the desk clerk. Instead, I went back to my office and wrote up a report. The following Wednesday, O'Malley drove to the motel and shot both his wife and the man she was cheating with."

"And you had no idea that man was your husband?"

"Stefan was handling a complicated land rights case and had to travel frequently. At least, that's what I thought." In truth, I'd barely noticed his repeated absences. Hadn't even realized his "out-of-town" trips took place every Wednesday night. After the last miscarriage, we barely spoke to one another, each of us trapped in a tangle of loss and anger.

Wright shifted his weight, resting his elbows on his rumpled pants. "You're an ex-cop. Pretty hard to believe you didn't notice something was up."

"I didn't." I resisted the urge to cross my arms over my chest. "Since Detective Reilly already gave you the case details, why are you really here? Just ask what you want to know or leave."

Wright's cheeks flushed an angry red. "The timing's suspicious. With your history, even you must see that."

"The timing of what?"

"It'd make me a lot more comfortable if you sat down."

Like I was supposed to believe I was making him nervous.

The man was six inches taller than me and outweighed me by at least eighty pounds. And he was armed. But rather than argue, I sank onto the cold stones of the hearth.

"Seems quite the coincidence, you finding the hand."

"I didn't find it."

"Right. The damn dog found it. And the timing of this 'discovery' is suspicious. You move here and a few days later, a severed hand washes up on the beach."

"Are you saying it did come from the ocean?"

Wright tsked. "What I'm saying is it's strange how you show up and the hand appears. I'm thinking maybe you had a score to settle and you killed the victim, cut her up, and took the remains to the beach a piece at a time. But the neighbor's dog screwed things up by finding the hand and carrying it back to you across the sand. All those people out there with their dogs, one of them might've seen you with it. Which meant you couldn't just chuck it into the ocean."

"Enough," Vasquez said.

Wright pursed his lips and shook his head. "You don't get a vote on this."

Vasquez's jaw tightened, but he remained silent.

Feeling sick, I finally caved to the impulse and crossed my arms. "Do you have an actual question?"

The detective gave another humorless chuckle. "You got any proof about when you left Massachusetts and when you got here?"

"Yep." Anger jerked me to my feet faster than I intended. "Hang on." I took my time climbing the stairs, then stalked into the office and stared at the piles of paper on the antique ship captain's desk until my heart rate returned to normal. After shuffling through the pertinent stack, I returned to the great room. "Here. Hotel bills. Restaurant receipts. Moving company invoice. I want them all back as soon as possible." Though I wasn't actually worried about losing the various slips of paper, giving Wright a hard time felt good.

"The gas and hotel receipts will show I arrived two days before Noodle found the hand. When would I have time to meet, kill, and dismember someone, then dispose of the parts?"

He handed off the stack to Vasquez, who took them with a mutinous scowl. Wright leaned back, looking way too relaxed for my taste. "Here's the thing. Who's to say the victim lived here in California? Maybe someone came with you from Massachusetts? Or maybe you moved to California to hunt the victim down. You could save us some time by telling us who she was."

Vasquez noisily squared the papers against the coffee table. I swore I spied sympathy in his eyes before he returned his attention to the receipts.

Wright frowned. "Was she another randy woman who slept with your husband? Or some poor motel maid who cut and ran after seeing your husband get killed?"

I bit back an angry retort. Even on a good day, insulting a cop was a bad idea. Especially since I wanted to live in Pier Point for the foreseeable future. "As fishing expeditions go, this is sad. All you've got is conjecture for bait. And I'm not guilty, so I won't bite."

CHAPTER 8

Once the detectives left, I climbed the stairs and hit the shower to wash away my interview-generated layer of sweat. Dressed in a fresh pair of shorts and T-shirt, I called Harlow into the kitchen and attached her leash. As soon as we stepped outside, I heard Noodle's deep barks coming from down the street.

I looked at my prancing Golden. "That poor dog. He's gotten used to having friends to hang out with." I broke into a jog and Harlow followed suit. When I unlocked the patio door, the Saint Berdoodle barreled through the opening. I bent to rub his mocha-toned ears. Saliva splattered my bare legs. "Ugh. Forgot my drool cloth. Never mind. Let's grab your leash and get out of here."

We headed down the alley to the beach. My time with the detectives meant we arrived later than usual. At this hour, no dogs ran free amid the sunbathers and body surfers. I bent and stroked the retriever's forehead. "Sorry, girl. Can't let you loose today."

While we walked, Noodle stayed close, seeming comforted by my presence. I felt bad he'd had to wait an extra hour before joining us today. When I'd had my one conversation with Sandy Johannson, I'd failed to ask what time he put Noodle outside each morning. I hoped the dog hadn't been stuck on the patio longer than ninety minutes.

Even on a lead, Harlow managed to show the shorebirds who was boss and bite several foaming waves. As we trekked across the sand, the smell of coconut-scented sunscreen rose from the baking sunbathers. I replayed the detectives' visit in my head. Detective Wright had confirmed at least one of my suspicions: the severed hand had belonged to a woman. He also made it sound as if the hand had spent some time tumbling about in the salty water.

At Marina Park, I stopped and stared at the children's playground. The colorful equipment reminded me how long it had been since I'd done any agility work with Harlow. I needed to start practicing with her again. Ocean walks were fun, but they didn't challenge her the way agility did. We turned back and I resumed dissecting the interview with Wright.

When we reached the house, the dogs guzzled water, seeming to splash as much as they consumed. I retrieved Harlow's weave poles from the garage and set them on the patio table while the dogs lolled on the lawn. The sun had been up for hours, but dew still clung to the outdoor furniture. I hadn't realized summer nights would be so foggy.

Pacing across the grass, I searched for a good location. Finding a flat area near the back of the yard, I placed the poles, leaving the required twenty-four inches between them. Dewy grass brushed against my ankles. Poor Butterscotch had to sleep outside in this damp. Which reminded me . . . I checked the time. I needed to be at Ava's in fifteen minutes. That gave me just enough time to finish.

The doorbell chimed. Though the dogs looked logy and hadn't bothered to bark, I still gave them a stay command before going inside.

Seville stood on the stoop, dressed in a fuchsia tank top, skintight jeans, and another pair of four-inch heels. "Morning."

"Hi."

"Sorry to drop by unannounced."

I held back a smirk. She'd never stopped by any other way. "No problem."

"When I left for work this morning, I thought I recognized a plainclothes cop at your door. What's going on?"

"Good eye." Being self-employed, Seville must be free to leave work whenever she chose. Otherwise she wouldn't be here right now. I glanced at the time again and didn't invite her inside. "A couple detectives did come by."

"Do they know whose hand it was?"

"I don't think so." Sharing the detectives' cover story was less troubling than giving Seville the real reason for their visit. "They had a few follow-up questions about the ring."

"What ring?"

"I didn't tell you?" I shook my head. "Guess I haven't seen you since Noodle found it."

"Frankendoodle found a ring?"

"Yep. We were at the beach and he dug up a wedding band. At least it looked like one to me."

"Oh my God. Did it belong to the hand?"

I shrugged. "Who knows? Lots of people lose stuff in the sand."

"If it's from someone else, that's a helluva coincidence."

"Agreed."

"And it was really a wedding ring?"

"I think so. I didn't want to handle it, but the band looked like solid gold. And it had this pretty vine-and-leaf pattern etched into the surface."

Seville frowned. "Wow."

"What?"

She pinched her lower lip. "I just . . . A wedding band's special. Losing it's sad—whoever it belonged to." Seeming to shake off the image, Seville looked over her shoulder. Her hulking red Yukon blocked the alley. "I better scoot. Thanks for the update."

"Sure. I've got to run, too. I'm helping Ava train her dog."

"The little girl with the big brain?"

"That's the one."

"Careful with her. She tried to kill me."

I looked at her face for signs she was joking but saw none. "What?"

"She ran up to talk to me while clutching a half-eaten PB and J sandwich."

"And?"

"I'm severely allergic to peanuts. Fortunately, I had my EpiPen. But I haven't trusted the rug rat since then."

"She's just a kid." With too few friends.

"Yeah, but she's a smart kid. She should've known better."

"Why? Had you told her about your allergy?"

Her cheeks grew pink. "No, but her parents knew."

Considering what I'd seen of Ava's mom so far, I was surprised Seville expected the woman to have absorbed the information, let alone repeated it to her daughter. But bad-mouthing any of my new neighbors seemed like a poor idea. Instead, I gave another shrug. "There's a good chance Ava didn't know."

Seville snorted. "Yeah well, good luck with your project."

"Speaking of Ava, she asked me to help with her dog because she saw one of your flyers."

"Oh?"

"Yep. She came here. To my home. Because my address was on the flyer."

"Oh, don't worry about that." Seville waved away my concern. "This is Pier Point. You couldn't live in a safer place. Well, safe except for the rug rat."

I opened my mouth but held my peace. The damage was already done. No need to pick a fight; I wanted this move to work out. And, even if I did expand on my complaint, I couldn't picture Seville running around town to take down the flyers. If I wanted them gone, that was up to me.

When she reached her SUV, Seville turned to face me. "I'm serious. If you're going to work with that . . . child, you'd better watch your back."

After a half-hearted wave, I hurried to the kitchen for my keys. I doubted Jemma would change Ava's schedule to accommodate any tardiness on my part. I checked on the dogs, then grabbed Harlow's old puppy crate and stowed it in my 4Runner. Though I didn't want to broach the topic in front of Ava, I hoped I could manage a conversation with her mother about letting Butterscotch spend her nights inside the house in a crate. If that didn't fly, hopefully she'd agree to put the crate in the garage. Even if both suggestions failed, I could still make a warm, dry space outside for the dog. To that end, I moved several empty boxes, searching for the spare tarp I used as a shade cloth for Harlow during competitions. Once I found it, I placed it in the back, along with one of her blankets.

I felt foolish driving the five-house distance to Ava's, but it was easier than lugging the crate on foot. Ava ran out her front door and down the walkway before I managed to pull everything from the 4Runner.

"Hi." A wide smile revealed a missing tooth.

"What happened there?"

Her smile broadened. "I lost an incisor. The tooth fairy brought me ten dollars." She gave a conspiratorial glance over her shoulder before continuing. "It's really my parents, but I play along." Her smile faltered. "What's that?" She pointed at the folded metal grid.

"It's a crate. I figured you could help me set it up and Butterscotch could sleep in it at night."

Her forehead furrowed. "It looks like a cage."

"Just wait until we get it set up. We're going to make it nice and cozy." I handed her the tarp and blanket. "Let's take this out back to the deck."

"Okay." She gave the metal pieces another suspicious look before leading the way through the house. Once again, I couldn't help but notice the men's clothes scattered on the floor and furniture. Rick was going to take a fair amount of training.

When we stepped outside, Butterscotch bounded over. I leaned the folded crate against the wall and gave the dog some love.

"Hey, Ava, ask her to sit."

"Butterscotch, sit."

The dog sat. I smiled at the girl. "Good job. Both of you."

Ava handed Butterscotch a treat as I began setting up the crate on the wood deck.

"It looks even more like a cage now."

"Just wait. Hand me that blanket." I filled the bottom of the crate with the fuzzy fabric. "Okay, now the tarp." I draped the waterproof cover over the crate. "This will protect her from the damp nights. Can you hand me those clips?"

Once the tarp was secure, I stood back. "Put a biscuit inside. Let's see what Butterscotch does."

Ava frowned but tossed a treat into the crate. Butterscotch hesitated on the threshold to sniff the blanket, then entered and scarfed up the snack. Once inside, the dog circled, then lay down.

"She likes it." Ava stared wide-eyed at the crate. "Why would she like being in there?"

"Dogs are den animals. The crate is like a den, providing a sense of security. It'll become her own personal refuge. When your parents are ready to let Butterscotch inside again, the crate can be moved into any room and she can continue sleeping in it. She can also curl up in it whenever she feels stressed or overwhelmed. Plus, if everyone's going to be gone, you can put her inside and close the latch. She'll be content and you won't have to worry about her chewing anything."

"You really are a dog wrangler." The girl's awed tone made the words sound like the highest compliment she could offer.

"Yep. Now let's do some wrangling."

She giggled, then called Butterscotch. We spent the remainder of her break working the sit, stay, and come commands. When our time was up, Butterscotch scampered into her den and Ava grinned.

"I know you need to get back to your schoolwork, but while you do that, I want to talk to your mom."

"Why?"

Not wanting to raise Ava's hopes about Butterscotch getting to sleep inside the house in a crate, I mentioned the second topic I had in mind. "The weekend's right around the corner. I want to see what time would be good for me to come over to work with you and Butterscotch on Saturday and Sunday."

"Yay!" Ava opened the slider and yelled for her mom, then skipped to her workstation off the kitchen.

I waited for Jemma by the open slider to the deck. Five minutes passed before she crossed the family room dressed in black leggings and a long teal tunic. She stopped a few feet behind Ava and watched her daughter work, then turned to scan the room.

I waved to catch her eye. Then I waved again. Finally, she honed in on me and wandered to the slider. Stepping onto the deck, I beckoned for her to join me. Once she did, I slid the door shut. Butterscotch lifted her head at the sound but didn't budge from her blanket nest.

The woman cocked her head, looking like she wasn't sure who I was or why I was in her yard.

"Hi. I'm Molly Madison."

Jemma continued to stare blankly at me.

I dropped a few more breadcrumbs. "I'm your new neighbor. We met two days ago. On Tuesday." Still nothing. "I'm helping Ava train Butterscotch."

"That damn dog. Rick never should've said Ava could get her."

Odd. According to Ava, it was Jemma who had okayed the dog. "Anyway, I wanted to talk to you about Butterscotch."

"What's she done now?"

"Nothing. I mean nothing bad. She's making amazing progress with her training."

She arched an eyebrow, managing to look confused rather than skeptical.

"Really. And I brought a crate for her to use." I pointed be-

hind Jemma and she seemed to notice the tarp-covered contrap-
tion for the first time. "The dog's content there. I think you can
move the crate into the house so she can sleep inside at night.
It doesn't have to be a bedroom or anything. A corner of the
kitchen or laundry room—or even the garage—will do."

Jemma turned back to me. Swaying, she placed one hand on
the glass slider and steadied herself. Balance regained, she
pursed her lips. "I don't think so. I'd need to talk to Rick first
and he's still . . . upset." She nodded at the crate. "I'm glad to
hear the dog is doing better."

Rats. "Okay. I also wanted to find out what time Ava's free
over the weekend. For more dog training lessons."

Jemma blinked slowly. "Oh, I don't think any time will work
then. Those are family days." On her second try, she managed
to open the slider. Crossing the kitchen, she stood behind Ava
for a moment, then drifted out of view.

I looked down at Butterscotch. Sensing my gaze, the dog
lifted her muzzle and stared back with sincere brown eyes. I
crouched and rubbed her ears, then whispered, "Is Jemma
stoned?"

Butterscotch rested her chin on her paws and closed her
eyes.

"You're right. Best not to answer that. I knew you were a
smart dog."

CHAPTER 9

The dogs and I were returning from the beach Friday morning when a familiar red Yukon pulled over to the curb. The driver's tinted window hummed down and Seville grinned.

"Harlow, Noodle, sit." Once they obeyed, I returned my attention to her. "Hi. How's it going?"

"Couldn't be better. I see you survived working with the Brainiac."

"Ava?"

Seville pushed her sunglasses up onto her tumble of blonde hair. "The very one."

"She and Butterscotch are doing great with training."

"And you walked away unscathed. Good for you." She stretched her arm out the window. "Glorious day, isn't it?"

The sun warmed my bare shoulders under a brilliant blue sky, but Seville's joyous expression seemed over-the-top for mere weather appreciation. "What's going on? You look practically giddy."

With a laugh, she beckoned me closer, then whispered,

"Love is in the air." Her left hand fluttered in front of my eyes. "A certain finger of mine will be sporting a huge rock soon. We're talking about a frigging iceberg. Titanic big."

Mixing shipwreck imagery with an expected proposal? Right. Not everyone's marriage ended in literal carnage. "Congrats. Who's the lucky guy?"

Seville shook her head. "I don't want to say anything until it's official. Can't risk jinxing things." She crossed her fingers.

"Is it someone you've been seeing awhile?"

"Long enough to know he's the one." Her hand disappeared inside the car. "And—though you didn't ask—he's loaded."

Yikes. How was that something I should've asked? "Uh . . ."

She waved me off and chuckled. "No worries. And I mean that literally. Like, none. At least moneywise. I'll probably still run my business after we're married, but I won't have to care whether it's profitable anymore."

Huh. Seville sounded more excited about his bank account than the man himself. Not an opinion I needed to share. "Good for you. And, again, congratulations."

"Thanks. Don't say anything to anyone yet. Not until I've got the rock."

I cocked my head. "Who am I going to tell?" I pointed at the dogs. "Besides these guys?"

"Good point." Seville chuckled, then revved off.

I took the dogs into the yard through the side gate and grabbed a towel. After drying Harlow's coat, I brushed her, then did the same with Noodle. The Golden settled in a pool of sunshine, fur gleaming, while Noodle sprawled on the shady deck.

When I went inside and checked my email, I found a new message from Mom. In addition to wanting to hear more about my new life in California, she reminded me to buy sunscreen. I couldn't help but smile. No matter how old I got, she was still my mom. Knowing she'd hear the stress in my voice if I called, I wrote back instead. By the time I finished sharing the non-worrying details of my life, it was time to head to Ava's. I peered through the slider. Both dogs were sleeping, so I left by the front door and hustled along the alley.

As I neared Ava's house, the girl ran down the front path to greet me. Cheeks flushed, she grinned broadly. "Butterscotch loves her crate. You must be the best dog wrangler ever."

As far as I knew, I was the only person claiming that title, but I gave a modest shrug.

"Come on." Ava grabbed my hand and scurried through the house to the deck. Once there, she pointed at Butterscotch happily snoozing in her crate. "See?"

"I do." After luring the Basset-Retriever from her den, we worked the sit, stay, come, and heel commands. "Good work, Butterscotch." I waggled my eyebrows at Ava and whispered, "You, too."

The girl beamed.

As clever as she was, I wondered how often Ava actually received praise for her accomplishments. Did knowing she was whip smart give her parents unrealistic attitudes about what markers were worthy of celebration?

I hoped not. No matter how bright the girl, she was still only eight.

When I said we needed to take the weekend off, Ava acted stoic. Apparently, her mother hadn't told her Saturday and Sunday were "family time." We wrapped up with a game of fetch, which led to teaching Butterscotch the "drop it" command.

———

The next two days passed in a pleasant blur. No visits from detectives. No worries about past rumors ruining my new life. Harlow, Noodle, and I continued our morning walks and training sessions, and I did some research on nose work for dogs. Each morning, I saw Hank the cyclist leave on his bike but missed his returns.

On Sunday, after returning from our beach walk and putting the dogs in the yard, I decided to take a closer look at the small garden in front of the ultramodern masonry-and-glass building on the far side of Seville's house. I wanted more than a patch of grass in my yard but wasn't sure what to plant. Standing in front of the mix of blooms and greenery, I breathed in the sweet scent of gardenia as I surveyed the vegetation. Very few houses along the alley featured lush plantings like this one.

"Hi there."

I jumped at the deep voice.

A broad man, just shy of six feet, dressed in neatly pressed jeans and a peach short-sleeve shirt, held out his hand. His hair was mostly gray and deep lines bracketed his mouth. "You're the new neighbor, right? I'm Doug Yamada." His huge hand engulfed mine.

"That's me, all right. I'm Molly Madison."

"Why don't you come inside? My wife and I have been wanting to meet you."

"Sure." I followed him up the flagstone path to the front door and into the soaring entryway. To the right a marble staircase spiraled upward. An abstract painting filled the wall to my left, its swirling teals and golds catching my eye.

"Let's sit in the solarium."

Trailing him along a wide hallway, I spied a cozy study and an airy living room on the left, to the right a closed door, and then the kitchen. We stopped in a glass room with a view of the backyard.

A petite woman, wearing a sleeveless dress that showed off well-defined arm muscles, sat in one of the wicker chairs. Her unlined face and obsidian-colored hair made me wonder if she was significantly younger than Doug or simply took good care of herself.

"Colleen? Could you pour another glass of iced tea?"

"Oh." I waved them off. "Don't go to any trouble."

"It's no trouble." Colleen stood. "I just made a fresh batch." She slipped from the room.

Doug led me to a teak table. Two tall glasses already sat on the glass top that protected the intricately carved surface depicting hills and a central valley with a meandering stream running through it. He gestured at the closest chair. "Please, sit."

I detoured by one of the floor-to-ceiling windows. "Your yard is amazing."

"The credit mostly goes to my wife. She does all the weeding and pruning." He pulled out one of the chairs for me. "You're from the East Coast, right?"

"Yep." I took the offered seat. "And I had no idea schefflera could survive outside."

He grinned. "We can't take credit for that. It's the climate. You like to garden?"

I nodded. "I've been looking around to see what sort of plants do well here. Most of the other neighbors seem to take a minimalistic approach to their yards. Lots of rocks and gravel. That's why I was studying your landscaping out front. But the back's incredible, too."

His wife entered carrying a pitcher of iced tea and another glass. She sighed. "It's the drought. Everyone's worried about water use. Fortunately, our garden is well-established and doesn't need as much as a young garden would." She poured tea into the glass and handed it to me.

"Thank you. I'm afraid my Massachusetts plant knowledge isn't going to help me much here."

"Oh, it's not that different," she said. "Sure, you'll be working with different plants, but caring for the soil, weeding and pruning, that doesn't really change."

I sipped the cool drink. "This is delicious. What type of tea is it?"

"I'm glad you like it. It's a special blend of mint and hibiscus. It's my favorite."

While we talked, Doug pulled a small pad of paper and a mechanical pencil from his shirt pocket, along with a pair of glasses. "Old engineer's habit." He waggled the notebook. "It comes in handy having paper and pencil. I'll put together a list of plants that'll flourish here."

"That'd be wonderful."

"Have you done any work in your yard yet?"

"No."

"Ahhh. When you do, you'll discover that under a couple inches of topsoil, it's mostly sand. Which means you'll need to improve the soil if you want anything to develop roots."

When I headed for the front door an hour later, he handed me a neatly printed list of twenty plants that would do well in my foggy coastal yard, along with the ingredients I would need to amend the soil.

"This is amazing. Thanks again. And it was great meeting

you. I've only run into half a dozen other folks who live on the block."

Colleen waved her arm toward the alleyway. "In another week, you'll see a change."

"What do you mean?"

"Now that the June gloom is passing—that's what we call these foggy mornings—the summer folk and weekenders will be opening up their houses."

I glanced at the expensive homes lining the alleyway. "People buy these places as weekend getaways?"

"That and for summers at the beach."

"Amazing."

After thanking her and Doug again, I left with the list, a small plate of cookies, and the prospect of two new friends.

The visit inspired me to head to the garden shop recommended by the Yamadas. I put a clean beach towel on the back seat to catch Noodle's drool, then loaded up the dogs. They nosed the air throughout the four-mile journey.

When I climbed out, I didn't bother locking the vehicle. Harlow was no deterrent, but who in their right mind would try to steal an old 4Runner with a huge dog like Noodle patrolling the back seat? "You two be good."

Near the entry, I stopped at a display of pavers along with a list of available gravel and stone sizes. I guessed some of my neighbors only got this far and never made it to the nursery. Power and hand tools filled a couple aisles; plumbing and electrical supplies—with a focus on irrigation-related goods—occupied a large swath of shelving. The central aisle focused on Fourth of July decorations. I shook my head. How could that be less than two weeks away?

Outside in the back, a covered area displayed patio furniture and firepits, indoor and shade-only plants, plus a colorful array of ceramic pots. I grabbed one of the red wagons provided for shoppers and continued on to the open-air section for sun-loving plants. A heady mix of scents filled the air—some familiar like the climbing roses, some not. I browsed my way through the entire collection, reading the plant labels and looking for the ones Doug Yamada had recommended. The shopping trip might have been overwhelming without his list. I grabbed a mix of six-packs: yerba buena, golden yarrow, artemisia, and lavender, as well as several bags of soil amendment. I was headed to the checkout when I realized I needed to replace the gardening tools I'd given away before moving from Massachusetts. Rolling to the tool aisle, I picked out gloves, clippers, a weeder, a kneeling pad, a trowel, and a shovel to start. Once everything was stowed in the 4Runner's cargo area, I drove to Hillside Park and took the dogs on a long hike.

When Monday rolled around, Harlow and I collected Noodle and took our regular walk to the beach. It was a clear, bright day, and the fog had already burned away. Maybe this heralded the end of the June gloom the Yamadas had referenced yesterday. The black labs, GiGi and JoJo, were galloping along the sand, as was Marge, the Boston terrier, though her pace could be more accurately described as a trot. There were also a handful of unfamiliar dogs and their people spread out across the tideline. Summer folk and their pets?

While Noodle walked by my side, I played catch with Harlow, the retriever racing through the water, pure joy on four paws.

After returning home, I toweled off the Golden, then brushed both dogs and left them in the backyard. I was eager to see Ava and find out how she was doing with Butterscotch's training. Halfway out the front door, I paused and shook my head.

Perhaps Murph was right about me needing some adult friends.

Unlike last week, Ava didn't burst from the house and race down the path before I reached the door. Was I early? I knocked and waited.

The door swung open. Ava's tangled hair hung loose and she wore black leggings with red polka dots and a green-and-blue-striped shirt. Did the girl dress herself? She gave a weak smile, then led the way inside.

I scanned the living room. Rick's clothes still dotted the sofa and carpet, but there was no sign of Jemma. No familiar sound of running water came from upstairs. A smell from the past filled my nostrils: burned pasta, spoiled milk, and sour wine. Just like my Aunt Lorraine's house. Thank God the woman had been funny and kind, because she'd been a disaster-level cook and housekeeper—to the point where I would've otherwise complained about staying at her home after school every day.

The normally pristine kitchen even looked like Aunt Lorraine's: counters covered with dirty dishes, a sauce-encrusted pan on top of the stove, a pot with congealed pappardelle noodles abandoned on one of the barstools. Something crunched underfoot. Small tan objects dotted the floor.

"Is your mom meditating?"

Ava shook her head.

"Where is she?"

"Crying in her room."

"What? Is everything all right?" Idiot. If everything was all right, Jemma wouldn't be crying and Ava wouldn't look bedraggled.

The girl seemed not to register the stupidity of my question. "Rick said some bad words before he went to work."

"Do I need to know which bad words?"

Ava nodded.

"Okay. Lay it on me."

"He said the S-L-U-T-T-Y neighbor was dead."

My stomach dropped. "What?"

"That's what Rick called Seville."

Pulse raging, I grabbed the counter for support. "Seville's dead?"

"Rick says she got drunk and drowned in the bathtub."

"Oh my God." I pictured Seville showing off her soon-to-be-ringed finger. Had she celebrated too hard? "This is terrible." Ava's stricken face brought me up short. Why would her parents say any of this within earshot? The kid would be terrified of bathing for the rest of her life. Still I had to ask, "You're sure?"

She gave an emphatic nod. "A detective came by last night to talk to Rick. Jemma got upset and had too much Jemma juice."

"Jemma juice?"

"It's what she calls wine. She doesn't think I know what it is. Last night she had a lot. Rick called her an L-U-S-H. She threw up in the hall bathroom." Ava wrinkled her nose. "Their yelling woke me up this morning. Rick called Jemma a B-I-T-C-H and said the thing about Seville being . . . you know."

"Dead?"

"S-L-U-T-T-Y. I stayed in my bedroom until lesson time, then went into their room. Jemma said she's resting today. But she's really crying."

"Right." This was all kinds of awful. Rather than focusing on the big picture, my brain kept circling back to how this was affecting Ava. "Do you know what those words mean?"

The girl's face grew red and she wouldn't meet my gaze.

I crouched in front of her. "When I was your age, I didn't know what any of them meant. But times change, right? Are kids your age familiar with those words?"

She shrugged, then finally made eye contact. "You won't tell Rick or Jemma?"

"Tell them what?"

"They spell words they don't want me to know. But . . ." She wiped a tear from her cheek.

"I'm not mad and you're not in trouble. I promise."

Ava sniffed, then spoke, her words barely audible over the hum of the refrigerator. "I look them up. In the dictionary. Or online."

Smart kid. "Of course you do." I surveyed the disaster that was the kitchen. "Did either of your parents make you breakfast?"

"No. I climbed on the counter and got the box of Cheerios. Some spilled on the floor."

That explained the mess on the tiles.

"The milk was on the top shelf in the refrigerator. I couldn't reach it, so I put water in the bowl." Ava pulled a face. "It didn't taste very good."

That explained the bowl of drowned Cheerios near the sink.

I didn't know what to do with all this information—at least not the parenting failure portions. But my cop instincts knew what to do with the rest. "Why did a detective want to talk to your father?"

"He said something about Rick, Seville, and the fair." Ava huffed. "Why would he go to the fair with Seville? Rick says the County Fair's a rip-off. Last year he wouldn't take me. Even though Mahala and Francine both got to go."

The fair? Had the cops said "affair" and Ava misunderstood? Made a far stronger reason for Jemma to drink to the point of vomiting.

"And why her? Seville wasn't very nice. She called me a rug rat."

Seville had said as much to me, but to tell Ava that to her face? "I'm so sorry." I wrapped my arms around her narrow frame and she huddled against me. "Hey, want me to make you a snack? Something better than Cheerios with water?"

Ava nodded.

"Okay. You start working with Butterscotch and I'll rustle something up."

She grabbed the bag of dog treats and flew out to the deck.

After checking the cupboards and fridge, I made Ava a BLT and took it onto the patio along with a glass of milk. While she ate, I swept the kitchen floor, then loaded the dishwasher. Figuring Ava needed some special attention today, I ignored the clock and we continued training and playing with Butterscotch until well past our allotted time. Finally, guilt over Ava missing her scheduled lessons got to me.

"Okay. This has been a ton of fun, but I think Butterscotch could use a rest and you need to put some more knowledge into that brain of yours."

Reluctantly, Ava called the dog, but by the time she settled at her workstation, she looked content. Of course she was. A smart kid like her probably enjoyed all her classes. As soon as she seemed engrossed, I backed out of the room. Part of me said I should butt out, but the part of me that was fuming propelled me up the stairs and through the double doors to the master suite.

CHAPTER 10

The pungent odor of bad breath and sweat greeted me when I entered Jemma's room. With the shutters closed, only a sickly light glowed from a bedside lamp. On one side of the bed, the covers had been thrown off, revealing a paisley-patterned sheet. On the other side, Jemma curled, nightgown twisted around her, wads of crumpled pink tissues scattered about like wilted flowers.

I cleared my throat but got no reaction from the slumbering woman. Stepping closer, I tried again. Still no response. Two amber vials sat on the bedside table. Maybe Jemma wasn't sleeping. My heart stampeded as I ran to her.

Grabbing the closest plastic container, I held it near the light. Xanax. The second was a prescription for Ativan. Made out to Rick Greenwood. Had Jemma combined them? Taken them with alcohol? I dug her arm free from the tangled bedding and took her pulse. I tried to block out my heavy breaths as I counted and watched the clock.

Sixty-two. Nothing alarming, but still I tucked the pill containers into the pocket of my shorts. I shook her shoulder. She mumbled something and I shook her again.

"Wha—?" Jemma squinted up at me. "Who are you?"

"The dog trainer."

"What are you doing in my room?" She sounded confused rather than alarmed.

"You need to get up and take care of your daughter."

"What's wrong with her?"

I resisted the impulse to shake her again and took a deep breath. "She's upset because her mother got drunk last night and has been sprawled in bed all morning crying. Oh, and you and her dad had a screaming match before he stormed off to work."

"How dare you—" Her outrage trailed away as she struggled to sit up.

"Listen, Ava may be brilliant, but she's still a little kid."

She pushed a dark tumble of hair off her face. "This is none of your concern."

"Wrong. You made it my concern when you and your husband talked about a neighbor—someone Ava knows—drowning in the bath. Loud enough for her to hear." Heat rushed up my face. "With no thought as to how that would affect her. Then you left her to fend for herself. You're supposed to be a parent, for God's sake."

Jemma's mouth opened and closed but emitted no sound.

I took a shaky breath. "I'll give you an hour to pull yourself together. Take a shower. Put on some clean clothes. Then come downstairs and look after your daughter."

As I stormed from the room, I closed my eyes. Great bedside manner there. Probably just ended my time as their dog trainer and Ava's only friend.

Crap.

Two hours later, Jemma tottered down the stairs dressed in sweatpants and a baggy T-shirt, hair pulled back in a barrette. Her face was pale, her eyes were red and swollen, but she was up. She beckoned me to join her in the living room. Voice low, she said, "Thank you for looking after Ava."

Deep breath. I needed to show the woman I could play nice. "Sure. I enjoy her company. Is what she heard correct?"

Jemma paled further.

Oh no. She probably thought I was referring to Rick's cheating. Or the name-calling. "I mean, did Seville really drown in the tub?"

She nodded as more tears seeped free.

"How? Ava said she'd had too much to drink."

"I don't know for sure. The detective wouldn't say. But that's what Rick assumed." She wiped her eyes with a tattered tissue. "I didn't realize Ava could hear us." She crushed the tissue in her fist. "But of course she could. We were yelling. I just didn't think . . . Did she hear . . . ?"

"She heard everything." The hope faded from Jemma's eyes. "But she didn't understand it all. She thinks Rick took Seville to the fair."

Her brow crinkled. "What?"

"The fair. Affair. She either misheard or didn't understand."

"Oh. Did she seem frightened to you?"

"I'm not sure. But you might have trouble with her at bath time."

"Right." Jemma bobbed her head. "Thanks again."

"No problem." As I let myself out, I hoped Jemma's attitude toward me would remain conciliatory. I'd hate for her to put a stop to my friendship with her daughter.

And I couldn't believe Seville was dead.

In contrast to my internal storm, the day remained sunny and clear as I walked home along the alley. Needing an antidote to the maternal disaster I'd witnessed, I unlocked the front door and called my mom.

"Hi, honey. It's good to hear your voice. I miss you."

"Miss you, too. What's going on with you?"

"Work's work. Nothing too exciting. The department bought me a new printer. So, I guess that's something."

"Nice to know they appreciate you."

She snorted. "The amount of money I bring in, they better. Oh, I almost forgot to tell you about my tomatoes. You should see these things. Huge, firm, and red. And the taste! This is the best crop I've had in a while. It's too bad you're all the way across the country and missing out."

There was no point telling her I could get fresh tomatoes in California pretty much year-round. "Glad the garden's going so well."

"I'm gonna have enough to can marinara sauce this year. I'll save a jar for when you come visit."

An awkward subject since my next trip back would likely coincide with the murder trial of Stefan's killer. "Thanks, Mom."

After making sure things were well with her, I hung up and paced the great room. Still feeling anxious and sad, I grabbed a beach towel and opened the slider. "Who wants to go to the park?"

Harlow and Noodle scrambled to their paws, tails wagging. I led them through the side door of the garage, placed the clean towel on the back seat, and then loaded them into the 4Runner. I cracked the rear windows before reversing down the driveway. As I drove, the dogs took turns sticking their noses out the windows.

Cross-town traffic was light and ten minutes later Harlow and Noodle pranced on the blacktop at Hillside Park while I dug in the cargo area for a water bottle and my knapsack. After slipping the straps over my shoulders, I headed into the park and across the grassy bowl to the hilly trails.

We started up an unoccupied track on the north side of the park, treading between the giant wild rye and sage. A cottontail darted halfway across the path and froze. Harlow and Noodle barked until the rabbit hopped into the underbrush. "Show's over. Let's keep going." Five minutes later, feeling I'd given the rabbit—and any other critter who'd heard the dogs bark—plenty of time to vacate the trail, I let Harlow off her leash. "Go on, girl." The Golden raced ahead.

By the time we reached the first crest, sweat dappled my forehead and upper lip. The park spread out below, its grassy center surrounded by dun-colored hills dotted with olive-green brush and trees. Noodle woofed and I followed his gaze. A Cooper's hawk surveyed the chaparral from a live oak branch. "Good find, boy."

I unpacked their bowl and filled it with water. After Noodle slurped and spilled, I called Harlow back. The Golden raced to my side, tags jangling, and licked my hand, then turned her attention to the water, lapping her fill. When she was done, I shook out the bowl, then guzzled from the bottle before packing both away. "All right. Let's get moving."

While the dogs explored, my thoughts circled back to Seville. She'd been so happy on Friday. Was that just three days ago? My cop brain had trouble accepting the idea she'd gotten drunk and drowned. It was possible, but that level of alcohol consumption—at least when done solo—was more often linked to depression than celebration.

Had the expected proposal failed to materialize? Or worse, led to a breakup?

Was Rick the man Seville had hoped to marry? My knees buckled. I landed on the soft dirt alongside the path. Noodle leaned against me and drooled on my arm. "I'm okay, bud."

But I wasn't. If Rick was Seville's hoped-for husband, did he object to that plan? To the point of murder? I'd never met him. Other than Ava's report about him hurling insults at Jemma and the fact he was a slob, I knew nothing about his character.

For Ava's sake, I hoped he'd had nothing to do with Seville's death.

As I pulled into the garage, my nerves no longer vibrated. The walk had helped—though sadness now pooled in my gut. I'd barely known her, but I'd liked Seville. In spite of how she talked about—and apparently to—Ava. Maybe that had more to do with her relationship with Rick than how she felt about his daughter.

It wasn't just that she was one of my few potential friends in Pier Point: she'd been way too young to die. What was she? Thirty? Thirty-one? There was so much I didn't know about her. She was single, but had she been married before? I didn't think she had any kids. Surely she would've mentioned them. I'd assumed she lived alone. But, then, who found her body on Sunday and called the cops? And what time was it when that happened? Ava said the police came by the house to question her father Sunday night. As irresponsible as her parents seemed, I couldn't imagine them letting an eight-year-old stay up past nine o'clock. If the police had swarmed Seville's house before then, why hadn't I noticed?

Right. Yesterday I had taken a two-hour hill walk with the dogs and gotten home around four o'clock. While the dogs napped, I'd dug out a twelve-inch-deep swath of grass along the back fence for a future garden. Then I'd come inside and mopped the drool-speckled kitchen and great room floors. Whipped, I'd taken Noodle home early. Dinner had been a nuked burrito eaten over the sink, before Harlow and I curled up on the sofa, her with a chew bone and me with a glass of wine and Bosch on my laptop. I fell asleep partway through the second episode.

At 2:00 a.m., I'd startled awake and dragged myself upstairs, tumbling into bed without giving a thought to what had woken me. Had that been the cops leaving Seville's? If she was already dead, there would've been no need for sirens when they first arrived.

Poor woman. What a way for her life to end.

I let the dogs loose in the yard and gazed at my plant packs and bags of amendment. My legs and arms protested at the thought of more digging. But the beds weren't going to dig themselves. The doorbell rang. The dogs barked and raced across the yard and sprang toward the slider. "I'm on it." I hustled inside, closing the door behind me.

A stocky man stood on the stoop, a boxy metal clipboard in one hand. Clean-shaven, with dark hair cut short, he was dressed in navy pants and a tan shirt with blue stripes. He smiled as if he knew me.

Nothing about him struck a familiar chord. "Hi?"

He held out his free hand. "I'm Efrain Hernandez. I'm here to measure your windows. For your new shades."

"Right." Trying to look like I hadn't completely forgotten, I shook his hand, then beckoned him inside. The scent of mint and coffee trailed after him. "The priority is my bedroom." I led the way up the stairs, speaking over my shoulder. "The first-floor windows all have shutters, but there are no window covers anywhere on the second floor."

"Gotcha."

I ushered him down the hall and pointed into the master bedroom. My cheeks grew warm. Of all the mornings for me not to have made my bed. Or put my clothes away. I threw the blanket over a pink bra. "I want to do the two windows in here." Moving on, I guided him to each room and pointed out the windows in need of measuring. The last room we entered was my office.

He set the storage clipboard in a clear spot on the antique desk. "How about I start in here?"

"Great. I'll leave you to it." In the hall outside my bedroom I paused, tempted to pull the bed together before the guy started working in there. But he'd already seen the mess, so how neurotic would tidying up after the fact make me look?

More than I was comfortable with.

I paused on the landing. This guy gave off a trustworthy vibe. Plus, it wasn't like I had a bunch of valuables he could pocket. I retraced my steps to the office. "Let me know if you need anything. I'll be in the backyard."

In spite of my whining muscles, I retrieved my trowel, shovel, and kneeling pad from the garage. After petting the dogs, I began turning the sandy soil along the back wall. Following Doug Yamada's advice, I mixed in the compost, peat moss and worm castings I'd bought at the garden shop. I finished prepping the back bed. Muscles looser now, I began to dig out a second bed along the side wall. I'd cleared out a two- by three-foot section of grass when the window guy knocked on the kitchen slider's frame. I looked up as he stepped outside onto the deck. The dogs roused themselves and trotted to the deck, barking.

"Stay." Dropping the shovel, I crossed the yard.

Gaze fixed on the Saint Berdoodle, he retreated a step. "I'm all done."

"Great." I reached the deck, pulled off my gloves, and shooed the dogs back onto the grass. Noodle continued to growl. Not one to discount a dog's instincts, I didn't shush him. But in the short time I'd known him, I'd noticed Noodle seemed leery of uniformed men. Granted, a striped shirt and blue pants wasn't a typical uniform . . . Unsure what to think, I placed myself between the Saint Berdoodle and Efrain.

"I'll take the measurements to the shop and someone will email a quote to you. If you're happy with it, they'll set up an installation date."

"Sounds good." I repeated the stay command before walking the man to the front door. We shook again; then I watched him climb into the Windows, Etc., van and drive off. Rather than returning inside immediately, I stared at Seville's tan two-story. Though she had just died, it already looked abandoned. Or maybe that was me seeing things that weren't there.

Doug Yamada hailed me from his driveway. Unlike the other day, his hair was mussed and dark circles shadowed his eyes. I crossed the street to join him. "Hi." I glanced at the adjacent house. "I guess you heard?"

"About Seville? Yes. Tragic." He tugged his earlobe. "Colleen found her."

"Oh my God. I'm so sorry. I take it you were close?"

"Colleen knew her better than I did. Even though Seville was younger, those two got on like a house afire."

"How old was Seville?"

"Turned thirty last month."

"I'm sorry for your loss."

He shook his head. "Seville tolerated me. I suspect she found hanging out with a retired engineer rather boring. But she and Colleen regularly went to yoga together. And they'd have coffee or tea in the mornings before Seville headed to work. They also liked going to lectures at the museum. That's why Colleen went to Seville's to check on her."

"Because of a lecture?"

"Sorry, no. My thoughts are still scattered. Seville missed the Sunday morning yoga class she and my wife usually take. I mean took."

"And you two have a key to her house?"

"For emergencies. Colleen had called Seville's cell several times. It wasn't like her to not at least text back." He sighed. "All through dinner, Colleen kept checking her phone, but didn't hear anything. A little before eight, she decided to go over and make sure everything was okay. I wish I'd gone instead." Pain etched his face.

"How's she doing?"

Doug rubbed the back of his head, further mussing his hair. "Terribly upset. Seeing her friend dead . . ."

"I can imagine." Actually, I could do more than that. No point going there. "Of course you wish you could've shielded her from finding Seville." I gazed into Doug Yamada's troubled eyes. "Is there anything I can do to help?"

"Colleen's not up to visitors right now. But maybe you could stop by tomorrow? It'd be good for her to talk to someone besides me. Or the cops."

"Have they been giving her a hard time?"

"Not really. But she wishes she could erase the image of Seville dead in the tub. With the cops constantly stopping by asking new questions, they're keeping that horrible moment alive."

"Are Seville's parents flying out?"

"No. Her father's quite ill. Pancreatic cancer. They've asked her ex-husband to take care of claiming . . . the body. And handling her cremation. He's supposed to ship the urn back to them in Martha's Vineyard. They asked us to handle any local memorial we felt might be needed."

"I didn't know Seville had been married."

"I'm not surprised she didn't mention it. The whole thing was a debacle. She'd known him forever and said she knew better than to marry the guy but did it anyway. She always referred to it as five years she'd never get back." He covered his eyes with his hand, then rubbed his forehead. "I wish they hadn't reached out to Beau. We would've been willing to take care of . . . those things for them."

"Is there a reason her ex shouldn't be involved?"

"She kicked him out three years ago. As far as I know, she hadn't spoken to him in a year and a half." Doug grimaced. "The guy's nothing but trouble."

"How so?"

He glanced over his shoulder at Seville's house. "I really shouldn't . . . It's not important now. I better get back inside. In case Colleen needs me."

"Sure."

As he walked up the slate path to the front door, his gait appeared unsteady. He seemed to have aged overnight.

Doug struck me as both meticulous and kind. What had Seville's ex done to put him off?

CHAPTER 11

I returned to the backyard, mixing peat and compost into the sandy soil until it looked like sugared coffee grounds and smelled of decaying plants and salt spray. My thoughts circled back to Colleen discovering Seville's lifeless body. I'd experienced more than the average person's share of DBs as a cop, but that was different. Not only was it my job, but I hadn't known any of the victims. Even when Stefan was killed, I hadn't seen him until his body had been made "presentable" by a mortician. Though I'd hated the idea, his parents and four siblings demanded an open casket ceremony. I'd been in no position to resist.

Poor Colleen. It must've been a terrible shock. Going next door to check on her friend. Walking through the house, calling Seville's name. Growing more anxious the longer the woman didn't respond. Then finding her in the bath . . . Had it been obvious she was dead? Or had Colleen needed to feel Seville's cold skin as she desperately sought a pulse?

I shook off the image, which left room for Seville's ex to wriggle into my brain. Her being out of contact with him for eighteen months didn't send up any red flags. Most couples didn't stay close once they divorced. But Doug had made his disgust with the man clear, his tone and expression hinting at a problem with Beau's character. Or behavior.

Why did Seville's parents reach out to him instead of to her friends?

The sky was streaked with peach and gold by the time I finished digging for the day. Standing, I pulled off my gloves, flexed my fingers, and whistled. "Come on, guys. Time to take Noodle home."

The two pranced as I washed up at the kitchen sink and then clipped on their leads. For a change, I took them into the alley by way of the side gate. The dogs did their usual inspection of the few shrubs lining the narrow road—acting as if they hadn't sniffed them twelve hours earlier. Each took a moment to leave a few liquid calling cards before we reached Dr. Johannson's.

When I inserted the key into the patio door, it swung open without me turning the knob. My nerves sparked.

Sandy stood smiling on the other side. "Hi there."

I gave my heart a moment to recover. "I didn't expect to see you. I mean, I know it's your home but . . . you're not usually here." When Sandy didn't move out of the doorway, Noodle pushed his way through the narrow gap, forcing the doctor to step back. I followed the big dog into the courtyard, unsnapped his leash, and set it on the bar.

"Finished an hour earlier than usual." Sandy shut the door behind me. "How's it going with the training? The dog's wolfing down his breakfast in record time—so I'm thinking he's getting lots of exercise. I take it that means he hasn't escaped again."

His jaunty tone jarred me.

Oh God. He didn't know about Seville. With the crazy hours he worked, who would've seen him to say anything? Even though the two weren't on speaking terms, he wouldn't sound this upbeat if he knew she'd just died.

"Noodle's doing great. No more escapes. He's been here every morning. And I can tell you more about his progress another time." I chewed the inside of my cheek. There was no easy way to say it. I found myself focusing on the small scar bisecting Sandy's left eyebrow as I resumed speaking. "Seville Chambers died last night."

"No." Disbelief laced his voice. "How? A car crash? I know she loved driving fast."

That was more than I knew. "No. She drowned. In the tub."

"Oh my God. I . . . Did she fall and hit her head?"

That thought hadn't occurred to me. "I don't know. All I heard was she had too much to drink and drowned." But Sandy's question made sense. Especially if she'd celebrated her engagement with a drink. Or two.

His face lost color. He took a step, then hesitated, seeming to move in slow motion toward the bar. Leaning forward, he steadied his forearms on the granite. "This is . . . Are you sure?"

I closed the distance between us. "I haven't talked to the police myself. I got the story from Jemma Greenwood."

"Is she . . . ? Did she find Seville?"

"No. Colleen Yamada did."

"Poor woman. And poor Seville, too." He gave an awkward shrug. "You may've heard she and I didn't . . . get along."

"Yeah. She told me about Noodle drooling on her silk blouse."

He straightened and smacked his fist against the counter. "Why didn't I just pay for the damn blouse?"

I placed a hand on his arm while Noodle and Harlow hovered nearby. "Truthfully, Seville seemed more amused than up-set when she told me about it."

"Really?"

The hope in his eyes made me feel bad for the guy. "Really."

He circled the bar. Lifting a bottle of tequila and two glasses, he clinked them onto the counter. "Can I pour you one?"

"No, thanks. Sorry to be the bearer of bad news."

"Not your fault." He uncorked the tall blue-and-white bottle, then closed his eyes and shook his head.

I retreated a step. "I need to get going."

"Oh. Of course." Sandy's brown eyes found mine. "I didn't mean to keep you."

"It's no problem." I walked to the patio door, Harlow and Noodle trotting alongside. I stroked the Saint Berdoodle's thick coat and bent to kiss his curly forehead. "Sorry, boy. I've got to head home. I'll see you in the morning. Sit." The dog sat. "Stay." I looked up at the doctor. "He's a smart fellow."

Turning, I grabbed the door handle. A sigh exploded from deep inside me and I revolved to face Sandy again. "The whole thing is awful. And she'd been so happy . . ."

He paused mid-pour. "Happy?"

"Seville was getting married."

His mouth dropped open. "To whom?"

"Some rich guy."

"How awful."

I raised my eyebrows.

Sandy shook his head. "I mean, the guy must be devastated. How's he taking the news?"

"No idea. I don't know who he is." Which raised the ques-tion: who did? Had Seville told Colleen about her fiancé-to-be?

"This is . . . Wow. She was getting married. But now . . ."

"Now she's not." I tightened my grip on Harlow's leash while blinking back a fresh crop of tears. "Did the police get in touch with you?"

"About Seville?"

"No. Noodle."

He bobbed his head. "Yeah. I told them I'd keep an eye on the dog's poop for body parts. But that was what? Twelve days ago? Anything he ate back then has passed through his system by now."

"Sure. But that's not what I meant. Have the cops talked to you about the ring?"

"What ring?"

"Right. I haven't seen you to tell you. Noodle found what looked like a wedding band at the beach. It might be related to the hand. Or it might not."

He picked up his partially filled glass and drained it, then thumped it on the counter. "How . . . ?" He shook his head, looking like he was at a loss for words.

"He dug it up."

"Were you with him?"

I nodded. "But if the cops haven't been in touch, maybe it's a good thing."

"How so?" He refilled his glass with the amber liquid.

"Probably means the hand and the ring aren't connected. I've got to go. It's almost time for Harlow's dinner."

He lifted his glass in a silent salute.

"Come on, Harlow." I shut the patio door behind me and headed down the alley.

Without the big Saint Berdoodle lumbering around, the house felt emptier. I double-checked the front and back door locks.

After canned food and kibble for Harlow and another micro-waved dinner for me, we settled on the sofa. Harlow rested her chin against my thigh, while I stroked her silky ears. "I'm so lucky to have you in my life."

She sighed and stretched, head slipping off my lap onto the seat cushion. I took advantage of my sudden mobility and grabbed my laptop. Turning it on, I stared at the screen. Seville's past was none of my business. Should I really be thinking about prying? No.

Fingers ignoring my conscience, I pressed keys and logged into my account at Trackers, the search service I'd used for my P.I. work. I input what information I had on Seville, then scanned the results. Her maiden name was Stuart. She'd attended UCLA and graduated in four years with a B.A. No real surprises there. I typed in her ex-husband's name. Ten minutes later, I was shaking my head. Harlow looked up at me. "This guy is dirty."

She nestled against my leg again.

According to the Trackers database, Beau Chambers currently lived in New Bedford, Massachusetts. I jotted down his cell phone number and address before opening another screen and searching for an image of his home. The real estate site listed the address as pre-foreclosure. The street-view photo showed a small Cape Cod with an overgrown lawn and shrubs. The wood siding needed a fresh coat of paint and the huge tree shadowing the asphalt drive looked like it had moved past shaggy a decade ago. The tail end of a car was visible in the gloom at the head of the driveway, but I couldn't tell the make or model.

Returning to my search service, I continued reading. Beau's assets included the house, an eight-year-old Corvette, and a checking account. No savings. He'd filed for bankruptcy twice after being charged with receiving stolen property. I made a note to follow up on that.

His work history showed him tending bar on Martha's Vineyard from 2007 to 2008. Did he and Seville meet before she moved to California? If that was the case, Beau was older than her by at least three years. When Seville moved to Los Angeles for college, she would've been about eighteen—which meant she came here twelve or thirteen years ago.

And boom. There it was: Beau bartended in 2008 at a club in Westwood, California. Conveniently close to UCLA. After a year, he began working as a sales rep for an alcohol vendor. Three years later, he was managing that company's warehouse. The firm filed for bankruptcy in 2014. The cause wasn't apparent, so I opened a search about the company. Established in 1999, it reported having eight employees. The number seemed low for a warehouse-based business, but what did I know?

Harlow sighed in her sleep and I stroked her head.

A news search generated an article about the bankruptcy. The owner stated he'd run into financial problems because funds had been illegally siphoned from his business. How many of his eight employees had access to the money side of things? And was Beau Chambers one of them? I found no information about any employees being charged with embezzlement. After filing for Chapter 11, the company stayed afloat, managing to pay off its debts in four years.

Further research showed the company had gone on without Beau.

The same year as his employer's bankruptcy, Beau started his own warehouse business—in the same town—competing with his former boss. That action didn't speak well for him. And where did Beau get the start-up money? A few years later, he sold that business. The time frame dovetailed with Beau and Seville's divorce.

After that, his employment trail resumed in Massachusetts, where he purchased another warehouse. Which was where he ran afoul of the law. Sixteen months into his ownership, he was charged with receiving stolen property. Known as a "wobbler," the crime could be charged as a misdemeanor or a felony. Beau got the lighter charge and never saw jail time. The man must have made a deal, named names so he could skate. Shortly thereafter, Beau filed for bankruptcy protection on his business. Five months later, he did the same for his personal assets.

I sat back and rubbed my eyes. More than ever, I couldn't understand why Seville's parents reached out to this guy to take care of their daughter's remains.

In spite of the warm summer evening and the furry dog snuggled against my leg, a shiver rattled my spine.

CHAPTER 12

Tuesday morning, the dogs and I were returning from the beach when my cell rang. Unknown number. "Hmmm." In my experience, that was rarely good. Still, I answered.

"Molly Madison?" The voice was low and female.

"Yep."

"The dog wrangler?"

"Yep." Other than Seville, I only knew one person who tossed around that job title. "Are you a friend of Ava Greenwood?"

"I'm her neighbor, Lupe Fox. I saw Ava walking her dog yesterday. That pooch used to be a holy terror. I couldn't believe how well behaved it was. When I complimented Ava, she told me about you. I have a Dalmatian I could use some help with. What do you charge?"

So far, all my dog wrangling had been for free. I did a quick calculation and threw out a modest hourly rate.

"Sold. Don't get me wrong; we did what we were supposed to. We tried taking Ulysses to obedience training after we adopted him. I don't know if he was too old, but he had some behavior problems and was larger than the other dogs. The instructor asked us to leave. She gave us some training tips, but nothing seemed to stick."

I unlocked the front door and the dogs trotted inside. "How old was he when you tried the class?"

"Eight months. He's ten months now."

Most people started puppy training when their dogs were around eight weeks. "Is there a reason you waited until then?" I crouched and unhooked the dogs' leashes.

"That's when we got him. There was this horrible man who ran a puppy mill. The police arrested him and called in the Humane Society. Over five hundred dogs were there in cages. Poorly fed, unclean, untended. The Humane Society needed a lot of people to adopt the ones who were healthy. We took one look at Ulysses and fell in love."

"Bless you, Lupe Fox."

"He's a sweet dog. He just won't do what we ask."

Though Lupe was obviously a wonderful person, in my experience when a dog's training didn't stick, most of the time it was due to operator error. "Dropping by to meet you and Ulysses is easy for me. I don't know if Ava told you, but I live down the street from her, too. Did you have a day or time in mind?"

We nailed down meeting at six-thirty tomorrow evening and Lupe recited her house number. My best guess said she lived in the Italianate two-story with all the wrought iron.

I hung up, then led the dogs into the backyard. After putting out fresh water and brushing them, I checked the time. I was due at Ava's in a few minutes. Inside the kitchen, I stared at the bottles of Ativan and Xanax on the counter. If Jemma was still acting emotionally fragile, returning them could be dangerous. I tucked the vials inside my pocket and decided to play it by ear. Before heading out, I put a handful of treats in a baggie for Butterscotch.

As I strolled down the alley, I breathed in the tangy ocean air, allowing myself to feel hopeful this move could still work out.

The house past Dr. Johannson's looked newly occupied. Bicycles lay scattered across the front walkway and beach towels draped over the rail of the second-floor balcony. Looked like the summer folk were returning to Pier Point.

While waiting for Ava to answer the door, I tried to prepare myself for potential awkwardness from her mother. The door swung open and Ava beamed up at me.

"Did you get my referral?"

I chuckled. "Lupe Fox called me. You looking for a cut of my earnings?"

She shook her head, then led the way through the house. Today her ensemble was again color coordinated: pink sundress with matching socks and hair ribbons. Rick's belongings were still scattered on the sofa, recliner, and carpet, but the kitchen had been returned to its usual tidy state.

"Where's your mom?"

"Upstairs, meditating. For real this time."

"Glad to hear it."

She gave me a shy glance. "I took your advice."

"What advice was that?"

"I asked Jemma to set up another playdate with Francine and Mahala. They came over yesterday afternoon."

"How'd it go?" I tossed a ball and Butterscotch scrambled after it.

Ava gave a little hop. "They loved Butterscotch. I showed them how she could sit and stay and then we all started running around the yard together and Francine put out her arms like a plane. Then we all flew around. Except Butterscotch."

"Of course. She'd need all four of her legs for that."

Ava giggled. "And I even complimented Francine for being able to fly so well with an unevenly distributed load. I told her only a skilled pilot could do that."

"And everyone had a good time?"

She nodded.

"That's great." We spent the next five minutes working with Butterscotch on sit, stay, and come commands, then we reviewed heeling. Butterscotch fell right into step with Ava. She bent to pet the dog. "What a smart girl. Good job, Butterscotch."

I nodded my approval of Ava's praising technique. "Let's try something new. The 'watch me' command."

Butterscotch had a little trouble with it, but Ava patiently repeated the sequence of steps, first holding the biscuit in her right hand, then shifting it to her left, making sure the dog's gaze followed. Then she moved the treat close to the dog's nose and raised it until it was near her chin. Butterscotch's eyes remained trained on Ava's every move.

"Great job. Both of you."

Butterscotch gobbled her reward.

I gave the remaining biscuits to Ava. "Is Rick still refusing to buy treats for Butterscotch?"

"Uh-huh. We're almost out of peanut butter for her Kong toy. But he's no longer saying we might have to get rid of her."

"Well, that's something."

"You're right." She grinned.

When our time was up, Ava skipped ahead of me to the door.

"Good job today. You guys are doing great."

"Maybe someday I'll be a dog wrangler, too."

I squeezed her shoulder. "I think that'd be a waste of that big brain of yours. Maybe keep it as a hobby."

Her smile faltered. "Maybe. I do like science and math." The grin was back.

"And you don't need to make a decision right now. You've got lots of time to check out all the options."

She gave an emphatic nod.

I strolled home, pill bottles still in my pocket. Since Jemma never came downstairs during Ava's lesson, I'd had no chance to return them to her nightstand. Maybe that was for the best. After setting the vials on my kitchen counter, I walked outside and made a fuss over the dogs, tossing the ball and running around the yard. As soon as Noodle's steps slowed, I kissed them both and resumed my gardening project.

My arm muscles began to complain at the one-hour mark. Shedding my gloves, I took the tools to the garage and grabbed one of the agility obstacles. The unused weave poles were still set up on the lawn from last Thursday. I stretched out the tunnel and positioned it twenty-two inches away from the final pole. "Wake up, you two. Harlow, Noodle. Come."

Seeing the tunnel, the Golden began to prance. Noodle joined in, though I was sure he had no idea what was going on. Accompanied by the sound of their happy panting and jingling tags, I ferried the rest of the agility equipment from the garage. Once I situated the jump and tire, I started Harlow on the most difficult task: the weave poles. The Golden took off perfectly, entering left shoulder first. She continued slaloming between the poles as I ran alongside, encouraging her. "Weave, weave, weave."

After she practiced her entry a few more times, I threw her the tennis ball. We played for a moment before Noodle ran over to join us. I let him drool on a second tennis ball while Harlow raced through the poles again. Then we moved on to the tunnel. "In, in, in." The Golden took off and I ran along the inside curve, doing my best to meet her at the exit. We worked on our blind crosses as we ran from the tube to the jump, then on our rear crosses from the jump to the tire.

"Good job, girl." I threw a dry tennis ball for her. Noodle galumphed over and nosed the tunnel. Though it looked like an easy obstacle, the tunnel intimidated many dogs at first. But the Saint Berdoodle seemed interested. Maybe I should give him a crack at it?

I straightened the curves so he could see all the way through, then guided him to one end. "Sit." Walking to the opposite end, I crouched to the side of the opening and held a treat where he could see it. "In, in, in."

The dog pawed the entrance and lifted his muzzle. Smelling the snack, he moved forward. A tight fit, he still managed to barrel through the nylon tunnel. It was like watching toothpaste leaving the tube as he burst out and hoovered up the biscuit. "Good job!" I patted his curly coat while continuing to praise him. Harlow nudged me with her damp nose and I petted her with my free hand.

"Okay, puppers." Standing, I found the drool-covered tennis ball and tossed it to Noodle and threw the drier one for Harlow. After recurving the tunnel, I had Harlow run through a few more times to the jump. Noodle stood panting near the opening. I got out a Kong toy to occupy him until we finished the task, then straightened one end and softened the curve on the other. After taking away the toy, I called to him, "In, in, in." He raced through and I gave him another treat, along with more praise.

Moving over to the jump station, I started Harlow with straight-ahead leaps. She knocked down the pole her second time around. After setting it back in place, I had her try again. She soared over it. "You are such a smart girl! Now, let's work on your threadalls." I moved her on to angled jumps, practicing figure eights. Her fur shimmied like a golden curtain when she leapt and landed.

"Come on, girl, let's do the tire. Go, go, go." Harlow flew through the opening like a dart. We repeated the task several times. It had been a while since we'd done this, and I reminded myself to point my feet where I planned to run. The last thing I wanted to do was confuse Harlow.

To wrap up, I threw balls for both dogs. Though the session had gone well, I needed to get Harlow to a real agility class soon so she could continue training on the A-frame, elevated dog walk, long jump, and seesaw. There was an advanced class in Camarillo on Tuesdays, but I'd been too late to make a reservation for today. Not wanting to miss out again, I'd signed her up for next week.

I wasn't sure what I'd do with Noodle when I took Harlow to Camarillo. He'd never be allowed to participate in an advanced-level class. And, with his size, I doubted all the jumping involved would be healthy for him. Not to mention the fact that I'd get more than a few raised eyebrows for spending that kind of training money on him. Saint Berdoodles weren't an AKC-recognized breed and he'd never be able to compete at their events. Still, I hated the thought of leaving him alone all morning at Sandy Johannson's. Maybe Noodle could come along and visit. Make some new friends. And if that didn't work out, we could find something fun to do on our way home.

While I started packing things away, the dogs sprawled on

the lawn, enjoying a well-deserved rest. The damp, salty air had already caused a minor rust bloom on the weave poles. "No more leaving these out overnight."

The dogs lifted their heads, but when I didn't say their names, they resumed napping. Once all the obstacles were stowed, I went inside and ate a quick lunch. I was rinsing the plate when my cell phone pinged. I checked the screen. Detective Wright had sent a text. My throat tightened. I tapped the icon and read: Your receipts can be picked up at the station.

"Jerk." He couldn't even be bothered to bring them back to me.

Shaking my head, I climbed the stairs to tackle my office. Though I'd removed all of the files from their packing boxes, only a handful had been put away. I set my cell on the windowsill and played Amy Winehouse as I got to work. Over the next two hours, Cherry Glazerr, Dayglow, and Mazzy Star serenaded me while I organized my papers.

Wiping the dust from my hands onto my shorts, I returned downstairs and pulled a cold root beer from the fridge. The soda hissed and foamed when I popped the top. I tipped back my head and drank.

Out front, someone shouted. A raised voice answered. Then both voices were yelling. Thumping the can onto the counter, I ran for the front door.

A red-faced Doug Yamada stood in the middle of the alley, hands clenched at his sides. An auburn-haired man with an equally flushed face mirrored his pose. Standing over six feet tall, he had a few inches on Doug. A scowl cut across the couple days' growth of beard covering his strong jaw.

"I'll stay where I goddamn want to." The man's voice carried the familiar accent of my home state.

"You . . . you . . ." Doug's face turned a deeper shade of red as he sputtered. "You should honor Seville's wishes. The woman kicked you out and told you to never come back."

"Tough. Her ma gave me a key and told me to make myself at home. And there's nothing you can do about it."

So, this was Beau, Seville's ex. The man obviously didn't care about making a good impression. I eased closer along the concrete walkway.

Doug grimaced. "Seville would never have let you inside the house again."

In my thirty-seven years, I'd learned the majority of disputes resolved themselves peacefully without outside intervention. This didn't look like one of those.

"What? You afraid I'll make a record of her belongings before that greedy wife of yours gets her claws into them?" Beau smirked.

Fist already cocked, Doug drew back his arm. I flew across the blacktop, launching myself between them. Years of training dropped me into a universal fighting stance, feet shoulder-width apart, my left foot toward the younger man. He was the unknown quantity. I planted one hand on each chest and pushed. Both towered over me, but I had enough attitude to make up the difference.

"Don't disrespect Seville's memory this way. I am not going to let you two duke it out in the street. You're grown men. Act like it." Breathing hard, I shifted my gaze between them, evaluating their body language. Inserting myself this way was foolhardy without a gun. Or at least a canister of pepper spray.

Doug gave in first. Shoulders sagging, he lowered his hands. He gave a rueful head shake. "Sorry."

The apology was directed at me, but I took it as a win. Turning, he plodded to his house. Once the door shut behind him, I narrowed my eyes at Beau.

He held up his hands in surrender. "You're right." Spinning on his heel, he strode toward Seville's, stopping by the red Porsche 911 parked in the drive. He pulled out an overnight bag, then continued to the front door. After unlocking it, Beau disappeared inside without a backward glance.

In addition to regretting his almost-street brawl, I expected Doug was sorry he'd encouraged me to drop by and visit Colleen today. My presence might help take her mind off Seville's death, but I was probably the last person—after Beau—Doug wanted to see right now. Maybe I'd wait a day before stopping in for a visit.

Though the crisis was over—at least for the moment—adrenaline still raced through me. Tucking my trembling hands inside my pockets, I studied the street, amazed no one else had come out to investigate the ruckus. Most of the homes must really be owned by summer people, as Colleen had said.

I stepped inside and locked the door behind me. What was that crack about Colleen's greedy claws? Where had Beau come up with that? Shaking my head, I crossed the great room and kitchen to the backyard. "Wake up, you dozy dogs." Harlow and Noodle raised their heads. "Who wants to go to the park? Nothing like a walk to make us feel better, right?"

The long walk on the hilly trails finally had my heart pumping hard for a good reason. While Harlow raced ahead, Noodle once again stayed close. I breathed in the scent of sage and pine drifting on the breeze. Far above, a red-tailed hawk keened. The Saint Berdoodle sat and barked at the soaring bird. I ruffled his coat. "Don't worry. You'll get him next time."

The trail split. Harlow led the way up the left fork. When we reached the crest, I called the Golden back and extracted the collapsible bowl and water bottle from my knapsack. After the dogs splashed and drank their fill, I crouched and petted them both. Straightening, I drained the bottle. "Come on, pups. Time to head home."

As we started downhill, my thoughts returned to the earlier scene in the alley. If it was uncomfortable for Doug and Colleen having Beau next door before, it must be a tension-fest now. From the level of rage in Doug's face, I was sure something more than the divorce had caused the rift between the Yamadas and Seville's ex.

The sun was headed toward the horizon. Time had gotten away from me. Bobcats and coyotes lived in these hills. For the dogs' safety, I needed to get them back to the parking lot before dusk. I picked up the pace. As we hurried down the trail, I kept an eye out for gopher holes while reviewing training techniques to share with my potential new client. To my surprise, I was looking forward to tomorrow's meeting with Lupe and Ulysses. It would be a fun challenge training another dog. Plus, it would get me out of the house and force me to interact with another grown-up.

By the time we reached the car, the sky was streaked with crimson and gold. Rather than walking Noodle to the doctor's from my place, I drove straight to Sandy Johannson's and parked my 4Runner beside his patio door. "Come on, Noodle." The big dog bounded out. "Stay, Harlow. I'll just be a second."

I deposited the Saint Berdoodle inside, refreshed his water, and kissed his forehead. "See you tomorrow."

After feeding Harlow, I ordered a pizza and then enjoyed a hot shower. Muscles loose, I dressed in sweatpants and a T-shirt and returned downstairs to await my dinner's arrival. I promised myself I'd shop for groceries tomorrow. Grabbing my laptop, I settled on the couch, legs tucked to the side. I patted the leather cushion. Harlow hopped up, circled, and curled up beside me.

I opened the computer and watched a few scent-training YouTube videos. Though getting Noodle to a class would be ideal, starting his training on my own looked simple enough. Because of the move, I had plenty of empty boxes to use as hiding spots on a homemade course. It'd be a fun activity for Noodle until I could take him to a real class. Ten minutes later, a sharp rat-a-tat-tat came from the front door. The retriever lifted her head and barked.

"That's right, girl. It's pizza time!"

Together we walked to the door. But instead of finding an underpaid teenager holding a cardboard box smelling of oregano and melted cheese, Beau Chambers stood on my porch, looking sheepish.

CHAPTER 13

Beau slouched against the pillar on my small porch. Behind him moonlight shone on the front yard and alley. Somewhere down the street, music played softly. He held up a bottle. "Peace offering."

I extended my hand and he moved the wine just out of reach.

"All I ask is that you share it with me. Don't worry, it's none of that cheap swill Seville drank. This is the good stuff."

"Really?" I crossed my arms over my chest. "You're taking this opportunity to criticize Seville's taste in wine? The woman just died."

"I . . . Hey, I didn't mean anything by it." He raised his empty palm. "I used to tease Seville about her taste in wine all the time. But I can see how what I said might sound . . . cold."

"You got that part right."

Beau cocked his head. "What say you forgive me for both this moment and this morning? Then we drink some fine wine?"

Good-looking as he was, I imagined a lot of women had forgiven him over the years. The desire to give him the boot warred with my curiosity. Was this a sincere attempt to make nice after today's almost–street brawl? Or would it devolve into a bad-mouth-Doug session? I didn't want to go there. I still hoped to become friends with him and Colleen. But, considering how Seville died, letting Beau drink alone seemed a terrible idea. And who was I to turn down a glass of "the good stuff"? Or a chance to find out more about Seville's life? Curiosity won and I waved him inside.

The entryway light limned the damp hair curling behind his ears. He'd changed into a tight T-shirt and jeans. The man was in shape and proud of it. I probably should've thought twice before jumping between him and Doug.

Harlow blocked the way, first sniffing Beau's boots, then his pant legs. Beau crouched and offered his hand to the Golden. She nosed his fingers, then sat on her haunches, tail sweeping the travertine.

He straightened. "Looks like I passed inspection."

"You did. Come on through to the living room." I pointed at the sofa, then continued to the kitchen. "Make yourself comfortable while I dig up a corkscrew and some glasses."

He scanned the room and sat. "I like the way you've decorated. Very minimalist. Most people can't leave well enough alone and let a room breathe."

I suppressed a chuckle as I pulled a second glass from the cupboard and wiped off the dust with a dishcloth. I wasn't going to tell him my decorating style wasn't a decision, but rather a failure to prioritize shopping since I'd moved in. Setting the glasses on the coffee table, I handed Beau the corkscrew. "Will you do the honors?"

Leaning forward, he drew a Swiss Army knife from his rear pocket and cut the necking foil from the bottle. Refolding the knife, he picked up the corkscrew.

Good thing I let him open the bottle; normally I jammed the corkscrew straight through the foil into the stopper. Not exactly classy. Or the right move when drinking "the good stuff."

The cork pulled free with a satisfying pop. After taking a moment to shift the glasses closer, Beau poured. Generously. "What part of Massachusetts you from?"

"Is it that obvious?"

He shrugged and handed me a glass.

I took a sip. "Mmm. You're right. This *is* the good stuff." While he focused on filling the other glass, I studied him. Large hands, calloused fingertips, grayish eyes—to go with the hint of silver glinting in his beard. The deep lines around his eyes and across his forehead made me think he was at least ten years older than Seville. I wished I'd thought to check his birthdate while running the background check on him. Stefan used to tell me I couldn't shut down the cop part of my brain. And he'd been right. While Beau seemed superficially pleasant, something about him struck me as off.

When he set down the bottle, I finally answered his question. "We lived in North Adams until I was six, then moved to Brockton."

"So, your folks weren't exactly upwardly mobile."

My shoulders tensed. Who was this guy to criticize the decisions forced on my widowed mother? "I had great parents and a loving home. Money may help grease the wheels, but it's not everything."

Beau's face burned red. "You're right. That was out of line."

Not ready to accept his apology, I felt free to be equally rude. "Is it weird staying at Seville's? Knowing she died there?"

"Damn. You play rough. Shoulda known. Brockton babes always go for the jugular." He held up his glass in a mock salute before drinking. "It *is* weird. And kinda awkward. Seville's ma told me to go through all the jewelry and bring back anything of value."

Not exactly what I'd call a maternal request. "Huh. That's got to feel a bit uncomfortable. Are you Seville's executor?"

"Yeah. Apparently, she never updated her will after the divorce. Though I'm one to talk. She's still listed as executor and beneficiary on mine, too. I'll be fixing that when I get back home."

Too? Did that mean Beau was Seville's beneficiary as well as executor? "I'm guessing you'll need to be here awhile."

"We'll see. I'm meeting with a Realtor tomorrow. Once the police give me the go-ahead, I'm putting the place up for sale."

It was like the remnants of Seville's life were being dismantled and erased as quickly as possible. But how had I been any different with Stefan's things? I tried to swallow away the lump growing in my throat.

The doorbell rang. I said a silent thank-you. Harlow barked, then escorted me to the door. Once sure I was out of Beau's sightline, I wiped my eyes. People weren't the sum of their possessions, but the way he talked about Seville's home and belongings felt unnecessarily rushed. And cruel.

This time when I opened the door, the anticipated pizza had arrived. I handed over the money, but tonight the smell of mushrooms and melting cheese turned my stomach. Beau may have spoiled my appetite, but my curiosity had yet to be sated.

Since dinner was already ruined for me, I might as well ask him to stay. The longer he lingered—and the more he drank—the better my chances of gleaning details about Seville's past. Holding the box, I returned to the great room. "Dinner's served. Want to join me?"

"Sure. All that Seville has in her kitchen is rabbit food." He winced. "Had. Had in her kitchen."

Not sure what to say, I placed the box on the coffee table, then retrieved paper towels and plates. "Dig in."

He took the makeshift napkin. "Thanks."

Hoping to expand on what I'd learned about him during yesterday's research, I said, "So, how did you and Seville meet?"

"We knew each other when we were teenagers. Back on Martha's Vineyard."

Unless he looked old for his age, I doubted Beau and Seville were both teenagers at the time—unless she was thirteen to his nineteen. Ick. "You moved to California together?"

"No. She came out for college. Then we bumped into each other when I was working as a wine importer and she was at UCLA studying business."

Had he really "bumped" into Seville? Or had he followed her to California? The timing of their separate moves had my gut leaning toward the latter option. The fact that Beau had edited out his years bartending and managing a warehouse left me wondering what else he might be altering in his story. The true surprise was that he thought he needed to change any of it for me. A stranger whom he never had to see again.

That alone told me a lot about the man.

I was nearing the bottom of my wineglass when I finally broached the topic I'd been curious about since I first spied Beau in the alley. "What's the deal with you and the Yamadas?"

A thread of melted cheese caught on his unshaven chin. He wiped it away with his hand. "The deal? That's the perfect word for it. I take it you know them both?"

"Yep."

"Know them well?"

"Not really."

"Lucky you." He grimaced. "Colleen Yamada used to be an investment manager. She started whispering in Seville's ear to move our money to her firm. So she could manage it." He wiped his hand before balling the paper towel and tossing it onto the table. "Seville was a businesswoman, for God's sake. And there she was soaking up an impossible earnings fantasy. When I complained to Doug, he told me I was getting worked up over nothing. But what the Yamadas didn't realize was I'd seen the results of Colleen's handiwork before. That woman ruined my boss's life. Lost him a ton of money. I wasn't going to let her do the same to us."

The boss Beau had competed against by opening his own warehouse? Not sure he would tell me the truth even if he knew it, I asked another question anyway. "When you told Seville you didn't want Colleen to manage your money, did she agree? Or still want to go ahead with it?"

His face turned red again. "She thought I didn't know what I was talking about. She had the fancy degree, but I'd been earning my way years longer than she had." He gulped more wine. "We were already in a bit of a rough patch and fighting a lot. The whole investment thing didn't help. Without the Yama-das, our marriage might not have fallen apart."

Classic—blaming others for your doomed relationship. "If that's true, would the next few years have been any good?"

He gave a humorless chuckle. "No." He lifted his glass and

drained the contents. "You're not one to hold back from asking the tough questions, are you?"

I refilled his glass, wishing I could've gotten suspects tipsy prior to questioning back in the day. Would've made the job a lot easier. Though I didn't usually toss down this card, I was curious to see Beau's reaction. "Old habit. I used to be a cop."

He sputtered and then began to cough.

"You okay there?"

"Sure. Wine went down the wrong way." Snatching the crumpled paper towel from the table, he wiped his eyes.

"So, did Seville go ahead and turn her money over to Colleen?"

"Couldn't." He gulped more wine. After another cough, he continued. "Our money was in a joint account and I wouldn't give the okay. Plus, the lawsuit kind of screwed things up with the Yamadas." He gave a wry grin.

"What lawsuit?"

"Doug sued me over some bogus dental bills."

"Excuse me?" I nudged the bottle closer to his half-empty glass. "How are Doug's dental bills your problem?"

Beau added a little more wine and swirled his glass, staring at the golden liquid as if it held the answers. Harlow's rhythmic breathing filled the silence.

"When he wouldn't make his wife back down with Seville, I punched him in the jaw. Doug claimed he needed to get a filling replaced because of it. Which was crap. He just wanted payback. And some free dental work. Me refusing to pay his bills . . . that was the last straw for Seville. She kicked me out the next day." He leaned back, crossing an ankle over his knee. The sofa sighed. "By the time our divorce was settled, Colleen had retired. I don't think she got the chance to mess with Seville's money."

After he had another slice and polished off the last of the wine, Beau clambered to his feet. "Thanks for the grub and gab. Didn't mean to take up your whole evening."

I stood. "No worries."

Harlow and I walked him to the door and waited until he made it across the alley to Seville's. Locking the deadbolt, I returned to the sofa, the Golden at my heels. I stared at the half-eaten slice on my plate, then down at her hopeful gaze. "You're lucky I ordered this with no onion." I held out the pizza. She wolfed it down.

"Glad one of us got to enjoy it."

After our beach walk Wednesday morning, I loaded the dogs into the back of my 4Runner. Ava had called and canceled today's training session. Though the girl sounded perfectly normal, I worried Jemma might be rethinking my visits. Had she realized I'd confiscated the bottles of Ativan and Xanax? Hopefully her mom only had an appointment she couldn't miss, as Ava claimed.

Since I'd made a big deal to the detectives about getting my travel receipts back, picking them up ASAP seemed like a smart move. The last thing I needed was for those two to think I hadn't been truthful when they questioned me. Located a few blocks shy of the drapery store, the police station was easy to find. Inside, the air-conditioning had been set to frigid. Wishing I'd worn something warmer than shorts and a tank top, I got in line for the desk clerk. When I reached the front and stated my business, the bored-looking blonde wrote down my name, then directed me to the waiting area. I rubbed the goose bumps on my arms and tried to get comfortable on the hard plastic seat.

Fortunately, the wait wasn't long. A broad-shouldered officer emerged from a side door, crossing the waiting area in four long strides. "Officer Gregory."

He gave me one of his room-brightening smiles. "Ms. Madison. I believe these are yours?" He handed over a manila envelope containing the evidence of my cross-country journey.

"Yes."

"Nice seeing you under better circumstances."

I was ten years too old for him, but my stomach still did a tiny flip. "Right. No violence or severed limbs for a change."

"Well, stay safe." He nodded and headed back toward the door.

"Thanks."

I strolled to my 4Runner, enjoying the warm sunshine on my shoulders. Behind me, someone called my name. Turning, I scanned the lot. Detective Vasquez was jogging my way. Wright wasn't trailing after him. Thank God.

He stopped a couple feet from me. Today he wore jeans and a tight polo shirt. "Ms. Madison."

"Detective Vasquez. You off duty?"

"How'd you— Right. My clothes. Yeah, it's my day off. But there's always paperwork to catch up on. You know how it is." He nodded back toward the building. "Do you need help with something?"

I held up the manila envelope. "Just retrieving my travel receipts."

"Look, I'm sorry my partner was a bit"—Vasquez rubbed the back of his neck—"overenthusiastic in his questioning of you."

I snorted. "That's one way to put it."

He gave a half smile. "It's the only way I can put it while I have to work with him."

Interesting choice of words. "Have to?"

"Anyway . . ." He pulled out his wallet and extracted a business card. "If you do need to talk to us, you can call me directly. Maybe I can run interference between you and Wright."

I took the offered card. Our fingers briefly touched. Vasquez's smile broadened and my stomach flipped again. Did Pier Point only hire good-looking cops? Detective Wright's face flashed through my mind, squashing that notion. "Thank you."

"No problem. Hope to see you around. In a non-crime kind of way." He grinned again, then loped back to the station.

On the drive home, I pondered the detective's words. Having been a cop, would I ever consider getting involved with one? Maybe. Especially one who looked like Detective Vasquez.

The dogs kept their noses out the back windows. When checking the side-view mirror, I saw a viscous length of drool break free from the Saint Berdoodle's flews. I hoped it didn't hit anyone's windshield. Or worse, a bicyclist. I entered the narrow alley from the west end and was about to pull into my driveway when I spied someone dressed in a white tunic and black capri pants cutting roses in the Yamada's front yard. Colleen. I braked and rolled down the window. "Hi there." She straightened, her wide-brimmed hat shadowing her eyes. "How're you doing today?"

Setting down her basket and clippers, Colleen walked onto the blacktop, bringing the sweet scent of roses with her. "Better. Thanks for asking." She glanced over her shoulder at Seville's house. "Doesn't help having that greedy creep here. First thing this morning, he had a real estate agent combing through the place. I heard him discussing bringing in an estate company to clear out everything." She pulled off one gardening glove and shuddered. "As far as I can tell, he just wants to sell her stuff as fast as possible. It's like he never cared about Seville." She dabbed her eyes with her sleeve.

"You and Seville were friends a long time?"

"Doug and I were the first to welcome them to the neighborhood. In spite of our age difference, she and I hit it off right away. Beau, on the other hand, struck both Doug and me as a liar and a cheat. The kind of person who cuts corners just for fun."

"That must've made your friendship awkward."

Colleen shrugged. "Not really. Beau wasn't around much. Seville seemed thrilled to have someone to do things with."

Harlow joined me in the driver's seat and nosed Colleen's hand.

"Hey, beautiful." She gently stroked the dog's forehead. Not wanting to be left out of the petting action, Noodle jammed his way into the front as well. Colleen gave him a misty smile. "You're beautiful, too."

"Okay, guys. Scram." I nudged the dogs into the back. My legs practically sighed with relief when all that weight lifted off them. "I don't mean to pry, but what's the deal with Seville's mother?"

Colleen's brow furrowed. "Sorry?"

"I talked to Beau yesterday. He said Seville's mother wanted him to go through her jewelry and bring back anything of value. That just . . ." I pictured my own mother's damp eyes when I told her I was moving to the West Coast. She understood the reason but, tough as she was, Mom was torn up about the physical distance it would create in our relationship. A cop's widow, she knew all about danger, all about risk. The whole time I was in uniform, I'd been sure she would manage to carry on if I died in the line of duty. But in that imagined scenario, she never gave a damn about rounding up my good jewelry. "Maybe it was the way he phrased it, but it sounded so . . . cold."

Colleen gave a noisy exhale. "Seville and her mother had a strained relationship. She usually got back to Martha's Vineyard once a year, but it always sounded like she spent the majority of the time visiting old friends. As for her mom wanting Beau to bring her any valuables, I wouldn't trust that man to bring in the mail." She seemed to study her nails. "If you talked to him at any length, I'm sure Beau mentioned me."

"He did. And that he slugged Doug."

She snorted. "I'm surprised he owned up to that. The two of them were having what my husband thought was a straight-forward conversation, then Beau punched him." She shook her head. "Like Doug had any control over my business decisions or investment recommendations."

"That logic struck me as odd, too. Beau excused his behavior by saying his boss lost a lot of money working with you."

"Pffft." Colleen waved her empty glove. "That same old song. Like I told Beau back then, it wasn't my place to discuss his employer's investment strategy with him. Suffice to say, his boss wanted money fast and chose risky investments. Investments that, for the record, I advised against. But, according to the forms the man filed, he was financially equipped to handle that level of risk. Of course, he failed to mention his gambling problem or include his gambling debts in his paperwork."

"And things went south."

"Exactly." She gave a tight nod.

I checked the street to make sure I could block the alley a bit longer. "Do you know if Seville's fiancé has been notified about her death?"

Colleen's brow furrowed again. "What fiancé?"

"Right. I mean her boyfriend. Seville said he hadn't popped the question yet. But she was expecting a proposal."

"Seville was seeing someone?"

My stomach plunged. What had started as a simple question was now something else. "You didn't know?"

"No." A breeze gusted up the alley and Colleen clamped a hand on top of her hat. "The only time she talked about dating was to lament the lack of good prospects."

"That's weird. The Friday before she died, Seville told me she was about to get engaged."

"To whom?"

"I've got no idea."

"You mean that whoever it is, he might not know she's dead?"

"Maybe." I rubbed my forehead, trying to make my brain work faster. "Did she have any other close friends around here? Besides you, I mean?"

"I don't think so. Every couple months she'd go to dinner in L.A. to hang out with some friends from college. But she wasn't what I'd call a girly girl. Didn't have a lot of women friends."

Sounded a lot like me. "Well, awful as it is, when she doesn't get in touch with the guy, he's going to want to know why."

"That poor man."

CHAPTER 14

I put the dogs in the backyard, then studied the pantry. Even a mouse would starve trying to scrape together a meal here. Grocery shopping couldn't wait any longer. Grabbing my wallet and keys, I detoured through the backyard and kissed the dogs before heading to the garage's side door. Both ran after me. "Harlow, Noodle, stay." I led them back to the grass and kissed them again. "I'll be back soon."

After turning out of the alley, I traveled along the main beach access road. I passed Pier Point's small business section and continued on to the shopping center near the freeway. The parking lot was jammed. I cruised several rows before I found a spot. Unfortunately, a seagull sat in it, beak deep in a potato chip bag. The bird turned. Appearing unimpressed, he returned his attention to the bag. "Really?" Losing patience, I leaned on the horn. After giving me one more blasé look, the bird flapped off.

The two-story bank stood out as the tallest building in the

complex and the grocery store as the largest. In between sat a range of shops: cards and gifts, dry cleaning, ice cream, and, of course, coffee. Fifteen minutes after I entered the sprawling grocery store, its layout still made no sense. I ended up wandering each aisle, tossing items into the cart as I found them: paper goods, dog chow, produce, frozen foods, dry goods. I picked up a jar of peanut butter and two extra bags of dog treats for Ava to use. When I headed toward the checkout, I remembered I was almost out of root beer. Backtracking halfway across the store, I located the soda section next to the bleach and detergents. I added a twelve-pack to the basket before pausing at the wine aisle. Should I buy a good bottle in case Beau dropped by and wanted to talk once more? No. I grabbed two bottles of inexpensive California chardonnay, then rolled my way to the front of the store and got in line.

Ava canceling today's lesson still bugged me. Did Jemma really have a conflicting appointment like the girl said? Or was her mom avoiding me because I'd read her the riot act? Considering the way she'd made herself scarce yesterday, it felt like Jemma was building toward ending my classes with her daughter.

"Bags?" The checker's voice snapped me back to the present. Head cocked like an inquisitive sparrow, the thin woman stared, obviously waiting for me to say something.

"I'm sorry?"

"You wanna buy some bags for your groceries?"

"Oh. Sure. Thanks."

By the time I turned into my alley, I couldn't stop yawning. I desperately needed a nap. The unmarked car parked in front of my house told me that wasn't going to happen. Clenching my jaw, I pulled into the drive. Vasquez climbed from the sedan. It took a couple minutes before Wright managed to shuffle his bulk from behind the wheel.

What now? I doubted they simply wanted to look at my travel receipts again. Dealing with more questions about the hand and ring wasn't a big deal—as long as they left Stefan's murder out of it. How likely was that? Not very.

I tapped the garage remote, pulled inside, and cut the engine. Dread pooling in my gut, I walked to the rear of the 4Runner to face Detective Vasquez.

"Stocking up on supplies, huh?"

Not a real question, so I didn't answer. Instead I opened the hatch and grabbed two grocery bags.

"Need some help?" Vasquez gave a concerned smile.

While I didn't want him to think I was swayed by his handsome face or charm, an extra pair of hands would make ferrying the bags inside easier. "Sure. You and your partner can grab the paper goods and the two other bags." Once Detective Wright had been conscripted, I shut the trunk and garage, then led the way in through the front door.

"Put those on the counter." I nodded toward the kitchen.

The detectives set down the bags and stared at me.

"I'm sure you've got a good reason for being here, but I need to get some of this into the fridge and freezer right away. If you want to have a seat"—I pointed at the great room sofa—"I'll be right with you."

In spite of my "be right with you," I took my time putting things away, even stowing the nonperishables before joining the detectives. Since they were on the sofa, I sat on the hearth. As much as I liked having floor space for the dog crate, I needed to buy an armchair for this room.

Today Vasquez wore a charcoal suit with a black-and-gold

tie. The dark fabric showed off where Harlow's blond dog hair had transferred from the sofa to his sleeve. After a couple swipes to remove it, he gave up. "Big grocery run. Guess that's part of getting settled."

I shrugged.

Wright again looked like he'd scrounged his ensemble from the dirty laundry. He waggled his bushy eyebrows. "Maybe she's throwing a party."

Vasquez ignored his partner's comment. "We—"

"And it looks like you stocked up on peanut butter, too."

Vasquez looked irked about getting cut off. Wright directed an unpleasant grin at his partner, then at me.

Why did Wright care? "I don't think you're here about my shopping list."

The rumpled detective leaned forward. "Tell us about your relationship with Seville Chambers."

My relationship? I crossed my arms. "Okay. What do you want to know?"

"I take it you've heard about her death?"

"Yep." The uneasy feeling washing through my gut swelled into a tidal wave. A deep breath helped me collect my thoughts but didn't quell the rising anxiety. "I thought it was an accident. Why are you involved?"

Vasquez cleared his throat, then spoke. "Someone wanted us to think that."

"What? Seville was killed?" My mouth went dry. "Are you saying she didn't drink too much and pass out in the tub?"

"She died from anaphylactic shock." Vasquez looked genuinely sorry to be breaking the news. "Her throat closed up and she suffocated. Then someone put her in the bathtub."

Pulse hammering in my throat, I licked my lips. "Wha—? I don't understand. Who would do that?"

"We're working on it. In the meantime, we're hoping you can tell us about last weekend."

"What about it?"

Vasquez set his phone on the coffee table, then lifted his gaze to meet mine. "I'll be recording this for our notes."

I nodded my understanding.

"Did you see anything out of the ordinary that Saturday or Sunday?"

I thought back and shook my head. "I didn't notice any strange cars or people in the alley. Or near her house. The only thing that stands out about that weekend—before I learned Seville had died—was her telling me she was getting engaged."

Vasquez's eyebrows shot up. "Engaged to who?"

"She didn't say. I got the impression it was kind of hush-hush. When I mentioned it to Colleen Yamada, she was surprised to hear Seville was seriously involved with anyone."

"Why didn't Seville tell you her fiancé's name?"

"I don't know. She acted like it might jinx things if she said too much."

Wright snorted. "Yeah, right."

Vasquez glared at him, then leaned back and returned his attention to me. "Where and when did this conversation take place?"

"The Friday before Seville died. I was walking the dogs home from the beach and she pulled over at the head of the alley to chat."

"About what time?"

"Uh . . . maybe nine-ish." Seeing his furrowed brow, I added, "In the morning."

"And other than this conversation with the deceased, you noticed nothing unusual? No odd comings or goings from her house?"

"No."

Vasquez seemed to study the shine on his brogues before continuing. "Seville's mother tells us she made an annual trip home to Massachusetts every year. That's where you're from, too. Right?"

Despite the warm day, the hairs along my forearms stood at attention. "Yep."

"When did you first meet?"

"Two weeks ago. The day I moved into this house."

Wright harrumphed. "I'm sure that's want you want us to believe." His partner shot him another warning look.

"Massachusetts may not be California big, but we don't all know each other." I turned to Vasquez. "How could Seville die from anaphylactic shock? She carried an EpiPen. If she had an allergic reaction, why wouldn't she use it?"

"Huh." The triumphal gleam in Wright's eye burned bright. "You claim the two of you just met, but she'd already told you about her life-threatening allergy?"

I resisted the urge to stand and pace. "She told me about an incident with a girl in the neighborhood."

"Ahhh. Young Ava Greenwood, right? Your protégé. She's got quite the big brain, hasn't she?"

Protégé? Where'd Wright get that? "She's also a nice kid."

Vasquez took the reins again, his voice a stream of calm after Wright's poorly hidden malice. "When we asked Jemma Greenwood if Seville Chambers had any allergies, she told us about her daughter approaching Seville with a peanut butter sandwich. She emphasized that she hasn't brought peanut butter into her home since then. Only almond butter. But Ava said you gave them a jar."

I wished I had a glass of water. Would it make me look too guilty if I got up?

Yep. I closed my eyes and counted to ten. "The Greenwoods were having a problem with their dog. The peanut butter is used to seal a dog toy. The toy engages the dog, focusing her chewing in a non-destructive manner." What was wrong with me? This was all kinds of bad and here I was sounding like a sales rep for Kong toys. "I checked with Ava about allergies before I gave her the peanut butter." Why was I playing Wright's game? When I should be asking if they were serious about me knowing Seville before I moved to California. And whether Rick's affair with Seville still had him in their crosshairs.

Wright leaned forward, looking like a bird dog who'd caught a scent. "Was Seville another of the women your husband cheated with?"

His smug expression stole my voice.

Here was the answer to my unasked question: the police's exploration of Seville's love life had expanded beyond Rick Greenwood. In a disturbing way. Did the detectives know something I didn't? As a teen, my husband had summered at the Cape and on Martha's Vineyard. Though a decade older than Seville, Stefan could have known her. Judging from her relationship with Beau, she had no qualms about getting involved with an older man.

Deep breath in. A long exhale. Finally, I stood. "I'm done answering questions without my lawyer."

Vasquez lifted both hands, palms up. "We're just trying to clarify things."

I directed my gaze at Wright. "Bull. This is another fishing expedition. I've never even been inside Seville's house. Which means you can't put me at the crime scene. So, whatever peanut butter I have in my home—or gave to Ava Greenwood—is immaterial. Now, unless you're going to haul me to the station, I'd like you to leave."

To my surprise, the men rose. Vasquez took a moment to pull down his shirt cuffs and brush off more dog fur before following his disheveled partner to the front door. Paragon of social skills that I was, I remained standing by the fireplace, icy hands clenched at my sides.

At the threshold, Vasquez turned. "Thank you for your cooperation."

Wright narrowed his eyes and added, "We'll be in touch." He tipped an imaginary hat, then walked out, leaving the door open.

I counted to ten, then closed the front door and checked my cell: ten after three, Boston time. I scrolled through my contacts and hit dial. After two rings, a woman with a smoker's rasp answered. "O'Brien, Peterson, and Allnut. How may I direct your call?"

"Molly Madison for Amanda Roosevelt."

"Please hold."

Watered-down pop music began to play. I set my phone to speaker and paced the perimeter of the great room. I was on my fifth lap when the music stopped. "Molly. I wasn't expecting to hear from you. You all tanned and relaxed out there in sunny SoCal?"

"A little bit of the first, not so much of the latter."

"Talk to me."

I explained the situation and Detective Wright's eagerness to tie me to Seville's murder. When I finished, the silence stretched.

I checked my phone screen; the call hadn't dropped. I leaned against the kitchen counter and waited.

Finally Amanda spoke. "In order to tie you to the crime, this Wright fellow needs to find a connection between Stefan and this woman . . . What was her name again?"

"Seville Chambers. Her maiden name is Stuart."

"Wright's trying to link you to the Chambers woman's death through your dead husband?"

"Yep. He asked if Stefan was involved with her—at some point in the past."

"Was he?"

Good old Amanda. Never avoided the blunt question. "I have no idea. The window of opportunity—when they were in Massachusetts at the same time—is pretty small. Seville moved from Martha's Vineyard to California twelve years ago. To go to college. She left when she was eighteen. Stefan was ten years older than her, so she was eight when he turned eighteen. By the time she turned sixteen, Stefan was twenty-six and a practicing attorney. Whatever his faults, he was smart enough not to get involved with someone underage. I checked and her birthday's in late June. That leaves two years and two months when she was of legal age and still lived on the Vineyard."

"That's a fair amount of time."

"I know."

"Checking my math here . . . She moved to California in 2008?"

"Yep."

"When did you and Stefan meet?"

"Uh, let me think. I'd graduated from the academy . . . so, 2004."

"And how long was it before you two got married?"

"Two years. We got hitched in December of 2006."

"And Seville would've been?"

"Sixteen."

"Hmmm. If you found out Stefan had cheated on you before you got married, would you have gone through with it?"

"Hell, no."

"Okay. And I'm guessing you would've noticed if something was off back then?"

"Yep."

"It's not much, but that might narrow the window by maybe six months. Do you know if Seville ever returned home after she left for college?"

I hadn't considered that. "A neighbor told me she made an annual trip back each year. Even after college. So, yeah, I guess there might have been other opportunities for them to meet."

"And the window opens up again. Still, it sounds pretty thin."

"With the way things ended, it's obvious our marriage was on the verge of collapse before Stefan was killed. But things were good with us at the beginning. I may be kidding myself, but I always thought Stefan was faithful during those early years." I sighed. "But, since I didn't know he was cheating during our last years together, maybe my opinion shouldn't count. The point is, even if Stefan knew Seville, even if he had an affair with her, I never had a clue. So why would I kill her?"

"And that's the entire supposed motive? Stefan cheating on you?"

"Yep. Especially since Alice O'Malley also wound up murdered."

"The detective said that? Accused you of directing O'Malley to murder his wife and Stefan?"

"He danced around it but made his point."

"The man sounds like he's desperate."

"He's not the only one."

"You'll be fine. You were never charged in the O'Malley case—as I'm sure the detective knows. His theory's weak tea. Look at it this way: Stefan's dead. Even if he slept with Chambers, it's not like he was going to step out with her again. Should the cops find some long-ago link between the two, there's no way they'll be able to convince a judge that you moved to California in order to buy a house on the same street as the woman Stefan slept with—how many years before?—so you could poison her with peanut butter. You hear me?"

"I do. Thanks."

"All part of the service." She cleared her throat. "It's good you called. I was planning to get in touch with you."

That was rarely good news. "What's going on?"

"The date for Wendall O'Malley's pretrial conference has been set for June 29."

"Next week? I don't need to be there, right?"

"Right."

"You hear any rumblings about him changing his mind and pleading guilty?"

"No, unfortunately. The man seems fully prepared to take advantage of his constitutional right to waste the taxpayers' time and money on a trial. Even though he's guilty as sin."

"He won't be the first. Any idea when the trial will be held?"

"Too early to say. There may be another court date scheduled for motions. I'll know more on Monday. I'll keep you posted."

"Thanks."

In spite of my lawyer's encouraging words, two hours after we'd hung up, I still felt like I was on an out-of-control roller-coaster. How could I learn whether Stefan's and Seville's paths had crossed? Even better, how could I prove they hadn't? And why did I have to? Why weren't the cops looking closer to home for Seville's killer?

Right. I lived across the street. Which made me pretty damn close to home, suspect-wise.

Back when I first met Stefan, he was a newly minted lawyer and I was fresh out of the academy. Focused on the future, he'd only shared the vaguest stories about his teen years.

I couldn't ask his family about life before me. Convinced I'd gotten away with murder, they all hated my guts. Before I moved west, I'd received countless "anonymous" threats. I knew who'd sent them, but the detective overseeing my husband's murder case wouldn't listen. I finally forced the guy to look at several birthday cards Stefan had saved. The writing samples from his father and brothers clearly matched those in the menacing notes. The detective's jaw tightened, but he agreed to give the family "a talking to." I'd stopped sleeping with a gun under the newly empty pillow next to mine when I left Massachusetts.

But Stefan's baby sister, Mona, had given me a sympathetic look at his funeral. Maybe I'd read too much into it, but she might talk to me about his summers as a teen. I pulled out my cell. It was a quarter to six back east. The mother of two small children, Mona was probably making them dinner. But at least her husband wouldn't be home from work yet. Though I couldn't prove it, I was sure Aldo was the one who shattered my front window with a brick two days after Stefan was shot.

I scrolled through my contacts, then took a deep breath and tapped Mona's name.

"Yeah?"

Wow. She sounded angry and I hadn't asked her for anything. Yet. "Hi, Mona. It's Molly."

"Yeah, I know. I can read my phone."

"Right. Sorry to bother you. I have a couple questions. About Stefan."

A heavy sigh filled the line. "Go ahead."

"Really?" Relief washed through me.

"Look, I don't mind talking to you. You ask me, everybody in this family went nuts after Stef died. The way they're still blaming you is crazy. But none of that matters. Aldo's gonna be home any minute and he won't like me talking to you. You got questions? Ask them fast."

"Thank you. Does the name Seville Chambers or Stuart ring a bell?"

"No. Why?"

"She lived on Martha's Vineyard from 1990 until 2008. She would've been about eighteen when she left. I thought Stefan might've run into her."

"I don't know. Though if he thought she could help him in some way, Stef would've managed a meeting. He always knew who to befriend. I mean, I loved him, obviously, but he knew how to work people. Seriously. The guy never had to get a job until after college. Not Stef. He got to spend summers with his buddies on the Cape and the Vineyard while the rest of us worked through every school break."

In spite of Mona's obvious desire to vent, I guided her back on track. "Did Stefan and his friends ever rent a place on the Vineyard?"

"Ha! Stef never had any money back then. Besides, the friends he stayed with already had places there." A high-pitched yell sounded in the background. "Quit it, you two. Can't you see Mommy's on the phone?" She continued at a lower volume. "Why are you asking whether Stef knew this woman?"

"She was my neighbor. Someone killed her. The cops thought there might be some connection between her and Stefan."

"You mean other than you?"

Maybe Mona didn't feel so warmly about me after all. "Yep."

"Stef wasn't one for talking about the girls he went with. Especially not to his younger sister."

"Right. Well, thanks anyway."

"Maybe you should talk to Charlie."

"Who?"

"Charlie Cooper. That's who Stef stayed with on the Vineyard. He and I hooked up a couple times. Pre-Aldo. He's some kind of bigshot in banking now. Oh. I gotta go. The garage door's opening. Aldo's home."

"Thanks, Mona."

She'd already hung up.

A quick online search told me Charlie Cooper of Martha's Vineyard was actually Charles Windemere Cooper III. The man was managing director of a private investment bank in Boston. Unlikely as it was that I'd get straight through to him, I looked up the number and called.

After five rings, a deep voice answered. "Sloan, Cooper, and Sloan. How may I direct your call?"

"I'd like to speak with Charles Cooper."

"Charles Cooper Jr. or Charles Cooper III?"

Good old nepotism. "The third."

"Please hold."

A symphonic rendition of a Beatles tune filled my ear. I put the phone on speaker and leaned my elbows on the kitchen counter.

"Charles Cooper's office."

I snatched up the phone. "Hi. I'd like to speak with Mr. Cooper."

"Regarding?"

"I'd rather talk to Mr. Cooper about the matter." A long silence followed. While waiting for a response, I checked to make sure the call hadn't dropped.

"I'm sorry." Her tone was anything but. "I can't put you through unless I know what the call is in regard to."

"It's a personal matter."

"Then perhaps you should call him at home." The line went dead.

Wow. What receptionist wasn't worried about angering a possible friend of the boss? Made me wonder about Charlie's relationship with her.

Through my Trackers service, I checked a little deeper into his background. His wife was a socialite and philanthropist who sat on the boards of several foundations. An image search revealed a striking blonde with sharp cheek- and collarbones and an icy smile. In one of the photos, she stood beside a tall, dark-haired man. The caption listed him as Charles Cooper. In spite of his well-tailored suit, he looked like a former athlete who was on the edge of becoming soft. The couple hosted frequent fundraisers for nature conservation. I found two home phone numbers for Charles Cooper III—one on Martha's Vineyard and one on the South Shore. I bet the South Shore address was their primary residence. Living on the Vineyard in the summer was one thing, but dealing with winter storms and the year-round commute was a different matter entirely.

I tapped in the South Shore number.

After two rings, a querulous woman's voice answered. "Cooper residence. How may I help you?"

Of course, the Coopers had staff. "Hi. I was hoping to speak with Charlie."

"You mean Mr. Cooper? Or Charles IV?"

Good grief, these men and their obsession with naming the next generation after themselves. "The elder."

"He's not home. May I take a message?" Her rapid-fire delivery seemed designed to show I was wasting her time.

Leaving a message was worth a shot. There was no reason for Charlie not to call the former wife of an old friend. "My name's Molly Madison. I'm Stefano Bellotti's widow."

A loud huff interrupted my spiel. This lady wanted me to know she had better things to do. Deep breath in. Then I added, "Stefano and Charlie were good friends. If you could ask him to call, I'd appreciate it." I rattled off my number, then hung up, hoping for the best.

After a couple minutes, I resumed pacing from the great room to the kitchen and back again. While it was true there was no reason for Cooper to ignore my message, there was also no compelling reason for him to call back. At least not without a more detailed explanation. I doubted his home secretary would be willing to take a longer message than the one I'd already left. Returning to my laptop, I searched for Charlie's email address and came up empty.

Rats. Even if I called back and asked as nicely as I knew how, that harridan wasn't going to give it to me.

Maybe I should go old school. Overnight a letter to Charlie and introduce myself. Ask if he or Stefan knew Seville Chambers when they were teens.

It took several minutes to compose the note. Once I had the right tone, I signed my name and added both my cell and email at the bottom.

A long shot. But doing something gave me a feeling of control.

CHAPTER 15

By the time I returned from the post office and another visit to
the garden shop, Harlow and Noodle were clamoring for dinner.
With everything going on, I still hadn't checked with Sandy
Johannson to see if he was okay with me feeding his Saint Berdoodle. But the dog was obviously hungry. I poured a handful
of kibble into two bowls and set them on the deck. After they
inhaled their snacks, we played catch in the yard. The Golden
outpaced the Saint Berdoodle every time, but Noodle didn't
seem to mind. Still, I grabbed a second ball and began tossing
it in the opposite direction. Ignoring it, the Saint Berdoodle followed Harlow to her ball of choice. "Well, I tried."

At a quarter past six, I left the dogs in the living room and
walked down the alley to meet Lupe Fox and Ulysses. The summer people next door to the doctor's house had added a tricycle
and a deflated raft to the play equipment dotting the small front
yard. Lupe's home was on the opposite side of the alley. A
smooth-finish stucco two-story, it had a striking carriage-style

garage door and a low wrought iron fence out front as well as wrought iron balcony railings upstairs. In contrast to the lovely lines and sleek elegance of the exterior, a snail-shaped knocker sat front and center on the arched front door. Fighting the urge to shudder, I rang the bell. A minute later, the door swung open. I held out my hand to the attractive woman standing inside. "Hi. I'm Molly Madison."

About my height, she was dressed casually in gray leggings and a loose sweater. "Lupe Fox." Her voice sounded melodic yet authoritative. We shook hands. "Come on in. Ulysses is sleeping in the living room." Lupe's dark ponytail swayed against her scarlet cable-knit sweater as she strode across the entryway. The Dragnet theme song began to play. She grabbed her cell off the coffee table and checked the screen. "Sorry. I've got to take this. I'll just be a minute."

"No problem."

She moved deeper into the living room, leaving me to study my surroundings. Soothing earth tones created a serene atmosphere in the high-ceilinged room. A fireplace filled one wall; a gorgeous oil painting of an empty lifeguard stand was centered on another. At the entry to the kitchen and dining area, the hardwood floor gave way to tile. The Dalmatian was sprawled on a fuzzy brown-and-tan pillow in front of the coffee table. A good-sized dog with large paws, he looked like he still had some growing to do.

Lupe crossed the room to my side. "Sorry about that. No more interruptions. Come and meet Ulysses."

"Any idea how big he's supposed to get?"

"About sixty pounds. That's why we've got to get his training straightened out. Soon he'll be too big for me to control."

"Mmm." The dog continued sleeping, chest moving in and

out like a bellows. What dog slept through a doorbell? "Is he usually so calm when a stranger drops by?"

Lupe shook her head. "He's actually pretty jumpy around people. Even us. You must give off a calming vibe."

"Huh." At the very least, Harlow raised her head when she heard an unfamiliar voice in her home. Eyes shut, Ulysses's head stayed on the pillow. "When you took him to class, what happened?"

"He played too hard with the other puppies. And he was already so much older and bigger, the instructor was uncomfortable having him there. She gave us some tips and techniques, but we haven't had much success."

I walked around the cushion. The dog continued sawing wood. "What sort of toys does he like?"

"All kinds of balls. He won't fetch but loves chewing on them."

I studied his white ears and the white fur rimming his eyes and nose. "Do you have any squeaky toys?"

"Sure." Lupe rooted around in a wood box by the sofa. "But he doesn't seem to care for them." She held out a plush moose.

Grabbing it, I squeezed it several times. The dog didn't stir. I put my fingers in my mouth and whistled. Ulysses still didn't wake. I clapped my hands. No reaction.

"What's going on?" A deep furrow marred Lupe's brow.

"I think Ulysses may be deaf."

"What?"

"Does he react when you call his name?"

Her forehead furrowed. "Sometimes."

"Think back. Is he facing you, looking at you when he does?"

"Um . . . Oh God, I think so. Ulysses? Ulysses?" She covered her mouth. "The poor dog. What are we supposed to do?"

"Well, first off, don't panic. Twenty-five to thirty percent of Dalmatians are born deaf."

"Really? That many?"

"Yep."

"I had no idea."

"With him coming from a puppy mill, it could be that his mother had some sort of infection that caused the deafness. The thing is, there are ways to work with him. And keep him safe."

She pinched her lower lip and nodded. "Okay."

"Most important, he shouldn't go outside unless he's on a leash or in a fenced area. And you need to add a tag to his collar that says he's deaf."

"Got it."

"He's also going to be jumpy if you wake him without warning."

"How do we avoid that?"

"If you've got a really bright overhead light, you can flick it on and off to get his attention. That or thump on the floor. He can feel the vibrations." I stomped on the wood floor.

Ulysses raised his head and looked around. Seeing a stranger inside his home, his hackles rose. I crouched, holding my hand low, and waited for him to come to me. Once he nosed my palm and arm, I gently stroked his back. "You can also buy a vibrating collar. They work with a remote control." Ulysses flopped onto his side and let Lupe and me rub his belly. "The important thing is, you can still train him. And he can have a great life. Believe me."

She looked up from the dog and nodded, brown eyes still worried. "His being deaf, is that why he cries at night?"

"Could be. Try putting a nightlight nearby. So he can see where he is."

"Okay."

"You'll need to learn some sign language. Until then, we can train him with simple gestures. When he gets something right, does giving him a thumbs-up work for you?"

"Sure."

"Because once you choose his 'congratulations' sign, you don't want to change it."

She nodded. "Have you worked with deaf dogs before?"

"No, but my good friend, Murph, had a deaf terrier. That dog was smart as a whip." I pulled a treat from my pocket and backed up three paces. Holding the biscuit low and toward Ulysses, I curled the fingers of my free hand in a beckoning gesture, repeating the motion as the Dalmatian scrambled to his feet and approached. When he reached me, I gave him a thumbs-up and patted his back before giving him the snack. Retreating a few more steps, I pulled out another biscuit and beckoned the dog. He hustled forward. Again when he reached me, I gave him the thumbs-up and stroked his coat. He scarfed up the treat. After two more successes, I backed up again, but this time summoned Ulysses without holding out a biscuit. The dog came. I gave him the thumbs-up, then pulled a treat from my pocket and offered it to him.

"That's amazing." Lupe stared at the two of us, hands on hips. "Can I try?"

"Of course. Why don't you do what I just did and beckon him without showing him a treat?"

"No problem." She shrugged. "I don't have one on me anyway."

"Oops." I patted the dog again, then walked around him and handed Lupe the remaining biscuits I'd brought.

She tucked the ziplock bag out of sight, held out one hand, and beckoned Ulysses. The dog cocked his head, then ran to her. Crouching, she gave him a thumbs-up and handed him a treat. Once he gobbled it, she wrapped her arms around him. "You beautiful, smart boy."

"How about trying it again?"

After three more successes, Lupe looked up at me. "I can't believe I didn't know he was deaf." Ulysses leaned against her. She continued petting him until he licked her face. Laughing, she straightened. "I feel like celebrating. Would you like a glass of wine?"

"Sure."

Ulysses seemed unsure what to do now. I caught his eye, walked to his bed, and patted his pillow. The dog came over and settled. I gave him another thumbs-up and he closed his eyes.

"Let's sit on the deck." Lupe opened the French doors.

Taking the offered glass, I stepped outside and sat in one of the Adirondack chairs. It was a gorgeous evening, no jacket required. Soft jazz came from the adjacent yard. We weren't the only ones enjoying the outdoors. The scent of honeysuckle wafted by. I scanned the yard. A flowering vine covered a large swath of the back fence.

Lupe sat in the chair opposite and leaned forward, glass raised. We clinked, then drank.

"Delicious."

"Right? Andy—that's my husband—he loves wine. Can be a bit snobby about it, but he brings home some great stuff."

"Go, Andy." I took another sip and closed my eyes. It was tart and fruity and rich all at the same time.

"Thank you again for today. This is going to make such a huge difference in Ulysses's life."

Wow. Lupe Fox really was one of the good ones, her concern focused on how sign language would benefit the dog, not her. I smiled. "The training will be the same for Ulysses as it would be for any other dog. When we get to the 'sit' command, the way you hold a treat over his head and push his butt down will be exactly like you do with a hearing dog. You'll just be giving the command visually."

Lupe leaned back and propped her feet on the firepit. "I keep going back to 'How did I not realize he was deaf?'"

"You've only had him two months and you knew he'd been raised in a puppy mill, so you were likely expecting behavioral problems. I imagine that's where your mind went."

"My God, you're right. Can we do this again tomorrow night? I won't be home until seven-thirty, though."

"Sure. I can postpone dropping off Noodle at Dr. Johannson's and come by a little before eight."

"You're taking care of Sir Drools-A-Lot?"

"What?"

"That's what Andy calls him. Sweet dog, but wow."

"The drooling—that's Noodle's Saint Bernard side. I imagine the dignified poodle part of him is appalled by it." I grinned. "If you can make time tomorrow morning to go over the 'come' command with Ulysses, that'll help him remember. Also, show your husband. The more practice Ulysses gets, the better."

She checked her watch. "Andy had a late meeting but should be home in a half hour. He's going to be thrilled to find out how we can communicate with Ulysses."

"Just keep his practice sessions to between five and ten minutes. No longer. You don't want him to get bored."

She nodded. "So is dog wrangling a full-time gig for you?"

"No. I'm an ex-cop and an ex–private investigator, but I'm done with both those careers. I've got some time on my hands and a whole lot of experience working with dogs."

Lupe grinned again. "We're like natural enemies."

"Huh?"

She tapped her chest. "Public defense attorney here."

"Ahhh. Well, the 'ex' means we should be able to work together."

Her musical laugh was infectious.

I took another sip of wine. "Do you like the work?"

"Yes." She brushed a loose strand of hair off her forehead. "I mean, sure, I'm overworked and underpaid. But I feel like I'm helping people. Of course, it doesn't always feel good. Let's be honest, some folks need to spend some time in prison. But I do my best to defend them anyway."

"When I met my husband, he told me he'd briefly considered a career in the DA's office while in law school. But when he heard about the pay and how brutal the hours were, he shifted his focus."

"Is he practicing locally?"

Why had I mentioned Stefan? "He died several months ago. Before I moved to California."

"I'm sorry. Was it sudden?"

Oh God. Here we go. It would be easy to blow her off, but I liked Lupe. I didn't want to lie. "He was murdered. The shooter's awaiting trial in Massachusetts."

"That's terrible. Will you go back? For the trial, I mean?"

Loaded question. "Not if I don't have to."

"Why? Never mind." She shook her head. "I'm going into

attorney mode. Which in private life is called prying. And we just met."

"It's okay. There's a good chance Detective Wright or his partner, Vasquez, is going to 'out' me to the neighborhood anyway."

"Miguel Vasquez?"

"I don't think he told me his first name."

"Good-looking guy? Sharp dresser? In his forties?"

"Yep."

"Sounds like Miguel. Don't worry about him. He's a good guy. And I should know. He's my older brother."

"Vasquez is your brother? Doesn't that make you natural enemies—like with ex-cops and P.I.s?"

"There's a family loophole for cop–defense attorney enmity. Besides, most of my family is involved in law enforcement. In some capacity."

"Really? Are the rest of them cops?"

She smiled. "My brother Diego is a probation officer. And Antonio provides counseling at the juvenile facility. Everyone marches to their own drummer." She leaned forward and spoke in a mock whisper. "The family shame? Antonio's twin, Alejandro. He's the black sheep of the family."

"Why?"

"Alejandro works in advertising."

I snort-laughed, chardonnay burning my nostrils. "Shocking. I hate to say it, but your brother and his partner aren't my biggest fans. But then, neither are the cops back home."

Lupe's brow furrowed. "Why's that?"

"Not to scare you, but I was a suspect in my husband's murder."

"Ah. The spouse is always suspect number one. I take it they figured out they were wrong."

I waffled my hand from side to side. "They still have their

suspicions. I'm hoping the trial will put an end to them. But, unless I'm called as a witness, I'm not planning to go."

"Is it likely you'll be called?"

"There's a good chance." No way did I want to tell Lupe how the killer hired me to follow his cheating wife. "But I'm keeping my fingers crossed."

"I will, too. Probably a lot of bad memories back there."

"Unfortunately."

"Talking about bad stuff: poor Seville."

"You knew her?"

Lupe cradled her glass between her palms. "Not well. Just to wave and say 'Hi' to."

"She was the first neighbor to introduce herself to me. But I didn't know her well, either."

"We've been having a run of bad luck in Pier Point."

"How so?"

When Lupe raised her eyebrows, I saw the resemblance to Miguel. "Seville's death, of course."

Bad luck? Big brother hadn't told her Seville was murdered? I kept my expression neutral and my mouth shut.

"And that hand." She leaned forward. "Did you hear about the severed hand that washed up on the beach?"

This I could talk about. "More than heard. Noodle found it while I was walking him."

"How awful! That hand was all anyone could talk about in class for a couple days."

"It's what brought your brother into my life. And his partner is looking at me like I'm a suspect."

"Huh." She rolled her wineglass between her palms. "You found the hand and reported it to the cops, but he's treating you like a suspect?"

"Yep."

"Odd. I'm sure Miguel will straighten him out. Wait." She sat up straight, feet thumping down against the deck. "I get it."

"Get what?"

Lupe clinked her glass onto the table, eyes boring into me. "As soon as Wright met you, did he come at you all suspicious and angry?"

"It's like you were there with us."

"I get why Wright's being a hard-ass with you." She picked up her glass and sipped.

"Want to share?"

"Messy divorce."

"I heard. Explains his grouchiness, but not the rest."

Lupe sighed. "He always been a chauvinist, but I hear that since the divorce, the guy's gone off the rails. Real anti-woman attitude. There have been formal complaints. I'm not sure how long he's going to be with the department."

"That bad?"

"According to the courthouse grapevine."

I picked up my glass and drank deeply. While I didn't want to spend my evening hashing out my problems with Wright, Lupe might know something that could actually help me deal with him. "I take it you work together a lot?"

"Not since he became my big brother's partner."

"Of course." Not sure how to get more information about the detective out of her, I shifted to an easier topic. "You mentioned a class. What're you taking?"

"Cooking. Neither Andy or I knew how. Growing up, as the lone girl among four brothers, my dad expected me to help in the kitchen. But Mom wanted me to have the same opportunities as my brothers."

"Good woman."

"Yeah. After Andy and I'd lived together six or seven months, we got tired of frozen dinners. Our first class was a one-day session on pizza making. We even made the crust. Then we got brave and took a tempura class. When that went well, we took several classes on sushi—learning the cuts of fish for sashimi, sushi, and rolls. How to make the rice. We're halfway through an Italian cooking course now. Next week we're supposed to learn how to make ravioli and cannoli from scratch."

"I'm impressed. Since moving to Pier Point, I've mastered the art of ordering pizza."

"Don't knock it. That's an important skill set."

A few minutes before eight o'clock, Lupe's shaggy-haired husband, Andy, slouched through the kitchen and joined us on the deck. He looked to be about five feet ten, and in spite of his rumpled suit, it was clear he had a swimmer's body. Lucky Lupe. Though warm and gracious, he seemed weary. That was my cue to leave.

As I walked down the alley, I realized I'd had so much fun, I hadn't thought of Detective Wright's insinuations about my involvement in Seville's murder for almost forty-five minutes. Not bad. I'd also completely lost track of the time and failed to take Noodle home at the usual hour.

When I opened the door, the dogs scrambled to greet me. After I fussed over both, Harlow and I walked Noodle to Dr. Johannson's, then returned home.

That night on the sofa, Harlow curled up beside me while I pulled out my phone and searched for information on training deaf dogs. Though I'd seen Murph in action with Digby, there were serious gaps in my knowledge. The first thing I looked up was the "stay" command. That one was easy enough. I found a brief video showing the ASL sign for "sit." I practiced, then found the signs for "down" and "drop it" and practiced them as well.

A new challenge would be good for me—and it would be fun spending more time with Lupe.

CHAPTER 16

Sunlight streamed through the bedroom window, waking me at five minutes before six. My eyes felt like I'd soaked them in bleach. But I was grateful to break free from tangled dreams of Seville turning blue while Stefan played harmonica and bled out. The mattress sagged on my left as Harlow put her front paws on the bed. That's right, I'd brought her upstairs last night. After climbing into bed, my conversation with Lupe about Stefan's death replayed, leading to worry over the upcoming trial. Unsettled and needing company, I'd thrown off the covers, gone down to the great room, and freed her from the crate. In spite of her company, I'd tossed and turned until the wee hours.

Her wet nose snuffled along my shoulder to my neck. "I'm awake, girl. Give me a second."

My first attempt at dressing had me wearing my shorts inside out. I managed to get them on right, then went into the bathroom and splashed my face with cold water. Feeling more alert, I followed Harlow downstairs. I sent her outside to do her business. For a change, when I let her back in, I got the coffee-maker going before filling her food bowl. The Golden looked at me with mournful eyes. "Sorry, sweetie. I need caffeine. Pronto. I'll get your breakfast in a minute."

When I put Harlow's bowl on the floor, she nudged me aside and went to work. While she ate, snippets of yesterday's conversation with my lawyer swirled through my brain. Amanda had helped me feel less worried, but even she couldn't answer two crucial questions: Who killed Seville? And why?

I hooked on Harlow's leash and we walked to Dr. Johannson's. Though we arrived earlier than usual, the house looked dark. ER hours must be brutal. Noodle capered while I attached his leash, and then we headed to the beach, the brine smell and crash of waves growing stronger as we neared.

About ten people were already running and walking along the sand with their dogs. The black Labradors I'd met last week lolloped nearby. "Hi GiGi, JoJo." They approached, and the four dogs sniffed one another, then the two raced back to their person. I gave him a wave. Farther up the beach we drew within hailing distance of the Boston terrier's companion and I called out a hello. Harlow and Noodle's joy over a simple walk gave me a much-needed boost. I found myself smiling as we crossed to the water's edge. The Saint Berdoodle even agreed to jog with us for a short stretch. When we stopped, the Golden charged into the churning surf. To my surprise, a laugh bubbled up.

"You guys are the best."

Noodle's curly tail swung like a pendulum set to high. I crouched and hugged him. He leaned in, breath warming my ear, drool trailing down my shoulder. Harlow galloped from the water to join us, adding fifty-five pounds of sopping wet love and kisses to the huddle.

When we returned home, I toweled off Harlow, brushed both their coats, and then hit the shower. After a breakfast of toast and orange juice, I sat on the back deck. Noodle strolled over to join me, soon followed by Harlow.

Ninety minutes later I woke, surprised to find myself curled up on the wood planks of the deck, my head on Noodle, and Harlow's head resting on my thigh. I disentangled myself. The dogs sat up and stretched, then relocated to the sunny lawn. "Guess I needed that."

A cold cup of coffee revived me. I checked the time. Yikes. I was supposed to be at the Greenwoods' house. Grabbing a bag of dog treats, I hesitated and then snatched the jar of peanut butter I'd bought for Butterscotch. As I'd told the detectives, possession of the stuff wasn't a crime. I jogged down the alley, arriving five minutes late. I knocked and realized I'd forgotten to grab Jemma's pill bottles. Maybe that was for the best.

Ava opened the door, eyes red, her yellow and white sundress looking far crisper than her sagging shoulders.

"Hey. You feeling okay? You look a little pale."

She nodded, then turned and led the way through the house without speaking.

Something wasn't right. Normally Ava was a chatterbox. There was no sign of Jemma downstairs. Had she dropped the ax on our training sessions? I followed the girl outside, where she called Butterscotch from her crate.

"Why don't you lead her to the lawn and run her through all of the commands you've learned?"

"Okay." Ava's gaze stayed glued to the ground, ignoring Butterscotch jumping and capering around her.

"Hey." I jiggled one of her hair ribbons. "What's going on?"

She chewed her lip. "Are you mad at me?"

"No. Why would you think that?"

"Because yesterday, after Jemma told the detective about Seville's peanut allergy, I told him you gave me a jar of it for my dog." She finally looked up, tears threatening to spill.

"That's fine. You told the truth. That's what's important."

"But—"

"Pop quiz, smarty-pants." I crouched so we were eye to eye. Butterscotch squeezed between us. I reached down to stroke the Basset-Retriever's silky coat. "How many people have peanut butter in their house?"

"I don't know."

"Okay. Let's say one thousand people live in Pier Point."

"I think the population is—"

"This is a hypothetical question. You know what 'hypothetical' means?"

She nodded.

"So, if one thousand people live in Pier Point, how many of those homes do you think have peanut butter?"

The sadness left her face as she began calculating. "Well, if fifty percent of the people are children, and half of those live in a two-parent family, that's maybe two hundred fifty homes. And if some are allergic like Seville or don't like peanut butter . . . maybe two hundred?" She looked at me as if expecting an answer.

"I don't have a number. I told you this was hypothetical, remember? What I'm trying to point out is: a lot of people have peanut butter in their kitchens. Just because I bought a few jars doesn't mean I'm in trouble. No matter what the detective said. Got it?"

A gap-toothed smile broke out. "Got it."

I pulled the new jar from my bag and handed it to her. "Okay. Now show me what you and Butterscotch can do."

Ava was walking Butterscotch at her heel when the deck slider opened. A man with slicked-back hair and at least a day's growth of beard stepped outside. Dressed in gray wool trousers and a white shirt with navy stripes, he looked ready for the office. I thought I recognized his tie as the one that had been tossed on the living room floor.

Ava told the dog to sit. "Hi, Rick. See how good Butterscotch is doing?"

He nodded, then turned his gaze to me and raised his eyebrows.

"This is my friend, Molly. She's a dog wrangler."

"Ah. You've been helping Ava get the mutt under control."

I bristled at him calling Butterscotch a mutt, but managed a half-hearted smile. "That's me."

"Watch this." Ava showed off some of Butterscotch's moves. Rick nodded again.

Ava crouched to pet the dog. "She's doing much better. Can we move her crate into the house? At least at night?"

"We'll see." He gave one more nod and then went inside.

Ava stared after him, then turned to face me. "That means 'no.'"

"Yep. But don't give up. Butterscotch has made amazing progress."

"This is the first chance I've had to show Rick what she can do." Her brow furrowed and she chewed her lower lip. "He's been staying at a hotel."

"Oh." Poor Ava. I crossed the grass to her side. "How do you feel about that?"

"Scared."

Jemma's angry voice blasted through the open upstairs window. "I'm not your laundry service. If you don't have any clean clothes, learn to wash them yourself. Or get one of your side pieces to take care of them."

Tears filled Ava's eyes. "Are they going to get divorced?"

"I don't know. They may not even know."

Rick's shouted answer was impossible to ignore. "If you'd get off your lazy butt and do something instead of gazing at your navel all day—"

"How dare you, you—"

"Hey!" I grabbed Ava's shoulders. "Want to come to my place and meet Noodle and Harlow?"

"Yes." Ava wiped her face and straightened. "Heel, Butterscotch."

After thirty minutes of tossing balls and watching the three dogs play, I walked Ava home again. Fortunately, all was quiet upstairs. Butterscotch went to her crate and Ava settled in at her workstation. I squeezed the girl's shoulder. "See you tomorrow, okay?"

"Okay."

I considered forcing another conversation on Jemma about looking out for Ava but decided against it. What did I actually know about the day-to-day work of parenting?

When I got back to my yard, the Saint Berdoodle and Golden were both napping. I went inside, opened the Tracker site on my laptop and continued researching Beau Chambers. This time I checked his birthdate: he was forty-five. Two years older than Stefan. Which meant my husband hadn't been too old for Seville to date. My stomach wobbled. I was glad I'd only eaten toast and juice for breakfast.

Wait. When I met Stefan, I was twenty-three and he was

twenty-eight. Seville would've been eighteen. The ten-year gap was huge—at least at that age. Though not inconceivable. Like I told Amanda, I was sure Stefan hadn't cheated during those early years. We'd been happy then. Until the miscarriages. I was chewing on this when my cell phone chimed. Unknown number, but a Massachusetts area code. Closing my laptop, I sat up straight. "Hello?"

"Molly Madison? Charles Windemere Cooper here. I just read your note."

Wow. Overnighting the letter worked. "Thanks for getting in touch."

"I can't believe Stef's dead. Your note was the first I'd heard of it. I would've tried to make it to the service if I'd known." Private bankers probably didn't keep up with tawdry South Shore love-triangle-turned-murder stories. "Was it sudden?"

How I hated that question. "Yes."

"His heart?"

Tempted as I was to lie, a simple Internet search would reveal the ugly truth. "No. He was murdered."

He gave a sharp intake of breath. "My God."

"They caught the guy. He's awaiting trial."

"I'm so sorry."

"Me, too."

"Does this Seville Stuart, a.k.a. Chambers, that you mentioned in your note have anything to do with Stef's death?"

"No. I . . . it's a long story. Does the name mean anything to you?"

"Not off the top of my head. Can you send me a photo?"

"Hang on." I opened my laptop and searched for her business website. Rats. IMPRESSions displayed plenty of product samples, but no headshot of Seville. There had to be one at her house. "I can't lay my hands on a picture right now, but I'll send you one soon."

After reciting his email address, Charlie apologized once more for not knowing about Stefan's death, then signed off with a promise to contact me after receiving Seville's photo.

"Huh." I'd missed a call during my earlier impromptu nap with the dogs. I played the message and learned the window people wanted to schedule an installation appointment. I checked the time. I'd tackle Beau first, then call them back.

I made sure the dogs had plenty of water before crossing the street to Seville's. An empty black and white was parked in the driveway beside the red Porsche and an unmarked car sat at the curb. If this was an active crime scene, why was Beau still here? I knocked, wondering whether a cop or Seville's ex would open the door.

Beau answered, hair standing on end, unshaven, dressed in wrinkled jeans and a stained T-shirt.

"Hi. Is this a bad time?"

"As long as the cops are here, every minute's a bad time."

"I heard yesterday that Seville's death wasn't an accident. I'm so sorry."

"You heard?" His eyebrows arched.

Busted. "Okay, I heard when I was questioned."

"Don't know why I'm hassling you." He gave a deep sigh. "I still can't . . ." He stared down with bloodshot eyes. "It doesn't make sense. Then, on top of receiving that news, the cops tried to hustle me out of here. No way I was letting that happen. They think they can stomp all over her life . . . I'm not gonna let them do the same to me." He rubbed his forehead. "Who would want to kill her?"

"I don't know."

"She was an amazing person. Positive, you know?"

I nodded.

"Even with the divorce, I never felt . . . angry with her. The Yamadas, sure. But not Seville. Everyone loved her."

Her murder said otherwise, but I kept that opinion to myself. "How're you doing with all this?"

"I feel like I'm trapped in a nightmare. And I don't trust the cops. Someone has to keep an eye on them. I'm sleeping on the floor in the damn laundry until they release the guest room back to me."

"Sounds uncomfortable."

"It is. The floor's tile. They only agreed to let me stay because I'd already 'contaminated' the kitchen, guest bath, and hall. Hell, I'd already slept in the guest room, so they're just being jerks kicking me out of there." He closed his eyes, took a deep breath, then pointed his gaze at me. "I don't think you're here to check on my sleeping arrangements."

"No. But if the cops have everything taped off, you may not be able to help. I was hoping you'd found some old photos of Seville when you went through her things."

"Nah. I didn't get around to looking at her computer before the cops came back. But I probably have a shot of her on my phone."

"Really?" Sounded like someone was still carrying a torch for his ex.

He pulled his cell from his back pocket and began swiping. "Here. The picture's seven years old. From our first anniversary. The waiter took it. Probably would've been smarter to delete it. No point hanging on to the past, right?" He thrust the phone toward my face. "But we both looked damn good in it."

Once my eyes had a chance to focus, I had to agree. "It's a good picture. You guys look happy."

"We were. Then."

"Can I get a copy?"

"Why?" His lips thinned. "You helping the Yamadas with the memorial?"

To lie or not to lie? "Yep." I gave Beau my phone number and he sent the picture. "Thanks. Have the cops told you how long they'll be here—or if they're looking for something in particular?"

"Nah. Far as they're concerned, I'm just in the way." He gave a sad shake of his head, then shut the door.

Had I'd misjudged him? Rather than acting from a lack of feeling, maybe his desire to dispose of Seville's possessions might be about protecting himself from more pain. Something I was familiar with. But keeping a photo of her on his phone— from their first anniversary, no less—raised a different set of questions about his feelings. Beau wouldn't be the first man who took a woman's rejection as an excuse to kill her. Plus, he'd hinted he was the beneficiary of Seville's estate. Another strong motive—especially when his own house in Massachusetts was in danger of foreclosure.

When Doug Yamada was yelling at Beau in the alley, he'd mentioned something about Seville not speaking to Beau for the last year and a half. But they'd been divorced for three years. What happened eighteen months ago?

I stopped on my front porch and opened the photo on my phone. It had been taken five years after Seville moved from Martha's Vineyard, so she'd still be recognizable to Charlie—if he'd known her. I scrolled through my contacts, then sent him the photo. Back inside my house, I called the window cover company.

"Windows, Etc. We'll cover your glass."

I repressed a groan. "Hi. Molly Madison returning a call. Someone was trying to set up an installation date for my roller shades."

"Let me check. Madison?"

"Yep."

"Uh-huh. Uh-huh. I see it here. We can come out Friday."

"You mean tomorrow? Not next week?"

"Uh-huh. Two o'clock. Would you like to take the appointment?"

Finally, some good news. "You bet."

CHAPTER 17

Clutching a cold bottle of beer, I climbed to the rooftop deck. Amber rays gilded the water as the sun sank toward the horizon. A handful of surfers sat on their boards waiting for the next decent wave. I snapped a photo and sent it to my mom with the message: "Another day in paradise."

Pulling my thoughts away from the beauty of my new hometown, I took a sip and tried to organize what I knew about Seville's life and death. As I pondered, a new thought hit: how did the cops find out about Rick and Seville's affair so quickly? They'd showed up at the Greenwoods' within hours of Colleen finding Seville dead. Had the cops stumbled across something of Rick's inside her house? Or had Seville told Colleen about the affair?

The doorbell bonged. Harlow and Noodle's barks reverberated as I trotted down the stairs. When I reached the foyer, they bounded to my side. "Good dogs. Sit." After rubbing them both behind their ears, I opened the door.

Detective Vasquez stood on my stoop, alone for a change. Tie off, top button undone, five o'clock shadow covering his jaw, he looked weary. "Sorry to drop by so late. But I've been going over the timeline around Seville Chambers's death. You're the last person who's admitted to seeing or talking to her before she died."

"How is that possible? When I spoke to her on Friday, I thought she was headed to work. Someone had to see her there."

Vasquez shook his head. "She ran a solo shop. No employees. We checked with the other businesses in the strip mall. No one admits seeing her. A kid from the ice cream place noticed the 'Closed' sign was still on her door when he parked in the lot at two o'clock for his shift. I'm trying to map where she went after you saw her. Can you tell me who else you encountered in the alley that Friday? And over the weekend?"

His expression appeared earnest, but my gut was still on high alert. "Come in and have a seat." I led the dogs out to the backyard, then returned to the great room. "Can I get you some coffee or a water?" I held up my beer. "I know better than to offer you one of these."

He gave a wry smile. "I'm good."

"Okay." Once again, he sat on the sofa and I took the hearth.

He pulled out his phone. "Before I begin recording, I just want to apologize for my partner. He has every right to question you, but . . ."

"He doesn't have a right to be a jerk about it?"

He chuckled. "In a word." He set his cell on the coffee table. "Why don't you start by telling me who you saw and where you went on Friday."

"That morning I had a lesson with Ava Greenwood. On my way down the alley, I waved at my neighbor, Hank. He was leaving for a bike ride. On Sunday morning I met Doug and Colleen Yamada. Doug introduced himself and invited me inside to meet his wife. As far as I can remember, all the other people I saw in the alley were in their cars. I didn't pay any attention to them."

"If you do remember a face, or the make or model of a car, let me know."

"Sure."

"What time did you leave the Yamadas'?"

Huh. Was his interest in me or Colleen and Doug? "About eleven-thirty. A little after that, I loaded up the dogs and went to the garden shop. I bought a bunch of plants. If you need it, I can get you the receipt. It should have the date and time of my purchase."

"We'll worry about that later. After that?"

"I worked in the yard."

"Front or back?"

"Back."

Looking disappointed, he rubbed his jaw. "You do anything else that weekend?"

"I walked the dogs on Saturday and Sunday. Saw Hank bicycling out of the alley both days. When we were at the beach, I saw other dog owners, but I don't know any of their names. I can tell you one of them has a Boston terrier named Marge, another a pair of black labs. The male is JoJo and the female's GiGi."

"But you don't know their owners' names?"

My cheeks grew warm. If my friend Murph were here, she'd take this moment to point out how socially stunted I was. "No. Dog lovers like me tend to pay more attention to the pet's name than the person's."

"I get it. Anything else?"

"Other than all of that, I'm pretty sure I didn't go anywhere. Except for picking up and returning Noodle to Dr. Johannson's each day."

"You see anyone while doing that?"

I closed my eyes as I thought back. "I don't think so. Other than waving at Hank, that's it."

"And Hank lives two doors down from you?"

"Yep."

Vasquez pinched the bridge of his nose. "He mentioned seeing you."

"I take it he didn't see Seville?"

"No. You talk to anyone on the phone?"

I pulled out my cell and scrolled back through my calls. "No." Seeing the time, I added, "Are we almost done here? I'm supposed to be at a neighbor's in two minutes." I watched his face. "I'm helping Lupe train her Dalmatian."

"She told me." A smile warmed his eyes. "She had quite a lot to say on that subject. I can't believe Ulysses is deaf. I've visited at least ten times since they brought him home and never guessed." He stood. "You like their door knocker?"

Thrown off base, I blinked and sputtered, "The door . . ."

"Knocker."

"You mean the snail?" I wrinkled my nose.

He nodded. "Gave it to them as a housewarming present."

"Why?"

"As a reminder to Lupe that justice moves slowly." Vasquez gave a half smile. "I'll show myself out."

I stared at the closed door. Had he said that to reassure me? Or to remind me the murder trial back in Massachusetts might not go the way I hoped? I didn't know him well enough to guess.

After adding water to their bowls, I gave each dog a kiss, then walked to Lupe's.

She welcomed me with a smile. "I really can't thank you enough," she said as she led the way into the living room. "Ulysses is much happier already. Much more engaged. Andy and I are so grateful."

"I'm sure you would've figured it out."

"I'm not."

"Well, how about I start by showing you the 'stay' command?" I demonstrated, then watched as she held up one hand like a cop stopping traffic. "Good. Now let's try it with Ulysses."

Lupe stomped on the floor to wake the Dalmatian. When he raised his head and saw us, he trotted over. After giving him some love, I stepped back and let Lupe take over. It took a few tries, but Ulysses figured out the stay signal. I grinned at Lupe while we both rubbed his belly. "So, we've got 'come' and 'stay' in his head."

"This is amazing. Right, Ulysses?" Though the dog couldn't hear her, he wiggled his butt and swished his tail across the floor.

On Friday, after bringing Noodle and Harlow back from our beach walk, I deposited them in the backyard, then crossed the alley to the Yamadas' house and rang the bell. After a brief delay, Colleen came to the door dressed in a loose shirt, jeans, lime-green clogs, and a wide-brimmed hat. I recognized the ensemble. "Did I interrupt your gardening?"

"I was ready for a break. Want to come in for a glass of iced tea?"

"Sure."

I followed her through the soaring entryway and down the hall to the glass room facing their lush yard.

"I'll be back with the tea in a jiff."

Rather than sitting on one of the wicker chairs, I walked to the nearest open slider and gazed out. Half-a-dozen sparrows darted about in the elderberry, azalea, and camellia bushes beyond the screen, chirps wafting in with the morning breeze. Colleen's footsteps drew my attention, and I joined her at the table. I hoisted a glass. "Is this your special mint and hibiscus blend?"

"It is." Her coloring looked better today, and her voice was steadier.

"How're you holding up?"

"Since learning Seville was killed?" She shook her head. "It's hard to wrap my head around it. That a murder could happen here. That it happened to her. I've been wracking my brain for any enemies she might have had. Any disagreements I witnessed. Or ones Seville told me about. Other than that awful ex of hers, the only conflict I can think of is the one she had with Sandy Johannson. Over his dog ruining one of her blouses. It probably sounds like I'm sugarcoating her life, but I can't think of anyone who didn't find her delightful." She lifted her glass but didn't drink. "It still doesn't feel real. So many times I've thought, 'I'll just pop over and tell Seville about—' Then reality crashes in again."

"It takes a while." I sipped some tea, then cleared my throat. "Beau told me you and Doug are in charge of the memorial."

"We haven't done anything yet."

I pulled out my phone. "He gave me this picture of Seville. It's pretty good. If you want a headshot for the service."

She took the cell and studied the image. "She looks happy."

"I figure you can crop out Beau."

Colleen returned my phone. "If only we could do that in real life."

"Has he been causing you problems?"

"No. But I keep expecting him to say or do something terrible. Which means I'm tense all the time. And not sleeping well."

I watched a hummingbird sipping at a sage blossom, sunlight bouncing off his iridescent throat. "Last Tuesday, when your husband and Beau were getting into it in the alley, Doug said Seville cut off contact with Beau eighteen months ago. Did something happen between them then?"

"Oh yeah." Colleen finally drank some tea. "Seville was heading to work and went into the garage. She climbed into her SUV and when she opened the door to back out, that's when she noticed a strange car parked in her driveway. She got out to investigate and found Beau asleep in the front seat of a fancy-pants rental. He just showed up. Flew in from Massachusetts without any warning. Seville told me Beau had been kind of 'stalker-ish' when they first met. She said back then she was young and dumb enough to be flattered by his behavior, instead of alarmed. Needless to say, she was far from charmed by his arrival on her doorstep."

"Ah. And she told him to get lost and broke off contact."

"Basically."

So, Beau hanging on to that photo of him and Seville was probably more than him liking the way he looked in it. "You're going to think I'm a total snoop, but with Seville being killed . . . my brain keeps coming up with new questions."

"About?"

"Like how did the police find out she was having an affair

with Rick? The same night you found her and called them, the cops were at the Greenwoods' asking questions. You have any idea what tipped them off?"

"Everyone knew about Rick. Except for Jemma. And, of course, Ava. Seville and Rick weren't exactly discreet." Colleen rolled her eyes. "Three nights a week—at seven o'clock on the dot—he'd park his Jaguar around the corner, then walk to her front door and ring the bell. I told her she shouldn't mess with a married man. But she claimed it kept things uncomplicated. That because he was married, nothing could get too serious."

"Huh." The crime stats in any city would disprove Seville's "logic." "And this was common knowledge on the street?"

"Pretty much." She pressed a well-manicured fingertip against her lower lip. "But I didn't say anything about it to the detectives that night. It didn't occur to me. I thought she'd had an accident. Who she was seeing wasn't relevant."

"So, who told them?"

She shrugged. "No clue."

"Have they talked to you about the affair since determining she was killed?"

"Yes. And I told them about Rick immediately. But they already knew." She thumped her glass onto the table. "I hadn't thought about it before, but someone must've told them about Rick that first night. There was no other reason for them to talk to him. Not then. Do you think the police suspected it wasn't an accident from the start?"

"Maybe." If the affair was common knowledge on the block, maybe Lupe had mentioned it to her brother.

"Unless Seville wasn't being candid with me, I can't see any reason for Rick to hurt her. She didn't want him to leave his wife for her. Said she liked being a free agent."

"Maybe he didn't agree."

"Maybe." She frowned.

"What?"

"I called the police right after I found Seville on Sunday night. As I understand it, they notified her parents the following day. Yet Beau was here by late Tuesday morning. I suppose Seville's folks could've called him right after they got the news. And he dropped everything and bought a plane ticket. Still, when you consider the time difference, he got here awfully quick."

"What are you thinking?"

Colleen pursed her lips. "I'm wondering if he was in town before Seville was killed. Is there some way we can find out?"

"Since you guys are barely speaking to him, leave it to me. I don't want things to get worse for you. I'll do some digging and let you know what I find."

CHAPTER 18

After leaving the Yamadas, I detoured by Seville's house and the empty patrol car parked by the mailbox to circle the cherry-red Porsche in the driveway. California license plate. Probably rented locally. Though Beau could've driven the car from Massachusetts in one of those "return the rental to its place of origin" deals. A long shot, sure, but possible. I peered through the tinted glass. Nothing in either cupholder. The floor mats were factory clean. No trash on the passenger seat. Unless he was a total neat freak, Beau hadn't driven this car cross-country. Which meant he'd flown here as he'd claimed. But when?

Short of going through the recycling bin—a foolish move with cops on-site—I didn't see how I could get a glimpse of Beau's used boarding pass. I gave the car one more go-round, then crossed the street.

I let the dogs in from the backyard and grabbed my laptop. The Windows, Etc., installer was due at two o'clock—which gave me a couple more hours to snoop. Since my initial search on Seville had been cursory at best, this time around, I'd go deeper.

Harlow jumped up beside me on the sofa while Noodle sprawled across a dog pillow. I logged into my Trackers account, entered Seville's name, and started reading. After sifting through links and sites, I had a clearer picture of her past. After graduating from UCLA in 2012 with a B.A., she earned a master's in business two years later. Her first job as a financial manager at a tech company only lasted six months. Must not have been a good fit. Next, she joined a private equity firm as a fund manager. Eight months later, she was working for a management consulting group. A repeat short-timer until she started her own business in 2017.

The same year her divorce became final. Was that where she got the seed money? Or did a bank loan make her dream possible? Or maybe a gift from her parents?

I rubbed my eyes, then looked at the time. I'd been down the research rabbit hole longer than I'd thought. The installer should've been here twenty minutes ago. I pulled out my phone, upsetting Harlow.

"Sorry, girl." I punched in the number for Windows, Etc., stroking the Golden's silky head as I waited for someone to pick up. When my call went to voicemail, I left a message, then shifted Harlow and stood. Noodle peered up from his pillow. "Come on, you dozy dogs. Who wants to play ball?"

"Ball" was second only to "walk" as a magic word. The dogs jumped up and raced to the slider. Harlow darted through the opening first, followed by a galumphing Noodle. I tracked down a tennis ball and tossed it. The Golden took off. Noodle trotted across the grass after her, seeming content to come in second. I tossed another ball and then worked the "hold" and "drop it" commands with both dogs. We were still working with the balls when my cell phone rang. "Hello?"

"Is this Molly Madison?"

"Yep."

"Hi. This is Adam at Windows, Etc. Your installer is running late."

No kidding. I tossed one of the balls. Noodle sank onto his haunches while Harlow dashed after it. "How late?"

"Should be there in another hour."

"Thanks for the update." Even if it took the installer two hours to get all the shades in place, I'd still be able to get to the Foxes' house in time for our five-thirty appointment. When Lupe suggested meeting earlier than usual—to accommodate a dinner out with her husband—it hadn't occurred to me the windows might not be done in time.

I leaned down and petted the Saint Berdoodle. "Looks like someone's tuckered out." After throwing the ball a few more times, I brought the dogs inside and picked up my laptop again. How could I find whether Colleen Yamada was right about Beau coming to Pier Point before Seville died? No rental company worth its salt would give out customer information. I opened the laptop and typed "exotic and luxury rental cars" in the search box. A list of companies popped up. A few were located at LAX. Starting with the ones at the airport, I scanned each company's inventory. All but one focused on luxury cars rather than sports cars. I browsed through the likely rental firm's inventory.

Interesting. Beau chose a Porsche instead of a 007-style Aston Martin. Not the direction I'd have gone. Who didn't want to feel like James Bond when they were behind the wheel?

I tapped the company's number into my cell.

"Smooth Ride Exotics and Luxury Car Rentals. This is Sasha."

She sounded young. Good. "Hi, Sasha. That's a mouthful to say to every time you answer the phone."

"I guess."

Even better. She didn't automatically defend the company line. "I'm hoping you can help me."

"Is there a problem with a car?"

"Oh no. Well, I hope not. Truth be told, I'm not sure if this call is even necessary." I did my best to sound flustered. "You see, five days ago, a man raced down my street in a bright red Porsche 911. Since it was Sunday, the neighborhood kids had their skateboarding rail in the street. The driver ran right over it, crushing one end and leaving a trail of plastic bits behind him. I figure he broke at least one of the parts protecting the undercarriage. He may've even damaged his suspension."

"Uh-huh."

"Then, earlier today, I see what I think is the same car parked across the street. I went over and chatted the man up. He's . . . let's just say he's not the most pleasant person I've ever met."

"Uh-huh." Sasha managed to weigh down those two syllables with an impressive layer of boredom.

"It's a beautiful car. My uncle had one just like it, so I know how important it is to protect the undercarriage."

"Uh-huh."

"Anyway, the man said he'd rented it from your firm. I thought you should know. It's not the sort of damage that might be spotted when the car's returned."

"What's the driver's name?" Suddenly Sasha sounded interested.

"Well, that's the problem. I got to thinking, maybe this isn't the same car I saw Sunday. I'm uncomfortable giving you the man's name in case it's just a big coincidence. I thought maybe you could tell me whether the person renting it now was renting it on Sunday. Then I'd know whether or not he was the driver."

"We can't give out any personal information."

"I wouldn't want you to. But if you could tell me what date the rental began? That would clear everything up. I don't imagine you have too many cherry-red Porsche 911s in your inventory."

The silence hung thick. Finally, Sasha spoke. "Hang on."

Success! While waiting, I paced the perimeter of the great room. On the first lap, the dogs lifted their heads, but by the third, neither bothered. I was on lap eight when Sasha returned.

"It's not our vehicle."

"How can you be sure?"

"The red Porsche 911 was on the lot last Sunday. We didn't rent it until Tuesday."

"I'm glad to know your car is fine. Thank you so much for your help." Hanging up, I felt the fizz of accomplishment. I still had the chops to pretext a civilian over the phone. Something I'd done frequently as a P.I.

Both dogs continued snoozing, unaware of my achievement. I sighed. I might still have the chops, but I no longer had someone to share these small triumphs with.

At ten after five, the sound of heavy bass began throbbing through the house. I opened the front door. Cars lined both sides of the alley. People stood on the small front lawn and porch of the house just past Seville's. More partygoers were visible through the open door and windows. A summer family must be celebrating their return to Pier Point. It looked like they'd invited everyone they'd ever met.

I retreated inside and called Windows, Etc., to cancel my appointment. The phone rang repeatedly. Finally, voicemail kicked in. "If you've reached this number between our regular business hours of 9:00 a.m. and 5:00 p.m., please leave a message."

It wasn't regular business hours. I left a message anyway.

Due at Lupe's in five minutes, I refreshed water bowls and petted each dog, then headed for the front door. When I grabbed the knob, the doorbell rang. I jumped. Noodle and Harlow began barking and scrambled across the travertine to join me. After giving my heart a moment to settle, I opened the door.

A dark-haired woman dressed in heavy-duty navy trousers and a short-sleeve shirt stood on the stoop. The name "Duchess" was embroidered inside a white oval patch above her left breast pocket. Seeing the dogs, she stepped back. "Hi. Sorry I'm late."

"You're the installer?" Slender and no taller than my own five feet six, her arms looked strong. Guess she'd have to be to do this job.

"Yeah." She looked at the huge Saint Berdoodle, wide-eyed. "Things went south at the last place."

Harlow and Noodle tried to push past me. I blocked their path. "Stay."

The installer took another step back, the heel of her work boot dangerously near the edge of the porch. "Anyway, I'm here now. Want to show me where the shades are going?"

"You want to start now?"

"Might as well. I've got all your supplies in the truck. Is that a problem?"

I scanned the jammed alley out front. "Where'd you park?"

"Two doors down. Someone left a spot open just as I pulled onto your street."

"I'm due somewhere . . ." I pulled out my phone. "Now." Impatience to leave warred with the seductive idea of not being woken by sunbeams. "You know what? Go ahead. Let me show you around so you can get started. I'll only be gone twenty minutes. Tops." I led the way inside, dogs at my heels. Leaving her here alone should be fine. It wasn't like I had a lot of valuables she could cart away—at least not without help.

"Your name's Duchess?"

"Yeah. Anglophile parents. I'm just lucky I didn't get named Princess. That was the leading contender until my dad said, 'No way.'"

But he was cool with naming her Duchess? As I showed her the upstairs rooms, the installer startled every time the Saint Berdoodle drew near. "Are the dogs making you uncomfortable?"

"A little." Her cheeks grew red. "I had a bad experience once."

"I'll put them in the backyard."

"Thanks."

While Duchess retrieved a ladder from her truck, I herded the dogs into the yard. Both still seemed unsettled by the throbbing bass. I gave them each a kiss and a hug. "I'll be back soon."

Duchess was hauling in more supplies when I left. Kicking myself for not thinking of it earlier, I said, "Want to put your truck in my driveway?"

"Thanks, but I'm almost done bringing stuff in."

I gave a quick wave, then jogged down the alley. When I rang the bell at Lupe's, the door opened immediately.

She smiled. "I was worried you weren't going to make it."

Tonight, she was dressed in designer jeans, heels, and a slinky off-the-shoulder satin top.

"I see you're already dressed for your evening out."

"Yeah. We have a six-thirty reservation."

"Sorry I'm late."

"No problem. Thought maybe you'd been lured to the party." She waved me into the living room. "With all the noise, Ulysses being deaf is probably a good thing—I mean, he should stay calm while we're out."

"At least the frequency's low. Still, my dogs weren't happy about the volume." Ulysses sprawled across his bed, the picture of contentment. "How's he doing?"

"So great. We put in a nightlight and he's not crying in the middle of the night anymore. Maybe it's my imagination, but since we started using hand signs it seems like he's sleeping less and eager to do new things."

"That's wonderful."

We started off running Ulysses through what he already knew. Then I introduced him and Lupe to the "down" and "sit" commands. The Dalmatian soaked up everything. Lupe was right: the dog was eager to learn. I looked at her grinning face. "You have time to try a couple more things?"

She checked her phone. "Let's do it."

We worked through the hand signs for "water" and "food," then took Ulysses outside, where I introduced him to the word "ball." Which led to teaching him the sign for "drop it."

"I know you need to go, but I also think that's enough for one day. It's still new and a lot for him to process. If you can go over all of this with him a few times tomorrow morning, that'll help cement things. Here." I handed Lupe a slip of paper. "I wrote down a great website for training deaf dogs. They have videos, so if you get confused about a sign or want to teach yourself some new ones, you'll have the info."

She took the note, a small crease disturbing her brow. "You're not done training Ulysses, are you?"

"Oh no. I'll keep working with him as long as you want me to."

"Great."

"You want me to come by tomorrow, or should we keep this a Monday-through-Friday thing?"

"During the week works best for me."

"You got it." As I headed to the front door, Andy emerged from the bedroom wing. Unlike the rumpled, exhausted man I'd met Wednesday night, his hair was neatly combed, his aloha shirt was crisp, and his eyes looked sharp.

"Hey, Molly. I want to thank you for figuring out Ulysses' problem."

"Don't even think about it. Lupe's already thanked me enough." I gave them a smile and stepped onto the front porch. "You guys have fun tonight."

"Will do."

Music continued to blast from the house just past Seville's. The sun still hung above the oceanfront homes, but the air held the promise of fog. Cars crowded both sides of the alley, some double-parked. One blocked the Greenwoods' driveway. Hopefully they weren't planning to go anywhere. The Windows, Etc., truck remained parked in front of Hank's. Duchess obviously hadn't absconded with my possessions.

A spark of irritation flickered through me. She'd left my front door ajar. Thank goodness the dogs were secure in the yard. After shutting and locking it behind me, I called out, "I'm back," then went to the kitchen and let the dogs in.

Harlow jumped up, nearly bowling me over. "Down. Honestly. I was gone less than a half hour." She didn't appear fooled by my pretense of being put out. Noodle moved past me, sniffing the air. The big dog growled. "It's okay. You're just smelling Duchess. She's upstairs."

Still looking stressed, he put his nose to the floor, tracking the offending smell.

"What is it, boy?"

He charged toward the stairs. Worried he'd terrify the installer, I called, "Heel." He froze. I caught up, then led the way to the second floor.

I hoped Duchess had gotten a lot done in the short time I'd been gone. The last thing I wanted was for the job to stretch late into the night. I stuck my head inside the office. "Hello? Duchess?"

A plastic-wrapped roll of what I presumed was a window shade leaned against one wall, but there was no sign of the installer. Noodle lunged for my bedroom. "Stay." Vibrating with urgency, the Saint Berdoodle managed to stop. This wasn't like him. The hair on the back of my neck rose. I peeked inside the master bedroom. "Duchess?"

The room appeared empty. Had I missed her outside? Impossible. Unless she'd gone into the backyard for some reason.

I hesitated. The air smelled off. I glanced down at Noodle's twitching nose, then gulped and took a cautious step forward. Something metallic glinted on the floor. A tape measure. My shoulders began to relax as I rounded the foot of the bed to retrieve it. "Oh no."

My heart jackhammered. Duchess lay on her side, a pool of blood spreading outward from her head.

CHAPTER 19

"Duchess? Can you hear me?" No reaction.

Noodle broke the stay command first. Harlow quickly followed. I pushed them back, knelt beside the woman, and gently shook her shoulder. Dampness seeped through the knees of my khakis. Blood spread across the carpet, the coppery scent turning the air rank. My fingers searched for a pulse along her carotid. Yes! There it was. Weak, but steady. With my free hand I pulled out my phone and punched in 9-1-1.

"A woman's been attacked in my home. She has a head wound and is unconscious." I gave my address. Noodle nosed Duchess's leg. "Stay. What? No. I'm talking to the dog. Whoever attacked her is gone. Uh-huh. She's breathing but her pulse is weak." Blood continued to ooze from her scalp. Head wounds usually bled a lot, but she'd lost a scary amount of blood. I scrambled to my feet and pointed at the dogs. "Stay."

I ran to the bathroom and grabbed a clean towel from the cabinet. After hustling back, I set my phone to speaker, dropped it on the carpet, and placed the towel against Duchess's wound. Afraid her skull might be fractured, I only applied pressure around the edges of the injured area.

The crisp voice announced from my cell: "Paramedics are on their way. Stay on the line until they arrive."

"Right." Why had I locked the front door? Biting back a curse, I removed my hand from the towel, picked up my cell, and raced to the stairs.

"Harlow, Noodle, come." I urged them to the ground floor and into the backyard, then sprinted through the house to swing the front door wide. I spoke to the dispatcher. "Tell the paramedics the front door's open and we're on the second floor." I flew upstairs and knelt by Duchess's side again, dropping my cell to the bloody carpet. One hand holding the makeshift bandage, the other her arm, I tried another gentle shake. "Can you hear me? I'm right here. You're going to be okay. Help is coming."

Time seemed to slow as I repeatedly felt for a pulse and watched her chest rise and fall. I strained for the keen of a siren, but the thumping bass from the neighbor's party made distinguishing a distant wail impossible. Howls and yips came from the backyard. Did the dogs hear the ambulance approaching?

Duchess's eyelids fluttered.

"That's it. Wake up. You're safe now. The paramedics are on their way."

She moaned. One eye opened. Wincing, she closed it again.

Finally, a siren pierced the music. Out back the dogs barked and howled. The siren stopped, but the bass pounded on. I willed Duchess to open her eye again.

A deep voice called out, "Paramedics."

"Up here!"

Heavy feet stomped on the stairs. A large man with a buzz-cut, dressed in a blue shirt and navy trousers, hustled into the room carrying a bulky canvas satchel. I scrambled up to give him space. He crouched at Duchess's side and checked her vitals.

"The paramedics have arrived?" The voice coming from my cell startled me.

I retrieved it from the floor. "Yes."

"You can hang up now."

A second man entered and took in the scene, narrow face calm. "Want me to bring up the gurney?"

"Yeah. Victim's floating in and out of consciousness." A penlight in his gloved hand, the first paramedic bent down and pulled up Duchess's eyelids one at a time. "Right pupil is fixed and non-reactive. Possible brain trauma."

"Got it." The other paramedic hurried from the room, then clomped downstairs.

Feeling useless, I chewed my lower lip.

"Looks like someone hit her from behind. You see what happened?"

"No. I was at a neighbor's. I found her like this when I came back."

Faster than I would've thought possible, the second paramedic returned with another man in a matching uniform, carrying a gurney between them. The first paramedic spoke again. "We've got a head wound, loss of blood. Get me a four-by-six dressing and some gauze, then we'll stabilize her neck and take her down to the vehicle."

The room suddenly seemed too small. I edged around the paramedics and waited in the hall. More voices came from downstairs. I looked over the pony wall. A cop, walrus-like mustache dominating his face, stood in the entryway. Feeling like my legs had been shot full of lidocaine, I made my way down to him.

"I'm Officer Lang. You live here?"

I nodded. "I'm Molly Madison."

"The victim still upstairs?" Lang's gravelly voice pegged him as a smoker.

"Yep. Paramedics will be bringing her down soon."

He pulled out a small notepad. "Victim's name?"

"Duchess."

He looked at me expectantly.

"That's all I know. She came by to install my new shades. She works for Windows, Etc."

Lang's eyebrows shot up. "They do nighttime installations?"

"The appointment before mine ran late." I stopped talking and watched the men ferrying Duchess down the stairs. Her face matched the white material covering the gurney. As they wheeled her across the entryway, her eyelids fluttered.

I realized the cop had been speaking to me. "What?"

"How'd you get the blood on you?" He pointed at my pants.

"I tried to stop the bleeding." I held up my blood-smeared hands.

"With your pants?"

"No. I kneeled down next to her."

"Uh-huh. Let's start at the beginning. What time did you get home?"

"Um . . ." I felt my pockets and retrieved my cell. Duchess's blood streaked the screen. Since my pants were already a disaster, I wiped it against them and checked the time. "I've been home about twenty minutes. Which means I got back from Lupe's a little after six."

He chewed his mustache, then said, "Did you notice any-thing out of the ordinary when you first arrived?"

"The front door was open. I was annoyed because I assumed Duchess had been careless, but . . ."

"Maybe not." Lang jotted a few words on his pad. "What'd you do next? I assume you entered?"

"Yep. Then I let the dogs in from the backyard." I stopped. The heavy bass continued to thrum from across the street, but the dogs had stopped barking. "I need to check on them."

"On who?" His bushy eyebrows met as he frowned.

"The dogs. The sirens really freaked them out. Just give me a minute." When I reached the slider, I froze. Blood splotched the white handle. I went to the sink and scrubbed my hands, then wiped down the handle and let the dogs in.

Harlow and Noodle circled me, sniffing the drying blood. Constantly turning to keep the stained portions of my pants inaccessible, I managed to pet both. "Everything's okay now. You did great." The Saint Berdoodle sat on his haunches, then woofed. "It's okay, Noodle. Now stay."

Lang had walked into the great room. I joined him and said, "Sorry, where were we?"

"You'd just let in the dogs." He frowned, turned toward the entryway, then spun back to face me. "If you let them in when you got home, how come they're outside now?"

"Once I found Duchess upstairs, I called 9-1-1 and tried to slow the bleeding. Then I remembered I'd locked the front door. I left her alone to run downstairs and put the dogs in the yard. And open the front door. After that, I stayed with Duchess until the paramedics arrived."

"And you didn't see anyone inside or leaving the house?"

"No. The dogs would've let me know if a stranger was here. As it was, Noodle knew something was wrong before I did."

Looking skeptical, he stroked his mustache. "You mentioned 'Lupe'? Who's that?"

"My neighbor. I was with her from about five-forty until six."

"Full name?" He took it down along with her address, then closed his notepad. "We'll be talking to her, but first I'm gonna check the place inside and out. Show me where she was attacked."

"Is it all right if I change when we're upstairs?"

"Just keep the dogs with you. We're gonna want to look out back, too."

"Right." Noodle gave the officer a low growl as he passed, but we all made it up the stairs without incident. The smell of blood filled the room. I pointed at the red-splotched carpet along the far side of my bed. "That's where I found her."

The officer nodded.

"Okay if I open the windows? To get rid of the smell."

"Sure." He walked around the room, examining the contents.

Wishing there was time for a shower, I grabbed a pair of sweats and retreated with the dogs to the hall bath. Once inside, my legs began to shake. I kneeled on the tile and wrapped an arm around each dog. Drool ran down my neck as I waited for the trembling to stop. Finally, I felt steady enough to rip off my stained pants and pull on the clean pair of sweats.

By the time I returned downstairs, Officer Lang was standing in the entryway with a second cop. The handsome man from the beach and police station. Officer Gregory held a large metal object in his gloved hand. Seeing me, his eyes widened, but then his poker face returned.

Lang pointed at the item. "You recognize this?"

My stomach dropped. "That's Harlow's GRCA Agility Trophy."

"His what?"

"Her trophy from the Golden Retriever Club of America. She double Q'd. Last year."

"Double what?"

"Double-qualified. In the 'Excellent A' category."

"What does any of that mean?"

"It's a dog competition." I pointed at the object in the other cop's hand. "That's the trophy."

Officer Gregory spoke. "Looks like the attacker tossed it under a bush when he reached the alley. Didn't even bother to wipe it down. Blood's still on it."

Lang peered at the object. "So it is. Good job."

Gregory bagged it, then gave me a nod before walking toward the squad car.

"Where'd you keep the trophy?"

"On my bedside table."

Lang pointed his pen at me. "Had the victim been inside your home before?"

"No. A different person came to measure the windows."

"Had you met her before tonight?"

The music from across the alley thrummed in time with my aching head. "No."

"So, you don't really know her."

"No."

"And you left her alone in your house?"

I shrugged. "I thought it'd be all right. It was just for a half hour. It's not like I've got a lot to steal."

"Uh-huh. So, for all you know, the victim invited her attacker inside your home."

"It's possible. But why? And why would someone attack her here?"

"Maybe to throw us off the scent. We'll know more after we're able to question her."

Technically, this was assault with a deadly weapon. Even if the weapon was a dog trophy. "Grabbing the trophy like that, it seems like the attack wasn't planned."

"Right. Weapon of convenience. Still a crime, though." Officer Lang huffed, his breath ruffling his mustache.

"Is it all right if I use my bedroom tonight?"

"Yeah. No point bringing the tech crew out. Paramedics stomped all over any possible evidence. So did you and the dogs." He gave me an apologetic glance. "I'm not criticizing. But, even I can tell there's dog hair all over the crime scene. We're not going to find anything worthwhile there. Our best bet is the weapon and the victim."

"But if she was hit from behind—"

"Ma'am. We got the weapon. I'm going to check out back now."

While the cops flashed lights around the yard, I waited on the sofa. Harlow curled by my side and Noodle guarded my feet. Lang seemed more than a little cavalier about not treating my bedroom as a crime scene. Not to mention the way he'd let me walk around the house unsupervised. I knew I hadn't clocked Duchess, but he didn't. He was counting too much on the trophy and the hope of a witness I.D. Duchess might not have seen her attacker. And if this was a burglary gone wrong, her attacker could've worn gloves. Lang was shortchanging the investigation. When I was on the job, we called lazy cops like him Sloppy Joes.

A tap on the slider launched me into the air, startling both dogs. After I soothed them, I hustled to the kitchen and opened the door.

Officer Lang stepped inside. "We've checked all the first-floor windows and it seems clear whoever hit the victim came in through the front door." He hitched up his duty belt. "We're gonna get going now. Here's my card. I've written the complaint number on the back. You have any questions, give me a call."

"Okay."

I locked the front door and made sure I'd locked the slider. Then I did the rounds, double-checking each window. Harlow watched from her pillow while Noodle accompanied me. Suddenly the air felt less pressurized. I looked at the Saint Berdoodle. "What just happened?"

Right. The music from across the street had stopped.

Filling a bucket with cold soapy water, I left the dogs downstairs and went up to deal with the bloodstains on my carpet. After scrubbing for ten minutes, the water in my bucket had turned red. I dumped the water into the tub, rinsed the porcelain, then refilled the bucket and got back to work. I scrubbed until my arms ached. When I stopped, the bloody footprints left by the paramedics were gone, but the splotch where Duchess collapsed was still visible. I'd need to rent a carpet shampooer. A wave of guilt crashed through me. Why was I worrying about some stains when Duchess had been carted off to the hospital?

Because the cleanliness of the wall-to-wall was something I could control.

I showered, changed again, then poured myself a large glass of wine. When I settled on the sofa, Harlow rested her chin on my leg. I took a sip and rubbed her silky head.

What the hell was going on? I'd moved to Pier Point for a fresh start. I'd chosen the place for its small-town feel and hang-loose beachy lifestyle. In only eighteen days, one person I'd met had been murdered, another assaulted. And I'd found a severed hand.

I contemplated retrieving my gun from the safe inside the office closet, but decided against it. Even though Pier Point wasn't as benign as I'd hoped, I had two big dogs to protect me.

In spite of the partygoers and their cars still lining the street, I felt too edgy to walk the big dog home. Instead, I left a message for Sandy telling him Noodle and Harlow were having a sleepover. By midnight, my eyelids were way beyond drooping. I headed for bed, hoping the memory of Duchess bleeding on my floor wouldn't infiltrate my dreams. "Noodle, Harlow, come." They scrambled up the stairs behind me. I patted the coverlet and Harlow immediately hopped up. Noodle cocked his head and looked perplexed, but then he jumped up to join us.

The dogs woke me at sunup. A low price to pay for feeling safe all night. Grumbling, I followed them downstairs and let them outside. I held off starting the coffeemaker, hoping that after they ate, we could all return to bed for a nap. By the time the two finished in the backyard, their bowls had been filled. Noodle inhaled his meal, then looked piteously at Harlow as she gobbled her chow. When she finished, the Saint Berdoodle sniffed the adjacent bowl and the surrounding floor for missed morsels, then joined the Golden at the screen door. "If that's what you want."

I let them outside again and trudged up to my room. I flopped onto the bed.

Ugh. I sat up and ran my hand across the sheet. I'd landed in a pool of Noodle drool. Surveying the bedding, I found other puddles. I got up, stripped the bed, and carried everything downstairs to the laundry room. While the washing machine did its work, I remade the bed with fresh linens and blankets, then took a quick shower. After coffee, I leashed up the dogs for a walk and we headed to the beach.

The sunny Saturday morning seemed to mock me. A clear, beautiful day, the weather didn't care that a woman had been attacked inside my home last night. I looked down at Noodle and remembered to check my phone. The doctor hadn't responded to my message. Guess he didn't mind me dognapping Noodle for the night.

When we reached the cul-de-sac, I stopped to stare. The summer tourist season had truly arrived. Family groups were out early, colorful towels and blankets marking territory on the sand. "Sorry, Harlow. Can't let you run free today."

Breaking from our morning routine, I walked the dogs north. Near Pier Point's small business section, we crossed to the bike path, then connected with the two-lane street. At this hour, the only eateries open were the smoothie shop and the taco stand. A smattering of pedestrians strolled the sidewalk, making it relatively easy to navigate the dogs around them. At the main intersection, we crossed and took a meandering route along narrow streets lined with a mix of homes that ranged from bungalow to mansion.

In front of a pink clapboard cottage, a young woman was strapping a surfboard onto the side rack of a bicycle. When she saw us, she secured the board and smiled. "What beautiful dogs. Can I pet them?"

"Sure." I let her come to them.

She first extended her fingers to the Golden, then patted her flank. Harlow's tail swung with joy. "And what kind of dog are you?" she said as she reached out to Noodle.

"He's a mix of Saint Bernard and poodle. His name's Noodle."

"He's adorable."

I'd heard the Saint Berdoodle called many things—Frankendoodle, Sir Drools-A-Lot, monster—this was the first time someone had described the one-hundred-eighty-pound pooch as adorable. And I had to agree. "He's a great fellow. And this pretty girl is Harlow."

"Hi Harlow, Noodle. I'm Wisteria."

"I'm Molly." We chatted a minute longer, then I called the dogs to heel. As we walked away, I congratulated myself for resisting the urge to ask if Wisteria was the name on her birth certificate.

We took the next right, which dead-ended near the water. Harlow barked. "Sorry, girl. Not today." I suspected Noodle enjoyed the leisurely pace of the walk more than our usual fast clip at the beach. Turning back, we continued exploring the neighborhood until Noodle began to flag. When we returned home, the Saint Berdoodle flopped down on a sunny patch of grass, while Harlow curled up on the deck.

"Rest up. We're starting your scent training in a little while." I went inside the garage and rooted around among the empty packing boxes, searching for small- to medium-sized containers. Retrieving eight, I scattered the cardboard boxes about the yard, open side down. Keeping my eye on the dogs, I crouched behind each box and lifted it an inch, but only hid a treat under one. When done, I said, "Noodle, come."

The dog shook himself and ambled over. I held a biscuit out of reach so he'd catch the scent and gestured at the boxes. "Find it, Noodle."

Smelling food, the Saint Berdoodle lifted his muzzle, then began tracking. None of the decoy boxes fooled him. He nosed a mid-sized box onto its side and gobbled up the biscuit.

"Good job."

The dog had an amazing nose. I reset the boxes and hid another treat. "Harlow, you want to be our control group?" When the Golden took a turn, she, too, found the treat, but not until she'd knocked over three boxes. After setting them upright again and hiding another treat, I had both dogs try to find it at the same time. Once again, Noodle immediately zeroed in on the correct box. We repeated the exercise several times. Each time, Noodle beat Harlow to the biscuit.

"Well done, both of you." I collected the boxes and returned them to the garage. The dogs settled in the sun to take a snooze while I went inside. Not sure how to burn off my restless energy, I paced the great room.

Feeling helpless drove me crazy. Probably why I became a cop. And the reason I'd moved cross-country. I couldn't stand living in a house haunted by memories of my dead husband. Nor could I stand feeling powerless about the angry jibes and judgmental looks from Stefan's family and my former co-workers. But right now I felt just as helpless as I had then.

That had to change.

Logic said Duchess getting attacked inside my home was a crime of opportunity. Maybe she forgot to close the front door when she finished bringing in supplies. Maybe one of the party guests from across the street decided to take a chance on scooping up some valuables? And ran into Duchess and panicked.

I strode to the front door. It was time to meet my new party-loving neighbor.

CHAPTER 20

Warm salty air greeted me when I stepped onto the porch. In front of the party house, a young man picked up red Solo cups and assorted bits of trash from the alley. Unshaven. Mid-twenties. Tanned, with sun-bleached hair, he wore faded yellow board shorts and a black tank top. Looked like a surfer. Though my short time in Pier Point had taught me many who couldn't actually ride a wave dressed the part. Was this the summer neighbor? I crossed to his side of the alley.

Straightening, he looked at me with bloodshot eyes. "Is the lady who got attacked okay?"

Did the whole block know? "You heard what happened?"

"Yeah. Cops were all over my party. Cited me for violating some noise ordinance. Gave tickets to a few of my guests for double-parking. A couple idiots blocked the alley." He shook his head. "The ambulance had to back out to Ocean Avenue. I couldn't believe anybody I knew would be that stupid. I was awake half the night worrying whether they got the woman to the hospital in time."

Okay, maybe not considerate where noise levels were concerned, but a good guy nonetheless. "She was regaining consciousness when the paramedics took her away."

He let out a whoosh of air. "Good to know."

"You get here yesterday?"

"Nah." He wiped beads of sweat from his forehead with the hem of his shirt. "I opened the house late Thursday and spent yesterday stocking up on booze and eats. I got a ton of killer guac left over if you want to take some home."

"Thanks, but I'm good."

"Excuse my manners." He freed his right hand from his work glove. We shook. "I'm J. D. Lennon. And that's home." He pointed at the two-story stone and masonry home behind him.

"Molly Madison."

"Like those little snack cakes?"

"Uh, no. That's Dolly Madison."

"Guess your parents didn't realize how alike the names sound. But it's not like I've got bragging rights there. My full name's Jagger Daltry Lennon. Saddling me with three of my dad's rock idols. Which is why I go by J. D."

"Got it." Curious how a guy his age could afford this place, I asked, "You're staying here by yourself?"

"For a while. When I was a kid, we'd come for the whole summer. Now my folks only join me for a month or so. I love it here and am thinking about making this my home base. I don't remember you from last year. This your first summer in Pier Point?"

"I'm a new year-rounder. Moved in a little over two weeks ago."

"Not much of a welcome to the neighborhood."

I thought about Seville's murder, the severed hand, and Detective Wright's barrage of questions. "You've got no idea."

"Look, aside from your friend getting hurt, I'm sorry about all the noise last night. I usually start and end the summer with a big bash, but . . . ." He sighed again. "A lot of people I didn't know showed. Didn't matter how many times I turned down the music, it was blasting a minute later. I may be getting too old for these parties."

I fought the urge to guffaw. "How old are you?"

"Twenty-five. But . . . I feel a lot older. The last year aged me."

Unsure whether to verbalize my question, I raised my eyebrows.

"Instead of finishing my master's, I took a year off. To do a service project. Just got back from Costa Rica, where I worked on turtle conservation. And surfed in my spare time. Living that way . . . the beauty of the place made me rethink my relationship with nature. And society. I've been back in the States eight days and still get overwhelmed when I walk into a store. There's just so much stuff. Too much stuff, really. I mean, who needs ten different flavors of corn chips?

"And there are so many people. Everywhere. Thinking I could enjoy my usual party was a huge mistake."

"You probably need to give yourself more time to adjust."

"Yeah. I'm just not sure I want to. My perspective has changed. Like about how I want to spend my time. And with who. About what's really important in life. When I e-vited people, I was anticipating a fun kickoff to summer. Instead the whole night felt strained and stupid."

I nodded. That was the way I felt at most parties. "When are your folks joining you?"

"Probably in late July or early August. They're traveling around the Greek Islands right now."

Rich parents. Of course. How else could they keep a four- or five-bedroom beach home as a summer getaway?

"Have you gotten an okay to visit your friend in the hospital?"

"I didn't actually know the woman who got hurt. She came to install my window shades. One cop was speculating that she knew her attacker and invited him inside. But when I left, she was carrying in supplies, so someone could've taken advantage of the open door. I don't mean to be a jerk, but do you think one of your uninvited 'guests' might've decided to let themselves in?"

"Like I told the cops, the guy I saw came on foot from the beach-end of the block."

My heart began to gallop. "You saw who did it?"

"I saw someone go in after you left. Obviously, I didn't know it was you leaving at the time."

"What'd you see?"

"Around half past five, someone kind of jogged away from the house down the middle of the alley. If I hadn't seen the other person after that, I would've thought you were the bad guy. Because you were running away."

"I was late. I'm helping Lupe Fox train her dog."

"Cool." He stared past me at the alleyway and pointed to his right. "About ten minutes later, someone approached from that end of the block and went inside your house. I told the cops he showed up around quarter to six and was gone like seven minutes later. Then you came back maybe ten minutes after that."

"How'd you know it was me?"

"I didn't. Until the cops told me you lived there. But I rec-ognized your clothes and haircut, so I knew it was the same person who left earlier. Plus, you're a lot shorter than the other person."

"Was it a man?"

"I think so. I couldn't see his face or hair. Even though it was still light, he kept his face pointed at the ground. And wore a hoodie. But my guess is a man—because of the height thing."

"Was he stocky or thin?"

"Not stocky, but not thin either. Average, I guess."

"Did any of your guests see him?"

"No clue. The cops questioned a lot of people. I don't know who saw what." He stared down at the asphalt. "I was hiding in my room. Too many people were in the house. I started to feel like there wasn't enough air, like my lungs were getting crushed." He turned and looked up at the second floor. "I was standing in front of that open window taking deep breaths and fighting off a panic attack when I saw you."

"And the police know all this?"

"Yeah. I told that cop, Lang, last night. And thanked him for shutting down my party. That's the last big blast I'm throwing." He gave a rueful shake of his head. "The other folks on the block aren't gonna be too choked up about that. Speak of the devil . . ."

"Hey, Molly."

I turned toward the voice and smiled at Lupe. "Hi. I didn't see you there." Crouching, I made eye contact with Ulysses before stroking his smooth coat.

Lupe's warm tone iced over. "Hi, J. D."

"Hi." He cleared his throat. "Sorry about the noise last night."

"We went out. Missed most of the soundtrack for your latest kegger."

"The final one." He held up both hands. "I swear. I'm done with that nonsense."

Lupe gave him a "we'll see" sort of look, then turned back to me. "Miguel told me about . . ." She chewed her lower lip before cutting her glance toward J. D.

He pulled his glove on again. "I know about the attack already. But I'll give you guys your privacy." He gestured at the litter-strewn alley. "Better get back to it. Nice meeting you, Molly." He nodded at Lupe, then resumed collecting trash.

Lupe gaped as she watched him. "Cleaning up? That's a first."

I tapped her arm. "Want to come over? Ulysses can have a playdate with Harlow and Noodle."

"You think he's ready for that?"

"I do."

The dogs were thrilled when they spied a potential new friend looking at them through the slider. Harlow swung her tail so hard it was a wonder she was able to stay on her paws. Equally happy, Noodle wagged and drooled. "Keep Ulysses on this side of the screen for a minute."

"Okay."

I went out and petted both dogs, then let them approach the screen. Noses pressed to the mesh, the three dogs got to know one another. Three shimmying tails told me this would go well. I slid the screen open. More sniffing was followed by jumping and running. I picked up the tennis ball and threw it. Harlow and Ulysses raced after it. Noodle sat on the lawn by my feet.

Lupe chuckled and rubbed his curly head. "You're more of a sitter than a runner, huh?" She straightened and watched the dogs. "This is good. Ulysses has never really gotten to play with other dogs."

We settled on the wood deck.

Fifteen minutes later, the dogs' energy began to flag. I dragged the hose over and refilled the water bowls, then rejoined Lupe on the deck. "Does your brother know how Duchess is doing?"

She nodded. "Conscious, but not ready to be questioned."

The tightness in my chest eased. Conscious was good. "Makes sense. If she has a concussion, her memory may be a bit scrambled for a while. He tell you about last night?"

"He already checked out your alibi. Me." She smiled. "And confirmed Duchess was there to install your blinds."

"Nice to know."

"He had to check. It's his job."

"I know."

Harlow and Noodle ran to the fence barking. The squirrel was back. Ulysses, seeing his friends' focus, looked up and spied the intruder. Yipping, he sprinted to join them. The squirrel bolted.

"Good job, guys." I gave the Dalmatian a thumbs-up. I turned back to Lupe. "Miguel share anything else with you?"

"Just that she was hit from behind. They still don't know if she saw her attacker. But he hoped she'd be able to talk to them this afternoon." The wood squeaked as Lupe shifted position. "You sleep okay? It must've been creepy being here after . . ."

"It was. I didn't even take Noodle home last night." Hearing his name, the Saint Berdoodle trotted back and rested his chin on my leg. Drool trailed across my knee. "By the time the cops left, it was dark. The thought of walking down the street—even with the dogs—made me edgy. And having another dog around helped take my mind off what'd happened. Not that this big kook seemed focused on home defense."

"But his size is intimidating."

"True. And he's pretty protective of me." I wiped saliva from my leg, then dried my hand on my shorts. "Worse-case scenario, if someone broke in, he could sit on their chest and drown them in drool."

"Sounds like a plan."

After Lupe and Ulysses left, I set up the agility equipment. Harlow's class in Camarillo was in three days and I wanted her to be sharp. We worked the various obstacles; then I ran her through my mini-course a half-dozen times. Harlow was flawless on the jumps and weave poles. I still needed to fine-tune my footwork. When we finished, I let Noodle tackle the tunnel again. "Good job!"

My cell phone rang. Unknown number. "Hello?"

"I'm out front. Can you open the door?"

The deep voice sent a ripple of alarm up my spine. "Detective Vasquez?"

"Yeah."

Leaving the dogs in back, I strode through the house. What could he possibly want? According to Lupe, he'd already confirmed my alibi.

Vasquez stood hands on hips, brow furrowed. "I knocked, but you didn't answer."

"We were out in the yard."

"We?"

"Me and the dogs."

Dressed casually today, he wore faded jeans and a light-blue guayabera shirt. But he sounded businesslike as he stepped past me into the entryway. "Mind if I come in?"

Shaking my head, I followed him into the great room. "Does that work everywhere you go? Asking for permission when you're already inside the house?"

"Pretty much." He cocked his head and pointed toward the kitchen slider. "What's going on out there? A canine carnival?"

"That's Harlow's agility equipment."

"Really." He walked to the kitchen and stared at the yard. The tightness left his jaw. "Would Ulysses be able to do something like that?"

"Sure. You can guide a deaf dog through all of the obstacles using hand signs. But even with a hearing dog, it's a big time commitment. I doubt Lupe's got that much free time."

"You're right. She doesn't. Speaking of time . . . I don't want to waste yours." He spun, walked to the great room, and sat on the sofa. Once again, I took the fireplace hearth. "As you probably know, I talked to my sister and confirmed your whereabouts last night."

"Yep. And I met my neighbor J. D. He told me he saw someone enter the house after I left."

Vasquez leaned back with a sigh. "Of course he did. Keeping information confidential in this town is next to impossible."

"Have you been able to talk to Duchess yet?"

A small smile played on his face. "We partners now or something?"

"Look, you already know I didn't do it. And the crime occurred in my house. Isn't it part of your job to make the public feel safe? I think sharing a little information would do a lot to help me feel safer."

"Well played. Though I'd say the police department's job is to ensure the public's safety. Whether or not you feel safe is out of my hands."

"Does that mean you won't answer my question?"

"The victim's still unavailable for questioning, but her physician thinks she should be able to talk to us in a couple hours. We'll know more then."

I opened my mouth, then snapped it shut.

"What?"

"Do you think Seville's death and Noodle finding that severed hand on the beach are linked? And what about this attack? That's a lot of crime for a small area."

"Since you've been the connecting thread through a lot of it, I'm surprised you want to bring that up."

"Why wouldn't I? I'm not responsible for any of it."

He pulled out his cell and waggled it.

"I know. You're going to record this conversation for your notes."

"Correct. FYI, we've sent Seville Chambers's photo to the Duxbury police so they can question your husband's friends and colleagues."

My stomach sank. Was that why Charlie Cooper hadn't gotten back to me? It'd been two days since I sent him Seville's photo. Sure, he had an important job, but did his lack of response mean he was unhappy about getting dragged into a police investigation? But would the cops even question him? Charlie and Stefan had drifted apart years ago.

"We'll know soon enough if there's a connection."

Enough of this nonsense. Time to change the focus. "What about Beau Chambers? Just because he got here on Tuesday doesn't mean he didn't fly out earlier to kill Seville, then fly home again. He was still carrying a torch for that woman."

"A torch?" Vasquez's eyebrows shot up. "You think the guy came here, killed his ex, and raced back to Boston, but agreed to return when his former in-laws asked for his help?"

"Probably not. But it's no more ridiculous than thinking I did any of this over some possible long-ago relationship between my dead husband and Seville."

"You may have a point."

Wow. An unexpected admission. Lupe vouching for me obviously mattered to her brother. "About the severed hand—were your techs able to get any usable prints?"

"They were able to print the lone remaining fingertip. But it was the pinkie and we didn't find a match on file. And don't think I didn't notice you changing the topic."

"Did anyone follow up on the flower tattoo?"

Vasquez rubbed his jaw, then shook his head. "I'm not going there with you."

"I'll take that to mean 'Yes.' Any luck identifying the hand that way?"

"You're persistent, I'll give you that. Now, getting back to why I'm here . . . Since the responding officer last night didn't see fit to call in the techs, is there anything you can tell me about the scene?" Vasquez rested his elbows on his knees. "It's your house. You'd be the most likely person to notice if something was off."

"Like I told Officer Lang, when I got back from your sister's, the door was open. I was annoyed Duchess had been so careless. That's what I was focused on. After the police left, I went through all the rooms but didn't see anything missing—or out of place—other than Harlow's trophy."

"You go through all your drawers, jewelry?"

"Jewelry, yes. Drawers, no."

He brushed his thumb across his lower lip. "Besides the front door being open, everything else seemed normal?"

"Yep. But Noodle knew something was off right away. As soon as I let him and Harlow inside, he growled and barked and started following a scent."

Vasquez stood up. "Let him in where?"

"From the backyard." I pointed at the kitchen slider.

"He started following a trail there?"

"Yep." I walked to where Noodle first put his nose to the floor. "He started weaving side to side, like he was pinning down the scent, then he bolted to the stairs."

"Did he track it from there?"

"No. I was worried he'd scare Duchess. I had no idea she was hurt. I told him and Harlow to heel and led the way."

Vasquez walked to the kitchen, stared out the slider, then studied the floor tiles. "I sure don't see anything."

"Neither did I."

"And nothing's been taken from the kitchen?"

"Not that I've noticed."

"No missing knives?"

I gestured with my chin toward the full knife block. "No."

He slowly spun, studying the cabinets and counters. "Why would the attacker come into the kitchen if he wasn't looking for a weapon?" He pointed at the refrigerator. "You mind?"

"Go ahead."

He pulled it open and stared at the contents. "How about food? Or liquor?"

"You think a kid did this?"

He shrugged. "It's possible. Teenager sees an open door, hunts for booze, maybe thinks he'll find some pills or jewelry upstairs, and winds up surprising the victim. You check the contents of your liquor bottles?"

I shook my head. "All I've got is a couple bottles of beer and some wine in the fridge."

"And?"

"I poured myself a glass last night. If there was less wine in the bottle, I didn't notice it."

He began opening and closing cupboards. "This is a weird one."

"One of the dogs could've started barking and the intruder wanted to—"

"What? Get a better look?"

"Make sure the door was secure?" Oh God. Vasquez was right. Something was missing. "The pills are gone."

"What pills?" His brow creased.

"I took them from Jemma Greenwood's bedroom."

His frown deepened.

"A couple days ago she had a bottle of Ativan and one of Xanax on her nightstand. It looked like she'd combined them."

"So, you stole them?"

"I-I was just trying to protect Ava. I planned to return them the next day—if Jemma seemed okay."

"And?"

"I didn't see her, so I brought them back here. And I left the bottles on the counter." I pointed at the area to the right of the sink.

"And now they're gone."

"Yep."

Hands on hips, he studied the room again. He pointed at the slider. "I take it you've used this since then?"

"Several times. As did Officer Lang."

"And that clown thinks he's going to do well on the detective's exam." He shook his head. "No point trying for prints now."

CHAPTER 21

I took it as a good sign Vasquez departed without further discussion of the pills I'd confiscated from Jemma Greenwood. If he was willing to let something like that slide, maybe I actually had a chance of building a future here in Pier Point. But believing that didn't make me feel better about doing nothing to prove my innocence. I paced the great room, foyer, and kitchen. For all the indoor wandering I'd done over the last few days, it was probably a good thing most of the downstairs remained unfurnished. I told myself to focus.

The biggest question: was there a link between Seville's death, the attack on Duchess, and the severed hand and ring Noodle found? My gut said some—if not all—were connected. But several differences stood out.

First, different weapons were involved. Using peanuts to kill someone took special knowledge about the victim as well as planning. The assault on Duchess looked like a crime of opportunity. Which could be why she survived.

Second—and another big difference—Duchess wasn't assaulted in her own home.

In spite of the warm day, a chill shook me. Last night when the installer arrived, I'd noticed the similarities between us. Same height. Same build. Her hair shoulder length and medium brown. Like mine. Had I been the intended target?

Knees weak, I staggered to the sofa and sat. Why would anyone want to hurt me? I hadn't lived here long enough to make any enemies. Had one of my vengeance-seeking in-laws traveled cross-country to bash in my head? A strong possibility. If I called Mona again, would she 'fess up to the fact if any of Stefan's male relatives were out of town? Doubtful.

Rubbing the warmth back into my hands, I rose and resumed pacing. I needed to take action. But what avenues could I pursue—without annoying the cops? As much as I wanted to question Duchess, I'd never be able to talk my way into her hospital room. Not with today's strict privacy rules. Besides, I didn't even know her last name. Snooping at Seville's house was out, too. Neither Beau nor the cops were going to let me poke around through her things. Which left the severed hand and the wedding band as the only possible investigative paths for me.

Asking questions about the hand was problematic. The logical place to start was with the tattoo. But the inked daisy hadn't been mentioned in the news—which meant the cops were withholding that tidbit. If I blundered into a tattoo studio the cops hadn't yet visited, I could screw up their investigation. It'd be safer to start with the ring. Since Vasquez hadn't admitted a connection between it and the hand, he couldn't claim I was stepping on any cop toes.

After completing an online search, I changed into drool-free shorts and a tank top and went outside to give the dogs some love. Though Pier Point's tourist shops sold abalone earrings and puka necklaces, there was no dedicated jewelry store. I climbed into my 4Runner and drove to the neighboring city of Ventura's small downtown.

On Main Street flocks of people were enjoying the gorgeous Saturday. Their colorful tank tops, shorts, and sundresses gave the four-block strip a festive air. Some folks strolled, some window-shopped, and others popped in or out of the brew-houses and wine bars. The early dinner crowd blocked the side-walk in front of several eateries as they gazed at the posted menus. With no available spaces on the main drag, I parked on a side street. The sun warmed my bare shoulders as I walked to Main Street and joined the throng. A line snaked in front of the movie theater. I checked the marquee but didn't recognize any of the titles. Moving and murder had done a number on my cultural awareness.

I crossed the street to Troy's Fine Jewelry. The shop sat between two narrow restaurants. The smell of curry made my mouth water. Three women stood mesmerized in front of the plate glass window, oohing over the sparkling rings and brace-lets. I moved past them to the door, a low chime sounding when I entered. I stopped and stared. A series of abstract paintings hung from the side walls. Brick red and maroon danced across varying shades of yellow and gold. "Wow."

Mentally shaking myself, I refocused on the job at hand.

The shop smelled faintly of linseed oil with an overlay of roses. A colorful arrangement of birds-of-paradise, palm fronds, peonies, and pale pink rosebuds frothed from a tall vase near the register. Wild yet controlled—like the paintings. Farther along the counter, near a couple studying diamond rings, sat a bowl of individually wrapped chocolates. I was savoring a piece and trying not to drool like Noodle when a perky voice spoke.

"Can I help you?" A thirtysomething blonde, dressed in a cobalt blouse and multicolored gauze skirt, faced me over the glass-topped case.

I swallowed and smiled, hoping my front teeth weren't coated with chocolate. "Hi." I nodded at the array of rings and earrings between us. "You have beautiful jewelry here."

"Thank you." She gave a prim smile in return. "In addition to what you see on display, we also design custom pieces."

"Really?"

She nodded.

Huh. I'd buried my wedding and engagement rings at the bottom of my sock drawer. Maybe I could repurpose the stones and gold into something I'd actually wear? "Good to know. I'll give it some thought. What I'm hoping for today is to see if you can tell me whether a particular wedding band was made or sold here."

Her gaze dropped to my bare hands and her brow puckered. "Do you have the ring with you?"

"No. But I have a photo." I pulled out my cell and scrolled through the pictures. Harlow. Harlow. Noodle. Harlow. Noodle. Good lord, I took a lot of shots of the dogs. I swiped faster. "Here it is." I enlarged the image of the ring nestled in the sand, then offered the salesclerk my phone. "I don't know if you can see, but there's a delicate vine pattern etched in the gold band."

"I can. Is this your ring?"

"No."

"May I ask why you're inquiring?"

No point ruining a pleasant conversation by bringing up the severed hand. "I found it. Or rather my dog found it on the beach. In Pier Point. I turned the ring over to the police but got to thinking I should check with local jewelers—find out if any of them know who it belongs to."

She moved my phone close to her face. "It doesn't look familiar but, even if it did, there are privacy issues. We can't give you any of our customers' names." She set my cell phone onto the display case.

I retrieved my phone. "What if I printed this photo on a flyer along with 'Found' and my phone number?" I looked at the gorgeous paintings on the walls. No way they'd hang something like that here. "Would you be willing to keep a flyer by your register in case someone recognizes it?"

"I can ask Troy. He isn't in today, but you can call me tomorrow and I'll let you know what he says. My name's Celia."

"Thanks. I'll do that." I took another piece of chocolate for later and headed out into the sunshine. Not exactly a rousing success, but not a failure either. If Celia and Troy agreed to put a flyer in their shop, there was a chance someone would contact me. Which might lead back to the severed hand.

I hesitated on the sidewalk, a stone in a river of pedestrians. The scent of turmeric and cardamom made my stomach growl, luring me inside the Indian restaurant next door. I placed a to-go order for garlic naan, aloo gobi, and saffron rice and spent the next fifteen minutes gazing at my phone while I boned up on training deaf dogs. A young woman approached the counter from the kitchen and cleared her throat. My stomach rumbled again as she handed me the bag of food with a brilliant smile. After thanking her, I wove between the pedestrians, gripping the heady-smelling meal with both hands. When I reached the car, my cell phone rang. I carefully set the food on the floor of the passenger side before checking the screen. Massachusetts number.

"Hello?"

"Molly. Hi. Charles Cooper here." The man sounded any-thing but miffed. Maybe the South Shore cops hadn't con-tacted him.

"How are you?"

"Sorry for the delay getting back to you. The picture . . ." He cleared his throat. "Sorry. I just feel terrible."

Oh God. He knew Seville.

"I was such an ass back then. Careless about other people. Especially women."

My appetite tanked.

"The truth is, I have no idea whether I met this woman when I was younger. And I know this will sound insensitive, but back then, there were so many teenage girls on the Vineyard. All of them ready and willing to party. Which made for count-less parties with pretty blondes."

Relief mixed with disappointment. I pushed both feelings away. "You're saying you don't know her."

"Right."

"Well, I appreciate you taking a look."

"I hope this wasn't presumptuous, but I forwarded the pic-ture to a few friends who had vacation homes near my family's place. To see if any of them recognized her."

My throat tightened. "And?"

"My friend Stater thought she looked familiar but couldn't come up with a name. Or why he might have known her. None of the other fellows recognized her."

"Oh."

"I'm not sure why you want to know about this woman—or whether what I'm about to say will help—but if Stef did know her, she wasn't important to him. If she mattered, she would've been around enough to be memorable. Though I still might not know her name, at least her face would seem familiar. And one of our crowd could've identified her."

I appreciated Charlie's efforts, but it didn't help. At least not in the way I'd hoped. In some ways it made things worse. Had those summer girls been disposable commodities to Stefan as well as to his pals? "Thanks for asking around. I appreciate it."

The drive home passed in a blur. I hadn't realized how much I'd been counting on a definitive "I've never seen that woman in my life" from Charlie about Seville's photo.

After stowing my dinner in the refrigerator, I hooked leashes on the dogs and headed out for our final walk of the day. The beach was still well-populated, but instead of lounging on towels, people stood near the water's edge, waiting for sunset. The cool air energized Harlow, and I had to stay focused on making her heel. When Noodle's pace slowed, we turned back.

Seagulls wheeled above, heading south to their nighttime colony as the sun dipped toward the horizon. When the fiery ball disappeared, a brilliant slash of orange and gold spread to meet blue. People began clapping. I paused and smiled. This was the first time I'd witnessed a crowd of strangers spontaneously appreciating nature. I looked down and noted Harlow's swishing tail. She'd always enjoyed applause. And tonight, it didn't seem to matter whether it was for the sunset or her. Interesting. And humbling. More than once I'd wondered if she excelled at competitions because of her applause drive, instead of my dog-handling skills.

Back at the house, I grabbed a towel, rubbed Harlow's coat damp dry, and brushed her. Then I gave the Saint Berdoodle some attention. I pulled out my phone and snapped a picture of each and sent them to my mom. Sharp as she was, I wondered if Mom had already figured out I was texting to avoid talking to her. I hoped not. If she suspected something was wrong, she wouldn't stop calling until she got through. And my tone alone would tell her there was a problem. Before I knew it, I'd be spilling my guts about the attack on Duchess, Seville's murder, and the severed hand. Leading to worry-filled days and nights for her in Massachusetts.

"Time to take you home, big guy." Noodle gazed up at me, drool dripping down his fur to the deck. I wiped his flews before leading the dogs out the side gate to the alley. They dawdled, sniffing shrubs along the way. Officer Gregory said he'd found Harlow's bloody trophy tossed in one of these bushes. I studied the ground around a few but saw nothing unusual. I watched Noodle. The big dog nosed every plant he encountered without giving one any more attention than the next.

Had Duchess's attacker really been after me? Or was the intruder merely hunting for booze and drugs as Vasquez thought? Feeling edgy, I looked over my shoulder. Except for parked cars, the alley was empty. When I neared Dr. Johansson's, the security lights along the fence clicked on. I jumped. Sensing my unease, Harlow leaned against my leg. "Thank you, girl." I unlocked the patio door and led the dogs inside. After topping off Noodle's water, I gave him a kiss and headed home, my head on swivel.

The next day, I woke again with the sun. How insensitive would I seem if I called Windows, Etc., and asked when someone could finish installing my shades? More callous than I was comfortable with. Besides, were they even open on Sundays?

After my usual morning routine with Harlow, we collected

Noodle. Though I doubted the jewelry store would be open this early, I was anxious to hear whether Troy had okayed putting a flyer about the ring by the register. I left a message for Celia and asked her to call back. It never hurt to nudge folks along. With that thought, I called and left a message at Windows, Etc., as well.

I tucked my cell into my pocket and walked the dogs to the beach. When we rounded the seawall, I froze. Empty sand stretched ahead. This was the first time since the move we'd had a totally unoccupied beach. I guessed the tourists were sleeping in today. I let Harlow off her lead. Noodle and I watched her dash across the sand, scattering birds and charging into the water.

Thirty minutes later, sunbathers and swimmers began to arrive. I called the Golden back and attached her leash. Soon suntan lotion competed with the scent of seaweed. Frisbees flew and laughter mixed with the crash of the surf. A small child raced across the sand, nearly colliding with Noodle. I pulled the Saint Berdoodle back and the girl stopped to stare. The dog was as tall as she was.

A harassed-looking woman stomped over and snatched up the toddler. "You don't go running off like that. Hear me?" The child began to wail. Without a word to us, she carried the crying child back to their beach blanket and umbrella.

I looked at Harlow and Noodle. "You guys had enough?" We reversed course and headed toward home.

When we reached the cul-de-sac, I checked my phone. Troy's Jewelry should be open by now. Why hadn't the clerk gotten back to me? "What do you think, you two? Would it be too pushy if I called Celia again?" Noodle looked up at me and drooled while Harlow smiled. "Got it. I'll wait."

We turned up the alley. Halfway down the road, I stopped. "Who's that on our front porch?" Harlow and Noodle ignored me, choosing to sniff the plants and gutter. The figure was hunched over, but still looked big. The auburn-haired man wore blue jeans and a dark T-shirt. As we drew closer, his features came into focus.

Beau's face looked pale. Bloodshot eyes with dark circles beneath testified to sleepless nights and unforgiving days. "Hi. You doing all right?"

He clambered to his feet. "Not really."

Noodle growled. I crouched and grabbed his collar. "It's okay, big guy." I patted his flank and glanced at the opposite side of the street. "The police cars are gone."

"Yeah. Cops said they're done. I can get my plans back on track."

Noodle settled and I straightened. "But?"

"But what?"

"You may not have said it, but I heard a 'but.'" I cocked my head and waited.

He rubbed the back of his neck. "Before getting here, I'd psyched myself up to go through Seville's stuff, clear the place out, and put it on the market. But . . . now I don't feel like doing any of it."

"Maybe you should wait until after the memorial. Saying goodbye might help you deal with what you need to do."

He cocked his head and seemed to study me. "I was thinking a second pair of hands might be what I need."

Wow. Did Beau know he was offering me what I wanted most—a chance to snoop through Seville's belongings? I tried to hide my excitement. "If you'd like some help, count me in."

"Yeah?"

"Sure." After telling him I'd be there in ten minutes, I took the dogs out to the backyard, topped off their water, dried and brushed Harlow, and then changed into even grungier clothes. Though the police would've taken anything they associated with the murder, clues might've been overlooked.

I crossed the street and knocked. Beau must've been waiting by the door, because it opened immediately. He waved me inside. Stepping into the entryway, my feet sank into the chocolate-and-caramel-toned rug covering the Saltillo tile. The smell of sour wine made me flinch. Was that Beau or the house?

The air grew fresher as we passed through the high-ceilinged living room. Furnished with a mix of tan leather and dark wood, it had an earthy feel. We continued through the dining area. The seven-foot-long metal table with matching bench seats gave the room an austere industrial look. In contrast, the kitchen was airy, light, and homey. Had Seville hired a different decorator for each room?

Beau leaned back against the granite counter. "If you could take the upstairs, go through her office, her bedroom, and the bathrooms, that'd be great. I can handle this and the guest room. But being upstairs depresses the hell out of me. Everything reminds me of her." His gaze dropped to the floor.

"Okay. What exactly do you want me to do? Are there things you want saved? Discarded? Items I should put aside for you to go through?"

The silence stretched. Finally, Beau looked at me and straightened his shoulders. "Get rid of any unimportant papers. But keep anything business related. At least until I meet with her accountant."

"Sure."

"Put all the jewelry you find on the kitchen counter. Or

anything else you think might have sentimental value to her parents. I have an appraiser coming in to look at the furniture and all the knickknacks."

"What about her clothes? And the bedding? Stuff like that?"

"Bag it all." He retrieved a box of plastic lawn and leaf bags from the kitchen counter. "Maybe save the towels. Might end up using them for cleanup when everything's out of here."

"Okay." I grabbed the box and headed up the carpeted stairs. This was the first time I'd been inside Seville's house. It felt weird exploring after she was dead. Hesitating on the threshold to the master bedroom, I told myself to buck up and went inside.

A king-size bed dominated the room. The floral comforter and matching drapes surprised me. I hadn't thought of Seville as a flowery person. Though she'd only been gone a week, the room already smelled musty. Dust coated the bedside table, each speck a marker of time's passage. The world didn't slow— much less stop—when we lost someone.

After opening both windows, I started with her walk-in closet. The shelves were filled with her trademark high heels, arranged by color. I couldn't bring myself to touch them. I turned my attention to her clothes, pulling out hangers full of blouses, slacks, flowing jackets, and vests and tucking them neatly inside several large plastic bags. At the back of the closet, a number of Halloween costumes hung. Witch, cheerleader, clown, nurse, hula girl. Seville hadn't struck me as being whimsical. But then I didn't get to know her well.

It seemed indecent to dump Seville's beautiful shoes into a bag, but with no shoeboxes available, I finally did just that. Once the closet was empty, I crossed to the sleek mahogany dresser. More dust. I dried my eyes and started at the top, emptying drawers and transferring the contents into the large plastic bags. In my short time in Pier Point, I'd never seen Seville in a dress—nor did I find any inside her closet—but she owned dozens of pairs of stockings in a variety of styles and colors. Way more than my one measly pair.

Not surprisingly, she had two drawers crammed with leggings and tank tops. When I cleared the last of her clothes from the bottom drawer, I froze. A ziplock filled with what looked like folded paper had been shoved into the back corner. I pulled it out and peered through the clear plastic. Seeing nothing helpful from that angle, I slid the seal open and shook the bag. Out fell the packet of paper along with a blister pack of pills.

The pills were something called carbinoxamine. I grabbed my phone and searched the name. An antihistamine commonly prescribed for allergies and hives. Why hide these at the back of her dresser? Had the cops missed these—or decided they were unimportant? I removed the papers and tossed the plastic bag, along with the rest of its contents, on the bed. The outermost sheet crackled as I unfolded the packet. Nested inside were more pieces of paper. Some lined, some plain, some crisp, others mellow with age. All of them love notes. Written by different hands and in different colors of ink. I sorted through the collection. The ones that looked oldest ripped off lines from Justin Timberlake songs. Two of the notes written in pencil on pale blue paper featured what I could only assume were original poems. The author inexplicably—at least based on their content—rhymed "my heart" with "Descartes" in one and, in the other, "desire" with "dessert."

Eight other notes, neatly printed in black ink, spoke of lazy days in the sun and moonlit nights on the beach, each signed "B." Was this group of letters from Beau? Feeling awkward and suddenly way too intrusive, I refolded the pages and returned them to the plastic bag.

Several torn bits of paper had fallen from the creases of the larger sheets. I gathered them together and scanned their contents. All of them had a simple "Love you, gorgeous," written in the same cramped hand. No signature. No other message. Bland and soulless. Not of the same caliber as the other notes. The Timberlake thief had used someone else's words to match his feelings. Not original, but heartfelt. And the poet had tried to say something personal. Maybe not well, but still a brave effort. The ink on these curt notes looked less faded and smudged than the rest. Were they from Rick? Had Ava's dad been afraid to put more in writing in case Jemma somehow saw them?

No matter who wrote them, why would Seville bother keeping them? There was nothing clever or touching. Nothing that hinted at a deep and abiding love. And their anonymous nature struck an off note. Why save messages from someone who hadn't bothered to own their sentiment with a signature?

If the notes were from Rick, had Seville hung on to them as proof of the relationship? Had she tried to use them as bargaining chips to secure a diamond ring? If so, did that mean Rick—or whoever the author was—had something to do with her death?

Rather than returning them to the bag with the other messages or dropping them in the trash, I tucked the scraps inside my pocket.

I ferried two bags of clothes downstairs. Seeing no sign of Beau, I set them on the dining table and returned upstairs for another load. By my fourth trip, I'd grown concerned about Beau. I walked into the living room, then back through the din-

ing room to the kitchen. Out the rear window, I spotted him
sitting on a concrete bench beside a giant blue agave plant. He
was smoking while tears streamed down his face. Feeling guilty
for spying, I retreated and hustled upstairs.

When I moved into the master bathroom, the sight of the
tub stopped me. Was this where Colleen found Seville? Deep
breath in. I turned to the vanity and started cleaning out drawers. I no longer wanted to think about what I was doing and
tossed item after item into the bag, leaving only the cleaning
supplies under the sink.

Two hours later, I had done all I could in the master suite
and hall bath. After bringing another load downstairs, I spied
Beau in the kitchen boxing up pots and pans. Relieved, I returned upstairs to the office. Piles of papers and files covered
the glass-and-steel table Seville used as a desk. I sat in the er-
gonomic chair. The smell of mint and lavender filled my nostrils. Remnants of Seville's perfume or shampoo? I jumped to
my feet. Sitting there felt wrong. I pushed the chair aside and
began sifting through paperwork.

Near the top of one pile, I found a doodle done in blue ink.
I turned it to the right, then right again. Serpentine line, with
duck feet alongside it. Drawing obviously wasn't one of Seville's
strengths. Still, I ran my finger along the wavy lines. Would
Beau want this? Probably not. I dropped it into the recycling.

I started by putting all the business-related papers and files
in a single stack. Junk mail went in the bin. There wasn't much
in the way of personal material: no correspondence, calendars,
address book, or journal. Next, I attacked her filing cabinet. The
drawers were only half full. Had the cops confiscated some of
Seville's files? Everything inside was clearly labeled. Beau would
need the tax files until her estate was settled, but things like old

utility and credit card bills could be discarded. Fortunately, Seville had a heavy-duty shredder. Three trips down to the recycling bin later and all the nonessential records had been dealt with. I washed up in the hall bath, surprised by how grubby my hands had become from sifting through paperwork.

Though Seville's bedroom looked naked and forlorn, her office didn't appear all that different. I realized I hadn't checked the closet there. Inside were more clothes. Mostly coats, jackets, and sweatshirts and a few full-length gowns. I bagged everything, hangers and all. I hauled the clothes and bedding to the ground floor, bringing down Seville's jewelry box last. I found Beau sitting on the kitchen counter drinking a beer. "Here." I handed him the burlwood box.

He set it beside him. "Thanks."

"The upstairs is pretty much done. You'll need to go through the remaining files. I may've kept some things you don't need."

"Will do." He held up his bottle. "Want one?"

"No thanks. I better get going. I need to check on the dogs."

"Sure. I owe you a bottle of wine. I don't think I could've done any of that myself."

"No problem. If there are any other rooms you don't want to tackle, or you just want company while you get the job done, let me know."

He nodded, gaze focused on his beer. "I really do appreciate it."

"You're welcome. I didn't know Seville well, but she was my neighbor." My cheeks warmed. I hadn't just helped, I'd snooped. Not wanting him to see the flush of shame, I kept my face pointed at the floor all the way to the front door. After letting myself out, I stood staring at the welcome mat. An unsettled feeling needled beneath my breastbone. I'd been off the job for a while but knew what the sensation meant: I'd missed something. Something important.

The love notes? I pulled them from my pocket. Without handwriting samples for comparison, they told me nothing. Shoving the scraps back inside my pocket, I looked up.

The unmarked car parked in front of my house set my heart racing.

CHAPTER 22

By the time I crossed the alley, Vasquez and Wright had climbed from the sedan. Wright looked his usual rumpled, dour self. Vasquez, sharp-looking as ever, had reverted to stone faced. Just as handsome, but not the easygoing cop who'd dropped by yesterday. Was that because his partner was here, or had something else changed?

A breeze barreled down the narrow street, whipping my hair in front of my eyes. I tucked it behind my ears, then stopped beside their vehicle. "What brings you here?"

Wright had missed shaving a patch of stubble along his jaw, giving him a more disheveled appearance than usual. He nodded toward the front door. "We'd prefer to talk inside."

Feeling other eyes on me, I looked over my shoulder. J. D. stared down from his open bedroom window. I gave a small wave. He saluted in return. Shifting my attention back to the detectives, I led them through the entryway into the great room. "Excuse me for a minute. I need to check on the dogs."

When I returned, Vasquez and Wright were still standing.

My stomach tightened. What was going on? They'd never been shy about making themselves at home before. "Have a seat."

Wright remained standing. He gave his partner a curt nod, and Vasquez took out his cell and started recording. Narrowing his eyes, Wright said, "Where were you last night? Between eight o'clock and midnight?"

I wiped a suddenly damp palm on the back of my shorts. "Why?"

A deep trench creased his forehead. "Answer the question." Wright cracked his knuckles.

Annoyed that I'd flinched, I took a deep breath before answering. "I took Noodle to Dr. Johannson's at around quarter past eight and was home with Harlow after that."

"Did you talk to or interact with Dr. Johannson when you returned his dog?"

Returned? He made it sound like I'd taken Noodle without permission. "No. I didn't see him and the house was dark. That's how things typically go."

"Did you see or talk to anyone along the way?"

I pictured the dark, empty alley. "No."

"What about visitors when you got home? Did anyone stop by? Or call?"

What happened last night to spark this interest in my whereabouts? "No. Is Duchess okay?"

Vasquez pulled off his sunglasses and opened his mouth as if to speak. Wright cut him off. "What's your relationship with Celia Danvers?"

"I don't know any— Oh. Wait. You mean Celia at Troy's Jewelry?"

"Yes."

Oh God. The ring. Even though I'd convinced myself I wasn't interfering with a police investigation, Wright must be pissed I'd gone to the store asking questions. "I . . . I wouldn't say we have a relationship. I stopped in at Troy's yesterday. Celia and I talked."

"About what?"

Time to face his wrath. "About the ring Noodle found on the beach. I asked if they had made it or sold it."

Vasquez took a step forward. "What did she say?"

Huh. He appeared eager for information rather than angry. "She didn't recognize it. When I asked if they would put a 'Found' flyer by the register, Celia said she'd talk to the owner. Said I should check in with her today."

Wright took over again. "How?"

"How what?"

"How did she know what the ring looked like? So she could tell you she didn't recognize it?" Anger laced his voice. "Did you draw her a picture?"

My face grew warm. "I showed her a photo."

The detective practically snarled, "That you took at a crime scene?"

"Hey, no one said anything to me about a crime. Noodle found the ring. I called you guys. And I took a picture while I waited. So far no one's admitted the ring has anything to do with the severed hand. At least not to me."

Vasquez frowned. "You put this photo on a flyer?"

"I showed it to her on my phone. But I told Celia I'd include the picture if they okayed putting a flyer in the store."

Wright snorted, then took the lead again. "You sure she told you to call her at work today?"

"I don't remember exactly how she phrased it, but that was the gist."

"Troy's Jewelry isn't open on Sundays."

"What? That's weird." I turned to Vasquez. "You think she was blowing me off? That would explain why I haven't heard from her."

He gave the hint of a head shake.

My stomach dropped. "Why all the questions? I figured you were mad I'd gone there and asked about the ring. But that doesn't explain you asking where I was last night. What's going on?"

Wright's lips pursed. After exchanging a long look with his partner, Vasquez spoke. "Celia Danvers was murdered."

"What?" I staggered back as if slapped. "How? I mean . . . Another murder?" I covered my mouth with icy fingers. "I can't believe it. What the hell is going on?"

Vasquez finally sat, settling smack-dab in the center of the sofa and placing his phone on the coffee table. Wright glared down at him. Before continuing, Vasquez scooched over, making room for the other detective. "We're hoping you can help us answer that question."

Dread washed through me. "You think I killed her?"

Another micro-shake of Vasquez's head. He leaned forward. "You said you called her today?"

My nails bit into my palms. "This morning. I thought if Celia heard my message as soon as she got to work, it might push her to ask her boss about posting the flyer." A lump formed in my throat. The poor woman would never hear another message. Never go to work again. Or look forward to a day off. Never pull on her favorite pair of jeans. Hang out with friends. Kiss her loved ones.

"What time was that?"

Vasquez's voice brought me back to the fact I was being questioned about a murder. Again. "Around eight."

"And what time did you talk to her yesterday at the store?" His brown eyes looked concerned, not accusatory.

"About five-thirty." I pulled out my cell. Stefan's friend Charlie Cooper had called me right as I got back to my car. Tears made the screen too blurry to read. I wiped my eyes. He'd called at ten after six. I backtracked from there. A fifteen-minute wait for my take-out order. Five-minute walk to my 4Runner. "It was more like ten to six." I set my phone beside me on the stone hearth. "I take it she was killed after she left work?"

Detective Wright spoke, voice gruff. "We'll ask the questions here."

"Had you spoken with the victim before?" Vasquez rested his elbows on his knees and steepled his index fingers.

"Yesterday was the first time I saw or spoke to her."

"Why'd you go to that particular jewelry store?"

"Pier Point doesn't have a high-end jeweler. I noticed Troy's when I was driving through downtown Ventura a couple weeks ago and remembered it. Figured it was worth a shot." I laced my fingers together to warm them. "I didn't put a lot of research into the decision. If Celia had said I couldn't leave a flyer there, I would've widened my search and contacted other jewelers—in Ventura or other nearby towns." I took a deep breath. "Look, I know you're the ones doing the interviewing, but can you at least tell me how Duchess is doing?"

The two men exchanged another look. This time Wright spoke. "She's regained consciousness."

"And? Is she going to be all right?"

Vasquez said, "She's experiencing some issues. But we've been told she's expected to make a full recovery."

"Thank God. Was she able to identify her attacker?"

Wright frowned and shook his head.

"Dammit. I tried to tell Officer Lang there was a strong chance she didn't see the guy who hit her."

"So, you know more about the incident than you claimed?" Wright gave a nasty smile.

Looking pained, Vasquez pinched the bridge of his nose.

"No. I don't 'know' anything about the attack. But I've got common sense."

Wright opened his mouth. Vasquez placed his hand on the other detective's forearm and nodded at me to continue.

"The wound was on the back of her head. Duchess being able to ID her attacker was a fifty-fifty proposition at best."

Wright sneered. "You sure you weren't here when it happened?" He shook off his partner and spread his hands wide. "I'd be happy to take your revised statement."

Count on Wright to act like a jerk instead of focusing on what was important. I shifted my gaze to Vasquez. "And now it's too late to bring in the crime scene techs to collect evidence."

"Unfortunately."

"Did you at least recover prints from the weapon?"

Vasquez straightened. "Look, I know you used to be a cop and a P.I.—"

Wright cut him off. "You're not licensed in California. I checked. You keep going around butting in and asking questions, I'll charge you with obstruction."

Heat rushed up my face. "I'm not the one who decided calling out the crime scene techs wasn't necessary. And I'm not the one who's been barking up the wrong tree from the get-go." I took a deep breath. Telling off Wright might feel good, but it wasn't going to help find the killer. I pictured Celia in her cobalt blouse with her prim smile. "It's not my questions that are the problem. It's the person attacking these women."

Wright scowled. "And I think they're one and the same thing."

Vasquez cleared his throat and shot an angry look at his partner. "Let's go over everything one more time." He reviewed my statement, rephrasing Wright's more obnoxiously posed questions, but getting the same answers. Finally, forty minutes later, he retrieved his phone from the table and slid it into his jacket pocket. "Thank you for your time, Ms. Madison." He stood and spoke to his partner. "We're done here."

Wright pushed to his feet. "For now." He glowered at me, then clomped to the door.

If looks could kill, I'd be as dead as poor Celia.

Tension coiled down my neck and shoulders. Needing to clear my head, I leashed up the dogs and walked to the beach. We strolled along the waterline, Harlow biting the foam and barking at birds while Noodle stayed glued to my side. Wright had basically accused me of murdering Celia. Wrong as he was, had my questions gotten her killed? Or was it some weird coincidence? No. As much as I'd like to believe that, too many people around me were getting hurt. But why Celia? What could I have said that led to her death? Did she lie about not recognizing the ring? I mulled the question on the outbound and return journeys.

When we got back, I removed the leashes, then pulled out my phone and scrolled through dog pictures until I found the photo of the ring. I'd never gotten a close look at it. When Noodle dug it up, I didn't touch the band for fear of smudging possible fingerprints. After uploading the image, I sat my laptop on the kitchen counter and leaned my forearms against the granite for a closer look. The gold band's vine-and-leaf design was lovely. Something about it struck a familiar note, but I didn't know why. Maybe I'd seen something similar when I went through all those swatches at Windows, Etc.? Or maybe it reminded me of something I noticed while walking with the dogs? I closed my eyes and pictured the pattern.

Nothing came to mind. I enlarged the photo again. Still no lightbulb flashed on inside my brain. Was the inside inscribed? I couldn't tell from the picture. But if it was, surely the cops had followed up.

After walking Noodle home, I carried a bottle of wine and a glass to the rooftop deck. After pouring a generous serving, I stared at the churning ocean. Seville was dead. Duchess had been attacked. And now another woman had been killed. And the cops had no idea why.

Logic said Celia lied about knowing who the ring belonged to. Which meant that for some reason, she didn't want me to learn that person's identity. Did she contact the owner after I left? If so, that meant the severed hand wasn't connected to the ring, right?

That made no sense. If Celia told the owner the police had her ring, why would that person kill the messenger? The cops still had the ring—even though, apparently, they didn't know who it belonged to. If Celia was killed to keep the owner's secret, whoever they were must have a reason. One they thought worth killing for.

Which made it all the more likely the ring had once been on that hand. And the person who wore it was dead. Who did that leave for Celia to contact? I took another sip of wine, savoring the semi-tart flavor.

Maybe it actually was a wedding band and Celia, in an ill-advised fit of helpfulness, called the victim's husband? And he killed her for her kindness.

An ugly theory. But one that made a sick sort of sense.

Detective Wright was eager to accuse me, but Vasquez didn't seem to share that opinion. Nor had he looked angry about my trip to the jeweler's. Maybe I should share my theory with him? He'd have the authority to visit Troy's Fine Jewelry, show them the ring, and get a straight answer. Two women were already dead and another recovering from an attack. In a small town like this, there had to be a connection. Besides me.

After going downstairs to put away the wine and crate Harlow, I headed for bed. The faint rose-colored stain from Duchess's blood still marked the carpet. I needed to rent a carpet shampooer ASAP.

A quick shower helped ease the tension in my neck and shoulders before I slid under the covers. My mind immediately returned to the murders. Though Vasquez hadn't dressed me down like Wright, he'd pointed out I was no longer a cop or P.I. Not exactly an invitation to keep digging. And who knew if Wright's threat to charge me with obstruction was sincere? I didn't need more problems with the police.

Murph always said I was like a dog with a bone when tracking a suspect, and she accused me of using my job to push people away. Told me I'd wind up with only a yard full of dogs and bones for company.

Maybe it was time for this dog to learn a new trick and drop the investigation. Listen to the detectives and mind my own business.

On Monday morning, the beach was once again crowded. Apparently, the summer folk only slept late on the weekend. I kept Harlow and Noodle close during the walk to Marina Park. After the dogs took a breather on the grass, I tossed them a tennis ball. Harlow beat Noodle to it every time. The good-natured Saint Berdoodle didn't seem to mind. Though I'd promised myself just yesterday I'd butt out of the case, my thoughts continued to dig for a motive.

As soon as we returned home, the dogs flopped in a shady patch of yard. Noodle's tongue lolled. I refreshed their water and gave them both some love. "Okay, guys, I've got to head over to Ava's. Be back soon."

Stopping in the kitchen, I shoved a handful of treats into a baggie. As I sealed it, the image of Seville's love notes flickered through my brain. Where had I put the anonymous messages I found in her dresser? Probably still in the pocket of the shorts I'd worn that day. Which were now in the hamper. I needed to retrieve the slips of paper before I accidentally washed and destroyed them. Gripping the bag of dog biscuits, I trotted upstairs and rummaged through the dirty laundry until I located the crumpled scraps. At least the writing was still legible. I tucked them inside the paperback mystery on my nightstand.

When I reached the Greenwoods' front porch, I was still wondering whether Ava's father could've been the author of those breezy notes to Seville.

Ava opened the door and beamed up at me, Butterscotch at her side. "You're early."

"I am? Great. That means more time together."

"Yay!" Ava turned and skipped through the living room, coppery braids bouncing against her shoulders. Butterscotch capered alongside.

Something about the place had changed. I moved from the entry into the living room and studied my surroundings. No sign of Jemma. Hardly unusual. Though, if she was still avoiding me, it was more than a little silly.

I halted halfway to the kitchen as the difference snapped into focus. The dog was inside. Did Jemma know? She must. The living room was immaculate. No silk ties or pricey loafers strewn where a young dog might find them to chew on. I caught up with Ava at the sliding door. "Did your parents change their minds about letting Butterscotch in the house?"

"Jemma did." Ava shrugged. "She didn't ask Rick. He's still staying at a hotel and she's pretty mad. She said Butterscotch could move inside and be our guard dog."

I watched the loose-limbed Basset-Retriever gambol onto the deck, tail wagging. "Makes perfect sense. That's one terrifying canine."

Ava giggled, but then her face turned sober. "I think Jemma changed the rule because I wanted Rick to come home." She shrugged again. "I still miss him, but it's less lonely now that Butterscotch is always nearby."

"Of course it is." With Jemma single-parenting for now, I was glad I didn't return the pill bottles before they went missing. No matter what Vasquez might think.

Over the next twenty minutes, we put the dog through her paces. Ava and Butterscotch performed flawlessly. "You've been practicing since our last session, haven't you?"

"Every day."

"It shows. Good work. Any more playdates with Francine and Mahala?"

"Not yet. They want to come by some day after school and help walk Butterscotch."

"That sounds okay. Why the crinkled forehead?"

"I've taken up chess. My online group meets from three until five."

"You can't miss a session?"

"I can. I'm just not sure I want to. Chess is fun."

"I never learned. But if you like it, I say do it."

We wrapped up by tossing Butterscotch a tennis ball for a couple minutes. Before heading inside, I gave Ava the remaining dog treats. "To be used as necessary."

"Like a prescription."

I chuckled. "Right." Ava might only be eight to my thirty-seven, but brain-wise, she was eight going on eighteen. "This was fun. I missed seeing you two over the weekend."

"Me, too. So did Butterscotch."

"Maybe Jemma will reconsider."

"Reconsider what?"

"About weekends being 'family time.'" Ava's blank expression told me Jemma had lied about how they spent their Saturdays and Sundays. Having me around five days a week must already be too much of a good thing for her. "Never mind. I'm just glad you asked me to train your dog."

Her face brightened and she gave another gap-toothed grin. "It was Mrs. Johannson's idea."

"The doctor's wife? I thought she and the doctor split up before I moved in."

"Yeah." Ava nodded. "But she came back one night. Jemma said she probably packed in a rush and forgot something."

With her own dad still banished to a hotel, I hoped this conversation wasn't hitting too close to home. "Well, I'm glad she took a moment to recommend me."

"She left your dog-wrangling flyer on the front porch. She

was always complaining about Butterscotch barking. I guess she figured you could help."

"Huh. How do you know Mrs. Johannson was the one who left the flyer?"

"I saw her." Jemma pointed at the ceiling. "From my bedroom window." She lowered her voice to a whisper. "I was supposed to be asleep but was reading by flashlight. When I got out of bed to look up a word, I heard a noise and went to the window. Mrs. Johannson was shutting their front gate. Then she crossed the alley to our house. I ran back to bed, turned off my flashlight, and hid under the covers."

"Why?"

"I thought she'd seen me out of bed and was coming to tell Rick and Jemma. But she didn't knock."

"And you found the flyer the next day."

"Uh-huh."

"Well, it's too bad she didn't get to know Butterscotch." I reached down and patted the dog. "Because you're a wonderful girl, aren't you?" The dog rolled onto her back and I rubbed her belly. Straightening, I hesitated on the threshold. "I'm glad she left the flyer. Even though I'm surprised she recommended someone she'd never met. Must be a trusting person."

Or incredibly naive.

CHAPTER 23

After a lunch of cold leftover aloo gobi, I hauled Harlow's agility equipment from the garage and set up the obstacles. It would save time if I could eyeball the weave pole layout, but training on an inaccurate obstacle would do the Golden more harm than good. I sighed, then found the measuring tape and placed the poles twenty-four inches apart.

To prep for tomorrow's class in Camarillo, I took Harlow through each obstacle singly several times, then ran her through the entire setup. When she knocked the pole down on the jump, I put it back in place and we ran the course again, with me calling out encouragement. As we repeated the course, Noodle seemed content to watch and drool. Midway through a run, my thoughts drifted to Celia's murder and Detective Wright's accusations. I miscued Harlow. Refocusing, I ran her through the course again.

Though appearing content to laze in the sun, the Saint Berdoodle scrambled to his paws and followed Harlow over the jump on her final run. "Look at you go. Good job, Noodle. Good job, Harlow!" I threw them each a ball.

The Golden charged after hers. Noodle pursued his ball at a more leisurely pace, stopping to inhale a mystery scent along the way. I carried the equipment to the carless side of the garage. Between trips, I paused to toss the balls again. Once everything was stowed, I retrieved the weeding tool, kneeling pad, and trowel.

While I turned dirt and dug out weeds, the dogs sprawled on the deck. The earth now had a rich humus scent from the soil amendments I'd added. I wondered how Noodle interpreted the scent, knowing my nose captured only a fragment of what his did.

In the week since I'd transplanted the artemisia and lavender, both showed new growth, and the blooms on the golden yarrow had opened. All the leaves and flowers looked healthy. I'd have to stop by the Yamadas' and thank them for their plant recommendations. And return Colleen's cookie plate.

When the fog rolled in a few hours later, I stood and stretched. So much for a warm night. The summer folk would be disappointed. I gathered my tools and was heading for the garage when the doorbell sounded. Harlow's ears perked up and she woofed. Noodle dropped the ball he was gnawing and charged toward the house. I set the tools on the deck and told both dogs to stay.

I wiped loose dirt from my knees and shoes before entering and closed the screen behind me. Crossing to the entryway, I opened the front door. Sandy Johannson stood on the porch. Was he here about my keeping Noodle the other night? If he was, he looked remarkably calm about it. Dressed in jeans, sneakers, and an expensive-looking pullover, he appeared ready for an evening at the yacht club. A bottle of wine was cradled in his arm.

"Hi. I take it you got my message?"

His brow furrowed momentarily. "Oh. About keeping the dog with you the night before last. I did. Not a problem."

"Good."

He held up the bottle. "This is the wine you liked . . . Was that two weeks ago?" Sandy shook his head. "I should've brought it by sooner as a thank-you. For training and looking after the dog."

"No worries. Want to come in?"

"Sure. I figured I'd collect him for a change."

That was a change indeed. "Everything okay?"

"Eh." He waggled his free hand from side to side. "Had a tough day at work. Not all that unusual, but I thought the stroll here and back might help me unwind."

I pointed at the bottle. "If you want, we can pull the cork on that right now. I'm pretty sure a glass or two will help you with the unwinding."

"Sounds good to me."

I led the way into the kitchen and retrieved the white wine goblets from an upper shelf. Noodle stood, nose pressed against the screen, but Sandy didn't acknowledge him. Once again, my heart ached for the dog. I scrounged in a drawer, then handed the corkscrew to the doctor. "Do the honors?"

"Glad to." He gathered up the glasses, then ambled to the sofa and sat before peeling the foil from the bottle's neck. I really needed to up my wine-opening game. Beau and the doctor had now both put me to shame. The cork pulled free with a small poof.

I looked back at the Saint Berdoodle. For the dog's sake, I

hoped Sandy's divorce would be finalized soon. Then Noodle could go to a loving home. I hoped Sandy hadn't already made arrangements for the big dog's adoption. The thought of him moving away hollowed out my heart. Maybe Sandy stopping by tonight was an unexpected opportunity. I hadn't yet thought it through, but I wanted to broach the topic of adopting Noodle. I hunted down a couple coasters and then joined Sandy on the sofa. He handed me a generous pour.

I waited until he'd filled a glass for himself before taking a sip. "Mmmm. You're right. This is good."

He sat back and rested his calf across his other knee. The image of a wealthy man totally at peace. I wouldn't find a better time to make my request. He spoke before I could gather my thoughts.

"I'm not normally a chardonnay drinker, but I have a sentimental attachment to this wine. It's my wife's favorite." He took a deep breath, then nodded toward the golden liquid. "Jessica and I stayed at the winery a few months before I proposed. Gorgeous hilltop location. Grapevines covering the land as far as you could see. The contrast between the rolling hills and soldier-like rows of vines . . ." He shook his head. "We stayed in one of the casitas with our own private deck. At night we'd sit outside with a bottle of wine and watch the sky go from gold to black. Just as the stars started to show, bats would come out and zip around chasing gnats. It was magical."

Not the moment to ask for his soon-to-be ex-wife's dog. I gulped more wine.

Sandy's glass clinked against the stone coaster. "I hate to say it but, like all beautiful women, Jessica always expected to get her way. That doesn't work in a marriage. Not a healthy one." He turned to look at me. "Have you been married?"

As he leaned in for my answer, he shifted closer, thigh stopping a millimeter from mine.

A flash of discomfort ran through me. Was I wary because of his proximity or the topic? I told myself to relax. The guy was smart, but obviously lacking in social skills. How else could he not be in love with Noodle?

"Yep. Back in Massachusetts." I hoped that would be enough for him. While I wasn't in the mood to hear what went wrong between Sandy and his wife, I had a far greater aversion to admitting how my marriage ended. Especially after being questioned by Detective Wright and learning my visit to the jewelry store might be the reason Celia was dead. Did all relationships—even the most casual of them—end in pain?

Enough. Sandy had brought good wine and I'd been stupid enough to invite him in to share it. Besides, I needed him to think well of me. Maybe listening to his lament was the price for top-quality vino. And it might warm him to my proposal about taking in Noodle. I took another sip.

The bottle was sweating onto my coffee table. Maybe I should get another coaster? My gaze lasered in on the label and I remained seated. The only other time I drank this wine, Sandy had poured it inside the house and brought a glass out to me on the patio. Twisted Vitis Chardonnay. The gold and green label featured a line drawing of a leafy vine coiled around the name. I sucked in air. Wine went down my windpipe. I choked, then coughed.

"You okay?" Sandy slid closer, placed his hand on my arm, and lowered his face to look in my eyes. "Need a thump on the back?"

I shook my head, the touch of his hand making my skin crawl. Another coughing fit hit before I could speak. Finally, I croaked out, "Went down the wrong pipe." I wiped my eyes. The undulating vine on the bottle matched the design engraved on the ring Noodle dug up at the beach. Now I knew why the design seemed familiar; I'd seen its twin on Sandy's finger the night I told him about the severed hand. Bile rose. I tried to scoot away, but his hand gripped my forearm.

"So, you do know."

Trying to hide my panic, I lifted my chin and met his watchful eyes. He looked like a normal person. But he wasn't. "It was your wife's ring. And her hand."

A furrow creased Sandy's brow. "I had the rings specially made. Inspired by the label of the wine she loved." He nodded toward my glass. "Drink up. I think you're going to need it."

"Why kill her? And chop her up? At least I'm assuming that's what happened."

"As I started to say, Jessica was a beautiful but difficult woman. We were heading for a divorce. Long overdue, in my opinion." He sighed. "I never planned to kill her. But one night she pushed me too far. I snapped. Her death was an accident. But who would believe that? Everyone knew our marriage was over. And an ER surgeon unintentionally hitting someone hard enough to kill them? If that got out, my career would've been ruined."

"Your career? What about her life?" I tried to pull my arm free, but his hold was like iron.

"The woman was a dilettante. She didn't save lives the way I do."

"You cut off her hand." I tried not to picture the bloodless trophy Noodle found on the beach. "She was someone you once loved and you . . . what? Chopped off all the identifying bits?"

He cocked his head. "Bodies are more fragile than we like to believe." He tightened his grasp on my arm.

I bit back a gasp.

"But they're extremely difficult to get rid of. Fortunately, I have access to the medical waste containers at the hospital. The problem is, you can't just bring in a body and dump it. I had to cut Jessica up and deposit the pieces over time." He placed his free hand on my thigh and leaned in as if sharing an intimate moment.

Hot breath touched my cheek. Revulsion washed through me.

"I kept her in the downstairs bath as I dismembered her, bagging parts and storing them in the freezer until I could take them to the hospital."

"Oh God." I'd seen plenty of careless cruelty on the job, but this struck at my core. I'd talked to this man and taken care of his dog. Never once had I suspected he was a monster.

"Wasn't easy. Since I didn't have any surgical equipment at home, I had to use our boning knife. While I was in the kitchen sharpening it, the damn dog grabbed one of Jessica's hands. I chased him but he was too fast. Stupid mutt thought it was a game. I figured he'd eventually get bored and drop it and went back to cutting and bagging parts. Next thing I knew, the dog was gone. Along with the hand."

"And Noodle buried it on the beach." Where was my phone? I shifted but didn't feel it in my back or front pocket. I scanned the table then looked at the kitchen counter. Nothing. Had I left it in the yard?

"Apparently. Now, I've answered your question. Have some more to drink." He picked up my glass and held it near my mouth. "Don't make me force this down your throat."

"Why do you want me to drink?" The room seemed to swim for a moment. Oh no. "You put something in my wine."

"I certainly did."

I needed to keep focused and fight whatever drug he'd dosed me with. "When you hit Duchess, you thought she was me, right?"

"Her name was Duchess?" He lowered the glass. "How odd."

I nodded. My head didn't feel properly attached.

"It seemed a perfect opportunity: noisy party, lots of strange people and vehicles in the street. Figured I'd find a weapon at your house. Make it look like a robbery gone wrong. I miscalculated. I didn't know you were having work done. Didn't even realize I'd hit the wrong person until after she collapsed."

In spite of the wine, my mouth felt dust-dry. "You didn't ask, but she's going to be okay. And she didn't see you, so she's no threat."

He chuckled. "Sweet you're worried about her."

His face multiplied, then regrouped. There was something I needed to ask him. Something important. "What . . . ?"

"Yes?"

"Um, what about Seville?"

He checked his watch. "You're lucky we have a little more time before I need to get going. I figure telling the cops we sat drinking and talking for thirty minutes is credible. Here." He pressed the glass to my lips. "Drink some more."

I clamped my mouth shut. Wine dribbled down my chin and onto my shirt.

"Go on. It'll help with the shock of dealing with your situation. And confirm my story when the medical examiner checks your stomach contents." He let go of my arm and peeled my lips apart with one hand while tilting the glass with the other.

Wine went down my windpipe again. I coughed and teared. Sandy sat back frowning. When I quieted, he gripped my arm and clunked the empty glass onto the table. "Guess that'll have to do. I'm going to tie you up before I walk the dog home. I'll come back after dark. Wouldn't do for the M.E. to decide you'd died while I was here. Especially since that nosey neighbor of yours saw me going up your walkway. Swear that guy's got nothing better to do than stare out his window all day."

"J. D.?"

"Who's J. D.?"

If J. D. saw me letting Sandy into the house . . . My mind went blank. How did that help? The bottle came into focus. "Did you bring the wine as a test?"

"Very good. I wanted to see your reaction. See if the gears engaged."

"Why?"

"Thought that was obvious. You've been poking around where you shouldn't."

"No." I shook my head and the room swam. When it stopped moving, I was able to form words again. "Why'd you kill Seville?"

"We had a little something going on the side. I'd made vague noises about marrying her. After my divorce was final. I may've meant it at the time. She could be quite . . . enticing. But let's face it, once Jessica was dead, those divorce papers were never going to be signed." His grip on my arm tightened further. "But Seville grew impatient. When I promised to put a huge diamond on her hand, that mollified her. I told her she could move into my home in a couple months—which also put her at ease. I did ask her to keep our engagement secret for the time being, but really didn't think she'd be able to keep her mouth shut."

If Seville hadn't been so discreet, would she still be alive? "She told me she was getting engaged, but not to who." My head felt like it might topple off my neck. On the plus side, my nerves were unnaturally calm.

He huffed out a breath, frown deepening. "Then you went and told her about the ring. She recognized the description."

I flashed back to the doodle I'd found on Seville's desk. "Those weren't duck feet, they were grape leaves."

"What?"

My head sagged forward and I jerked it back. The world twirled again. I closed my eyes. "Seville knew you'd killed your wife."

He grunted, then spoke. "She told me about the ring. Said how odd it was you'd found one that sounded like the twin to mine. I played dumb. But later, I realized things in my dresser were out of place. It was obvious she'd rifled through the contents. The next night I caught her going through my knife drawer."

"Maybe she needed a knife."

"We'd brought sushi home for dinner. No knife required. After that, I knew it was just a question of time before she put it all together. Seville was a smart woman."

"How'd you do it?"

"Do what?"

"Get her to eat peanuts?"

He chuckled again. "Got takeout from her favorite Chinese restaurant. They knew about her allergy and were always scrupulous about keeping her order peanut-free."

I tried to raise my eyebrows but wasn't sure I managed. "What happened?"

"Before bringing it to her house, I went home and added peanut oil to everything. One bite and Seville reacted. Sweat popped out on her forehead, ran down her face. Her makeup got all smeary." He pursed his mouth as if tasting something nasty. "When she started wheezing, I acted alarmed and asked where her EpiPen was."

"And didn't give it to her."

"Oh, I got the Epi from her purse. And switched it for one I'd dosed with peanut oil. She injected herself. Went straight into anaphylactic shock."

"You stood there and watched her die?"

"Not exactly something I haven't witnessed before, but no. Once she'd collapsed, I went into the kitchen and washed the plates, glasses, and silverware. Wiped down everything I might have touched. By the time I finished, she'd stopped breathing."

"And you put her in the tub."

"First I carried her to the bathroom. While the tub filled, I scrubbed off any trace evidence I might have left on her. Then I put her in the tub. I hoped the hot water might muddle the time of death, make it look like it happened later. After that, all I had to do was collect the food and containers and take the long way home."

Dizziness warred with my fury. "Three women are dead because you lost your temper with your wife."

"It'll be four soon." Sandy gave his watch another look and nodded. "I've been here long enough."

If he tied me up, it was over. Maybe if I used his big ego against him, I could keep him talking. At least until I figured a way out of this. "You wrote those notes."

"What notes?"

"The 'Love you, gorgeous' notes."

A sharp V appeared between his brows. "She showed you those?"

"No. I found them in one of her drawers. When I was help-ing Beau."

Voice tight, he said, "Where are they?"

"I gave them to Detective Vasquez. When he came by yester-day." That ought to scare him.

Sandy's face burned red. "Why would she save . . . ? There was nothing personal, nothing special . . ." His hand fell away from my wrist.

My arm was free. I shifted my weight forward. "Seville saved all her love notes."

"She thought 'Love you, gorgeous' actually meant some-thing?"

"Who knows? Maybe they were her insurance policy. On some level, she had to know you're crazy."

Sandy drew his hand back as if to strike me, then froze. "Nice one. Try to get me to mess up the timeline by hitting you now. It's not going to work. I'm smarter than that. But don't worry, I won't forget when I come back."

Jerking forward, I grabbed the wine bottle by its neck with both hands and swung. Chardonnay gushed over my wrists as the bottle connected with Sandy's jaw. He gave a muffled cry and fell back. Brain suddenly sharp, I pictured the gun safe upstairs. Too far. The knives in the kitchen. Too dangerous. This maniac could overpower me.

Dogs. In the yard. Yes.

Dropping the bottle, I stumbled on rubbery legs toward the kitchen. The short distance felt like a marathon. I reached the screen and lunged for the handle. Pain erupted from the back of my skull and fireworks flared before my eyes. I managed a guttural cry before my knees gave out. My chin smacked the tile. Hot coppery blood coated my tongue.

Noodle barked and jumped against the screen while Harlow whimpered. "Come," I choked out.

The Saint Berdoodle broke through the screen as if it were made of tissue paper and charged inside. Sandy swung the wine bottle at Noodle. The dog came in low, then leaped. Nearly two hundred pounds of fury landed on the man's chest, knocking him to the floor. The bottle clattered from his hand and rolled across the tile, stopping when it bumped against the sofa.

Dizzy and shaking, I struggled to my feet. "Noodle, hold."

Sandy tried to shove the dog from his chest. Noodle bared his teeth and chomped down on the doctor's arm. Maybe it was a good thing I'd never explained all the training I'd done with his dog. Drool dripped from the Saint Berdoodle's mouth as he growled. Damn, he looked menacing. I told him to hold again. Harlow circled them, barking. "Good dogs."

Where was my phone? No time to search for it now. I turned and staggered across the great room to the entry, then tottered up the stairs to the office. Opening the closet, I kneeled on the carpet in front of the safe and punched in the code. Something dripped from the side of my mouth. I wiped my hand along my chin. Blood. Right. I'd bitten my tongue. I retrieved my Glock and checked the clip. Fully loaded. Hoping the dogs had Sandy under control, I pushed to my feet.

Wobbling down the staircase, I death-gripped the railing with one hand and the gun with the other. Growling and frenzied barks still came from the great room. When I entered, Noodle remained on Sandy's chest, jaw gripping his arm, snarling. "Good boy."

"Get this damn animal off me."

Gun in hand, I felt safe enough to search for my phone. I scanned the room. There. Sticking out between two sofa cushions. I gave Sandy a wide berth, retrieved my cell, and pressed 9-1-1.

"What's your emergency?"

The calm voice helped me focus. "I need the police. A man assaulted me inside my home. My dogs attacked him. I've got my gun and he's under control, but I've been drugged. I need the police." I gave my address, set the phone to speaker, and thunked it on the counter. Unwilling to point the gun anywhere near the dogs, I called, "Harlow, come." The Golden barked at Sandy one more time, then moved to my side. "Sit." I felt her shift onto her haunches. "Noodle, out! Come."

The Saint Berdoodle continued growling.

"Out! Come. Now!"

Noodle opened his mouth and shook his head, flinging drool on his prisoner before trotting to my side. "Good dog. Sit." Using a two-handed grip, I aimed the gun at Sandy. "You stay, too."

"Can I at least sit up?" A long tear in his sweater showed where Noodle's teeth had seized his arm.

The man was a killer. Crafty and cunning. "No. Stay right like you are." I took a deep breath, then another. The adrenaline spike was fading. Wooziness seeped into my brain. I leaned back against the counter for support. "Tell me about Celia."

Sandy gingerly touched his jaw, then opened and closed his mouth. "The clerk from the jewelry store?"

"Yep."

"You know I'm just going to deny I ever said any of this."

"Tell me anyway."

"She recognized the ring. I couldn't have her blabbing to you—or the cops—about it. Might make them wonder whether the hand was Jessica's."

"Celia told me the ring didn't look familiar. Why'd she lie?"

He propped himself up on his elbows. "Not to—"

"No. Down."

"I'm not one of your stupid dogs."

"Don't care. Lie down." When he complied, I said, "Why didn't she tell me the truth?"

"Not to sound egotistical, but I'm considered a catch. A soon-to-be divorced doctor who's easy on the eyes. Single women like that. And they like me. You didn't, which was odd." He rubbed his jaw again. "Why didn't you like me?"

This was what he wanted to know? "You weren't nice to your dog."

"You've got to be kidding." He winced as he raised his arm and looked at the damage Noodle had done. "That dog's a menace."

"That's not how I see it." The gun wavered. I tightened my grip. Fortunately, the doctor looked as shell-shocked as I felt. "What happened with Celia?"

"When she called, I got the impression she was trying to get on my good side. So, I told her Jessica tossed the ring into the ocean in a fit of anger. Told her how much that hurt me. Celia was very sympathetic. As a thank-you for her being so understanding, I offered to stop by her place with a bottle of wine from my personal collection."

I hoped the emergency dispatcher was hearing all this. "And you killed her."

"Is that such a surprise?"

I shook my head. Dizziness hit again. Before I realized what was happening, Sandy rolled and grabbed my ankles. I tumbled onto my side but kept my grip on the gun. Noodle jumped into the mix, snarling. Sandy shrieked as I kicked my legs free. Afraid I might shoot the dog, I crawled away from the melee. When I looked back, blood drenched Sandy's pant leg and arm. The drool from Noodle's flews dripped red.

"Good dog." I held out my free hand. "Come." He ran to me. I wrapped my arm around him, then trained the gun on Sandy. "Harlow, come." The Golden moved to my side and licked my face. "Good girl."

Sirens sounded outside. Harlow barked and Noodle began to howl.

I sagged against the wall. "Good dogs."

CHAPTER 24

I managed to keep my gun hand and gaze firm. At least until the police burst in. As the uniforms swarmed, I set the gun beside me on the floor and finally let my heavy lids close. A hand gripped my shoulder and shook. I opened my eyes again. A blurry uniformed officer crouched in front of me. Mustard clung to his walrus-like mustache. Officer Lang?

"Are you injured?"

I understood the words, but my tongue wasn't cooperating with my brain.

He yelled over his shoulder. "Need a paramedic." Then he turned back to me. "Help's here. What happened?"

Slowly, I put one word after another. "Sandy attacked me. He killed his wife. Jessica. Killed Seville. Killed Celia, too." My head kept getting heavier. I couldn't hold it up any longer. Slumping forward, the world went dark.

A bright light pierced my brain. "Wha—?" I couldn't move my legs. Or arms. The back of my head hurt. So did my chin.

And tongue. What had happened? Images flickered. Sandy Johannson showing up with the wine. I'd been drugged. Right. And when I ran for the door, he hit me from behind with the bottle.

"There she is." A man with a broad forehead and receding hairline bent over me. "Welcome back. We're taking you to the hospital."

I lifted my aching head. I was in the great room, strapped to a gurney. My mouth tasted like dirty pennies. Right. I'd bit my tongue hard enough to make it bleed. "Why?"

"You were unconscious. You may have a concussion."

"Just like Duchess."

"What?"

I shook my head. Mistake. Nausea roiled my stomach. I clamped my lips shut and waited for the sensation to fade. "Think I passed out from the drugs."

"What drugs?"

"Don't know. Sandy slipped something into my drink. Maybe the Xanax or Ativan he stole."

"All the more reason to get you to the hospital." They rolled me out the front door.

"What about my dogs?"

"It's okay, Molly. I'm here." A messy blonde head appeared over the paramedic's shoulder.

"J. D."

"I'll look after them until you get back."

"Thanks."

The siren reverberated inside the ambulance. The ache in my head shifted into high gear. Fortunately, the ride didn't last long. The paramedics jostled me and the gurney out. My head throbbed and I was grateful they'd strapped me in. They wheeled me through the emergency entrance. I closed my eyes against the harsh overhead light.

Someone opened my right eye. Dressed in baby blue scrubs, he shone a piercing light into my brain, then repeated the process with my left. The strong smell of rubbing alcohol and ammonia made me tear up. He wrote something on a chart and left it on top of my stomach. I went to lift it up and realized I was still strapped in.

The next time I opened my eyes I was being rolled into a noisy alcove. Wordlessly, the attendant parked me and strode away. I nodded off again.

An icy hand touched my arm. "There you are. I'm going to draw some blood now. Find out what you were given."

"Okay." My voice sounded like I'd run a cheese grater over my vocal cords.

The woman swabbed the inside of my elbow. "Can you make a fist for me?"

"Uh-huh." The rubber tourniquet around my bicep was more uncomfortable than the needle's pinch.

She removed the band and swiftly filled two vials with my blood. Applying a cotton ball and covering it with a bandage, she gave a tight smile. "All done."

The vibration of the gurney's wheels woke me. An orderly bumped my gurney along the hall. "What time is it?"

"Time for your X-rays." He rolled me into Radiology, where a petite redhead in pastel scrubs took over. Once they were done taking pictures of my aching head, I was trundled into a curtained cubicle. I still had no idea what time it was, but the urge to sleep was fading. The drugs must be wearing off. I stared at the ceiling. When that grew boring, I risked turning my head. No dizziness. That had to be a good sign.

A hand parted the pale green curtains surrounding me, followed by Detective Vasquez's head. "You're awake."

"Yep. Sore but conscious."

"Okay if I come in?" For a change, he waited for permission.

"Sure."

He approached the right side of the gurney, looking like he'd come straight from working in the yard: grass-stained jeans, faded T-shirt, and a day's growth of beard. He tucked his hands into his front pockets. "No chairs, huh? Guess they don't really want visitors in this area."

"You're visiting? Not questioning?"

He shrugged. "Doing a little of both. Good work back at your house. If you were still on the job, the Johannson collar would be yours. Smart move putting your phone where dispatch could hear everything. They got a recording of Johannson confessing to Celia Danvers' murder."

"That's a relief."

"My partner's working on getting a search warrant for his home. Based on you telling the responding officer the severed hand belonged to Johannson's wife."

"I did?"

"You don't remember?"

Was Vasquez pushing the envelope to suit the investigation's needs, or had I said that? "I remember Sandy admitting it, but not telling you guys. But the last couple hours are fuzzy. What time is it anyway?"

Vasquez check his phone. "Eight-thirty."

"And Sandy came by around five. Wow."

"Yeah, your noggin took a wallop. Anyway, now that we know Johannson killed his wife, I expect finding a print to match the remaining fingertip on the hand will be a snap."

I raised my eyebrows. Oooh. The muscles in my face were working again. "A snap? Is that the best choice of words when talking about a severed hand?"

He grimaced. "Good point. What I mean is, Johannson couldn't have wiped down everything his wife ever touched. We'll find a print somewhere. The guy's going down."

A harassed-looking nurse bustled in and checked my vitals. After scribbling onto the chart, he gave a curt nod and left.

I stared at the detective. As friendly as Vasquez seemed now, he'd only pushed back lightly when his partner accused me of murder. "I can't help but wonder about my future."

"I know your doctor. She says you're going to be fine."

The back of my head still ached. I resisted the urge to shake it. "No. I mean here in Pier Point."

"Why?" His brown eyes looked concerned.

"I lived in Massachusetts thirty-seven years before I was suspected of murdering anyone. I beat that record in California by thirty-six years and fifty weeks."

"Yeah, but we got the guy."

"They got the guy in Massachusetts, too. The doubts about me there are still lingering."

"But that's back east. Things are different here." He spread his hands wide. "It's not that we don't believe in history, we just don't let it define our futures. You'll be fine."

"So, all of Detective Wright's theories and suspicions are going to blow away like the fog?"

"Can't speak for him, but mine are gone. And everyone I've talked to in the department thinks you're a bona fide badass. Scout's honor."

"I guess that's a start. Oh!"

"What?" Vasquez lightly touched my arm. "Need a nurse?"

"No. I just remembered something. You should talk to Ava."

"The whiz kid from your block?"

"Yep. She told me it was Sandy's wife who left one of my dog-wrangling flyers on her porch."

"Your dog . . ." He cocked his head. "What?"

"The flyers Seville made—and handed out—without telling me."

He continued to look perplexed.

"About me being a dog trainer. The thing is, Jessica Johannson couldn't have left that flyer for Ava. She was already dead. Days before Seville made the flyers."

"I'll talk to the girl."

"Good. It was probably Seville who left it. Ava saw a woman leaving Sandy's place late at night and thought it was his wife. But it had to be Seville."

"Because she was having an affair with Johannson."

"Right."

His phone vibrated. He checked the screen and smiled. "I've got to take this." To my surprise, he didn't move out of earshot. "Hi. Whoa, take a breath. She's doing great. No. She's— Uh-huh. Uh-huh." He held out the phone. "Feel up to talking to my sister?"

"Sure." I took his cell. It was warm from his hand. "Hi, Lupe."

"You're really all right?" Her voice was loud and shaky.

"Yep. Bloody but not beaten. Oh. I guess I was kind of beaten. But I got in the first hit. So I think I can still say that."

Vasquez took the phone from my hand. "I think you're confusing instead of reassuring my sister." He lowered his voice and spoke into the phone. "No. She's okay. Really. Bruised and rattled, but she's going to be fine. All right. Okay. I promise. Talk to you later." He tucked the cell into his pocket. "According to my sister, she's holding me responsible for your full recovery."

"Does that mean I can go home now?"

After another two hours where I alternated between sleep and staring at the ceiling, the hospital finally released me. I told the orderly I could walk. He smiled but put me in a wheelchair anyway and trundled me out the front door. Vasquez stood on the concrete apron under the starless sky.

I thanked the orderly and stood. My leg muscles felt alarmingly spongy. "This is a surprise."

"Figured you'd need a ride home." He led the way to an unmarked sedan in the No Parking Zone. "It's the least I can do for our local hero."

"Thanks." He helped me into the car. I'd never been so grateful for an arm to lean on. I pulled the shoulder belt across and strapped in as he walked around the car and climbed in. When he pulled out of the lot, I was surprised by the amount of traffic. Resting my head against the seat, I stared at the streetlights blurring by. I closed my eyes.

"We're here." Vasquez gently shook my arm.

I gazed out the windshield. We were in my driveway. I'd slept through the short ride. The detective looked worried. I couldn't remember what I'd already told him about my injuries. "The doctor said I might be dozy and a bit fuzzy for the next few hours. From the drugs and a mild concussion. But no fractured skull. So that's something."

Vasquez rounded the car and helped me from the passenger seat.

"Thanks." The simple act of standing tired me out. I leaned

against the car and looked at the place I now called home. "I hope the dogs didn't give J. D. a hard time."

"Got to say, I'm impressed the party boy came through for you."

"Party boy?"

"My sister's told me the stories." Vasquez guided me to the front door and tried the knob. "Locked."

"A party boy never locks the front door. Pretty sure that's part of their code. I think J. D.'s an ex–party boy now."

Vasquez raised his eyebrows, but it felt like too much work to explain.

The door swung open. A flurry of fur and paws barreled past J. D. Before I could react, Vasquez crouched between me and the dogs.

"Hi there. Yes, she's happy to see you, too. But you need to calm down. You don't want to knock her over."

Though Vasquez hadn't given an actual command, the dogs settled.

I appreciated the assist but didn't say so. The dogs were the ones who needed reassurance. I bent down and kissed each in turn. "Thank you, thank you, thank you. You two were amazing. Such good dogs. Yes." Noodle licked my face until drool ran down my neck. "Guess you're really part of the family now, big guy. Is that okay with you?" Harlow joined in on the lick-fest. I laughed. "You guys are the best." When I straightened, J. D. handed me a towel.

"I've been using this to keep the big one's drool under control."

"Thanks. And thanks for stepping in to look after them. They seem fine. Like what happened earlier didn't faze them."

"They're just happy you're home. Both of them were doing a lot of whining and pacing while you were gone."

"Then I'm extra-grateful you were here."

"No problem. I saw you had wet and dry food, so I gave them a mix of both for dinner."

"Perfect."

J. D. squeezed my hand and grinned. "You take care now." He nodded at Vasquez, then left.

"Let's get you settled in." He touched my shoulder. "You want to be on the sofa or would you rather go up to your room?"

I looked at the staircase. Way too much work. "Think I'll stay down here for now."

Vasquez guided me to the sofa, then went to the kitchen. Glass clinked, followed by the sound of running water. My head hurt too much to turn and see what he was doing.

"Here. In case you get thirsty."

I hadn't heard him return.

He put a tumbler of water on one of the two coasters I'd brought to the table hours earlier for wine with Sandy.

A shudder ran through me.

"You okay?"

"I'm going to have some flashbacks and bad memories for a while. But I'll get through it."

Vasquez sat on the opposite end of the sofa. "I'd like to help you do that."

"Don't you need to get back to work? Big case and all that?"

"Wright can handle it. I'm fine staying here and helping you feel safe. If that's okay with you."

"It is." I curled my legs under me. Harlow jumped up, circled, and then rested her head on my thigh. I stroked her silky coat. The Saint Berdoodle lumbered over and sat in front of me. I looked at Vasquez. "I'm lucky Noodle was here."

"Got to say, I don't think it was luck. You spent more time

caring for that dog than Johannson ever did. Why else do you think Noodle defended you against him?"

We talked a bit about the horror show with Johannson and what Vasquez expected would happen next. Somewhere during our conversation, I nodded off. When I woke, sunlight streamed through my bedroom window. Right. I needed to follow up with Windows, Etc., and see when they could finish installing my shades.

Wait. The last thing I remembered was sitting on the sofa with Vasquez. After a surge of panic, I realized my shoes were off, but other than that, I was fully dressed. Interesting that sex with the detective was where my mind went first.

The sun was much higher in the sky than when I usually woke. Gingerly propping myself on my elbows, I saw Harlow and Noodle weren't in the room. Probably part of the reason why I'd slept late. Though my head was still sore, the throbbing had stopped and my vision was clear. After a hot shower, I dressed in clean clothes and ventured downstairs. The smell of coffee and buttered toast wafted from the kitchen like an irresistible invitation.

Vasquez must've had a change of clothes in his car. Dressed in jeans, an aloha shirt, and running shoes, he sat on the sofa reading an article on his phone. A plate with breadcrumbs sat on the table next to a mug of coffee. Harlow's head was in his lap and Noodle lay at his feet. The detective looked up and grinned. The thickening stubble shadowing his strong jaw looked good. "There's fresh coffee in the pot and the dogs have been fed. I opened a couple cans of that turkey stew for them. Hope that's okay."

"Perfect. Thank you."

He gave a modest shrug.

After filling a mug and taking a sip, I saw my cell still sitting on the counter. I checked the time. I'd missed taking Harlow to agility class. Oh well, there was always next week. I planned to make Pier Point my home for a good long time. I joined Vasquez on the sofa. Noodle rose and stretched, then padded over to me. I leaned down and rubbed the Saint Berdoodle's mocha-toned ears. The Golden opened her eyes but didn't move. "Looks like you've got yourself a friend."

"I'm hoping I've got a human friend here, too."

"You do."

ACKNOWLEDGMENTS

A huge thank-you to my agent, Melissa Jeglinski, for her encouragement and for seeing the potential in this series. Another big thank-you to my wonderful editor, Kristine Swartz, for believing in Molly and her world, and for asking the tough questions that made the story stronger. Thanks also to the amazing team at Berkley, who helped make each page shine.

Special thanks go out to my good friend Nancy Withrow, who introduced me to the world of agility training, helped me better understand dog training in general, and walked me through the ins and outs of competition. Any mistakes on this topic are my own!

A big thank-you to Wrona Gall for reading and providing feedback for this novel—in all its iterations. Her keen eye and insights helped ground the story. Big thanks also go out to the Sunday Morning Writers—a warmhearted, talented, and perceptive group—who read my ramblings over the years and helped me hone my writing: Ann Brady, Kathleen Coatta, Barry Falck, Sue Falck, Anne Riffenburgh, and Howard Rosenberg.

Keep reading for a sneak peek
at the next Peggy Rothschild mystery

PLAYING DEAD

Harlow hung her head out the back seat window, golden ears flapping and tongue lolling. The Saint Berdoodle nudged his way into the opening behind her. Drool broke free from the big dog's flews. Though I loved Noodle, three months living with him hadn't yet numbed me to his faucet-like slobbering. Hoping the stream of saliva hadn't hit anyone, I signaled and turned the 4Runner onto a two-lane, following the instructions provided by my GPS.

Ten minutes later, I turned onto another narrow road. A sturdy windbreak rose on my right along with a string of phone poles. To my left, avocado groves alternated with orange trees. The air smelled of eucalyptus, citrus, and hay. I noticed a flyer was stapled to each phone pole I passed. Slowing, I read the posted message: "$1,000 Reward for Information on Our Missing Golden, Freddy." Below the words, a photo of a smiling retriever along with a phone number. The flyer's edges were curled, and the picture looked sun-bleached. How long had

Freddy been missing? Or had he come home and no one bothered to pull down the flyers? Hoping it was answer number two,
I sped up again.

Near the road's end, the GPS voice said to turn right. I
bumped onto the single dirt lane. Dust swirled around us, and
I tapped the brake. "Heads back inside, guys." I powered up the
windows and turned on the AC. Another half mile along the
driveway, Noodle began to bark.

"Can you smell the other dogs already?" This would be our
first time at Playtime Academy for Dogs' training facility. Mem-
bers of my Tuesday agility class swore by this place and its staff.
In addition to agility, they had scent work classes, rally, and
barn hunt. Only Harlow did agility, but I was eager for Noodle
to take part in his first barn hunt. Everything I read assured me
the rats were kept safe. An animal-loving vegan in my agility
class swore the rats looked like they were having a good time.
Who was I to argue with that sort of testimony?

Noodle was a gentle giant. But having adopted him from a
sociopath, I often worried how he'd interact with others. I'd
spent the last three months introducing him to new people,
animals, and experiences. So far, the Saint Berdoodle had done
great.

I guided the 4Runner around a pothole. The slope turned
steep. Slowing, I continued up the winding incline through the
tawny, rolling hills. Though the day was warm, friends assured
me it would feel like fall soon. I missed the autumn leaves of
Massachusetts, but doubted I'd miss the snow and ice when
winter rolled around.

A metal sign arching over the drive—and the GPS voice—
told me I'd reached my destination. I pulled into the gravel
parking lot on the right. About a dozen vehicles were already

there. I chose a spot a few feet from a large SUV with an "I Heart Boxers" bumper sticker. When I cut the engine, Harlow woofed. "That's right, girl, we're here."

I reopened the windows and climbed out. It was at least ten degrees warmer here than on the coast. I pulled off my hoodie and told the dogs to stay. A group of about twenty people were gathered near a fenced field. Beyond that sat a second grassy enclosure plus two sizable dirt arenas. Wow. The arenas even had lights for night classes. Though I'd assumed the name "barn hunt" was figurative, there was also a big red barn.

The closest grass field was set up for standard agility competition practice, the unoccupied field beyond it for jumpers. An angular woman dressed in a khaki shirt dress and running shoes stood inside the first field, her Akita already off leash. Instead of being dialed in on her person, the dog looked bored. An Akita on the course meant I'd timed my arrival well; the small dogs had already run. A cowboy-looking guy clutching a clipboard approached the woman, but they were too far away for me to overhear any pointers.

Instead of checking in, I walked to the field and leaned against the railing. I scanned my surroundings while waiting for their run to begin. The buildings looked freshly painted, and even from here, I could see that the agility equipment was rubberized. Playtime obviously ran a quality operation. Movement pulled my attention back to the ring as the woman took off.

Arriving late had its downside. Though I'd spend less time waiting, I'd missed the course walk-through. I watched the woman and her Akita carefully. Tight right after the first jump, already heading to the tunnel. Straight run to the third obstacle. A sharp left to jump number one in the reverse direction followed by a softer turn toward the next jump. Then, the elevated dog walk and a quick reverse for the second tunnel. Straight run to the tire jump. After the A-frame, the course became less complicated. The Akita narrowly cleared the long jump and trotted to the finish. She and her handler completed a flawless, if moderately paced, run. The cowboy approached and spoke with her again. He placed a hand on her shoulder before she departed the ring, head down.

An auburn-haired woman entered along with a fawn-colored boxer. I wondered if hers was the SUV with the bumper sticker. She had a brief exchange with the cowboy before beginning her run. The boxer soared through the course looking joyful. Much faster than the previous pair and another fault-free run.

Watching was fun, but my dogs needed to stretch their legs. I spied the crating area on the far side of the parking lot and hurried back to my vehicle. Leaving the dogs in the back seat a moment longer, I loaded their supplies onto my cart and rolled everything to an empty patch. I assembled the crates and draped a tarp over each to shade them from the sun. Returning to the 4Runner, I opened the rear door. Harlow pranced with excitement while Noodle drooled onto the beach towel protecting the back seat.

I hooked on leashes and let them explore the area on the way to their crates. Once there, I pulled the water bottle from my knapsack and filled their bowls. When they'd lapped enough, we wandered to a small group of live oaks and the dogs decided which ones were worthy of their use. "All set?" They wagged their tails. "Okay then."

After urging each into their crate, I walked to the check-in table located under a blue pop-up canopy. I smiled at the stunning woman staffing the table. "Hi. Checking in."

She looked up. Her dark hair was gathered into a big puff,

and the orange company polo gave her skin a warm glow. "Name?"

"Molly Madison."

She ran her finger down a printout. "You're here with a golden retriever?"

"Yep."

"You'll be up after the standard poodle."

"Thanks. I also brought along my Saint Berdoodle for the barn hunt later today. Speed isn't his strong suit, but he's got an amazing nose."

She flashed her dimples. "See, this is how people should be. Recognize their dog's strengths and lean into them. Way too many folks can't seem to see that." Holding out her hand, she said, "Simone Beaulieu. I teach scent work."

We shook. "Nice to meet you."

"You know, barn hunt courses are designed with eighteen-by nineteen-inch tunnels. A couple of our tunnels are thirty-six by eighteen. Will your dog be able to fit?"

"Yep. He squeezes through Harlow's agility tunnel just fine."

"Perfect. If he's got a good nose, you might also want to bring him to a scent class. We have one later in the week."

"I'll think about it."

"Saint Berdoodle, you say?"

"Yep."

"Smart to get a dog like that into nose work. The combination of those breeds . . . Have you done any nose work with him?"

"Yep. Haven't been able to fool him yet."

"For classes here, we work with the usual four target odors: birch, anise, clove, and cypress."

"I've just been hiding treats."

"That's a good start. Looking forward to seeing you later at barn hunt, Molly Madison."

"Me, too." I returned to the agility ring. Another woman stood inside. Short and stocky, she wore capri pants and a shirt that matched the black and mahogany colors of the Rottweiler by her side. She unleashed the dog and spoke to the trainer. After a moment, she gave an emphatic nod and moved into position in front of her dog. When the cowboy signaled her, the woman started running. The Rotty took the first half of the course in stride but missed the final contact point on the A-frame. Instant five-point penalty. But the handler held it together, and the rest of the course went smoothly. Releashing her dog, the woman had another word with the trainer before exiting the ring.

Didn't any men take agility here?

An anxious-looking bottle blonde entered with a German shepherd. A brief conversation with the cowboy followed, then she got into position. It looked like she was talking to herself.

Almost as soon as she began, things went haywire. She miscued the dog on the way to the first jump. The shepherd hesitated, looking for guidance. Turning, the blonde urged him forward and he made it over. She darted toward the tunnel, and the dog plunged through like an otter in water. He soared over the next obstacle. An audible groan rippled through the crowd when she ran the dog the wrong way. Figuring it out before her shepherd back-jumped, she corrected their course. Obviously frazzled, she lost control of the dog at the following jump. She circled around to get him over it in the correct direction. After that she completely fell apart. When her dog balked at the see-saw, the woman froze and covered her face.

Yikes.

"Yeah, Ashlee's a train wreck on the course." The auburn-haired woman who had run the boxer joined me at the fence with her dog. "Don't get me wrong, Siegfried can do the work. And Ashlee's athletic and smart. But when a run is timed, she falls apart. Maybe it's a throwback to some sort of testing anxiety, but she absolutely loses it." The woman puffed out her cheeks, took a deep breath, then crouched to stroke her dog's fawn coat. "But not you. You did great. Yes, you did. You're such a good boy. Yes, you are."

Straightening, she tossed her long braid over her shoulder. The dog sat on his haunches, tail swishing an arc in the dirt, gaze on his person. "I haven't seen you here before. First time?"

"Yep. I've heard a lot of good things."

She looked back at the crating area. "The Saint Berdoodle here for barn hunt?"

"Yep. He has a great nose. I only adopted him three months ago, but he's shown real promise."

"And I'm guessing the Golden does agility?"

"You got it."

"Terrific."

Her dismayed tone surprised me.

"Sorry. I'm in a mood. Another large dog running agility won't help me advance." Grimacing, she gestured at the field. "You see my run?"

"Yep."

"Forty-five point six seconds. Royal did great. And I ran my ass off on the home stretch, but I can't seem to get under forty-five. To get to nationals, I need to get down to at least forty. Royal's good enough to win. He deserves to. I can't figure out what's holding us back."

"That why you're here today?"

"Ben's a great trainer."

"The guy in the cowboy gear?"

"That's him."

"And you want to cut five to six seconds off your time?"

She raised an eyebrow. "Why? Think it's impossible?"

"Not from what I saw."

"What? You think you can help?"

"I don't know about six seconds, but I saw how you can cut two or three."

"Three seconds?"

"Yep."

"How? Wait." She held out her hand. "I'm Felicity Gaines. And, of course, this is Royal."

"Molly Madison." We shook, then I held my hand out to her dog. The boxer sniffed and continued wagging his tail. "Don't see many boxers doing agility."

"Well, if you go to county meets, you'll see at least see two of them."

"You have another dog?" I scanned the area.

"Nah. Celeste liked Royal so much, she got a boxer of her own. She's been doing agility two years less than I have and getting better times. Pisses me off."

"I'll bet." I didn't recall seeing any boxers at the local trials I'd attended. "What's Celeste's last name?"

"Simmons."

"Never met her."

"Lucky you. What makes it worse is I'm the one who suggested she try agility. I was new to the neighborhood and ran into her while walking Royal. She told me she owned a couple gyms but was looking for something to do in her spare time. If I'd only known what she was like, I never would've suggested agility. Now she's got plenty to do. Of course, she still has no friends. But that's on her."

Finished with her rant, Felicity took a deep breath. "So how can you get me three seconds?"

"Two or three. It's your hair."

"My hair?" She fingered her braid.

"Not that. The loose hairs around your face."

Felicity ran her palm from her forehead to her plait. "What about it?"

I put my left hand up to my temple, then stroked it back. "Twice during your run, you touched your hair like this. With the hand you weren't using to guide Royal. It distracted him. Just a bit, but I'd say it added up to a two- or three-second delay over the course of your run."

"No. When?"

"First time was when you were heading away from the see-saw. The dog didn't go for full speed until you brought your hand down. Lost at least a second there."

"And?"

"During the run to the final tunnel. When your back was to him—same thing. You seem to do it when you break eye contact with him."

"Crap. Why hasn't anyone told me this before?"

"You come here a lot?"

"Yeah. Why?" Her brow furrowed.

I shrugged. "They know you. They probably don't see it. Like a tic they've grown used to. It stood out to me because I've never watched you run a course before. You're doing it now."

"Sweet fancy Moses." She tucked her left hand inside her front pocket. "How do I stop if I don't know I'm doing it?"

"Maybe wear a hairband? It'll feel different and hold your

hair in place. Or wrap masking tape around your hand? Something like that might call enough attention to itself to keep you from unconsciously doing it."

"Worth a shot. I think I'll wear one of Royal's bandannas during my next run. I should have a few extra in the car." Her jaw dropped open and she froze. "What's she doing here?"

I followed her gaze to a petite woman sporting a white-blond bob with one side of her head shaved down to stubble. Dressed in designer jeans and a black tee bedazzled with rhinestones spelling out the letters "KIP," she looked all bone and muscle. She led a brindle boxer from the crating area. The dog probably weighed only twenty-five pounds less than she did. "Is that Celeste?"

"Yeah, and she's supposed to be in Hawaii. For two weeks. Told me she'd miss the next regional competition."

"Giving you and Royal a leg up in your category?"

"God, I'm transparent, but yes."

The blonde spied Felicity, gave a finger wave, and headed our way. When she drew near, she said, "I was hoping I'd run into you here." Her boxer lunged toward Royal. Felicity pulled her dog back. Not to be completely thwarted, the blonde's boxer lodged his nose in my crotch. The woman did nothing.

Bad manners all the way around. I nudged the dog back. "Off."

Felicity moved Royal behind her. "I thought you'd be on your way to paradise by now—or at least packing."

"I couldn't let Buster miss the upcoming meet." Celeste gave a smile that was all teeth, no heart.

"You canceled your anniversary trip?"

"No. I convinced Del that joining him at the resort a couple days late would be good for him. My husband will get time to watch all the sports he can stand, and I'll get a chance for Buster to win and earn us an invitation to the championships."

"How? The entries are closed." Felicity looked at me. "I checked for a friend."

Even though I'd just met her, I was sure Felicity was lying. If she'd checked, it wasn't for a friend.

Celeste gave a carefree flutter of her hand. "Oh, I entered over a month ago. Just in case." She bent to adjust Buster's harness, then stepped closer to Felicity. "Even Del couldn't say no when I told him how that blue ribbon was calling me. And Buster's been running like a god lately. It'd be a shame to deny him another win." She gave one more toothy smile and touched Felicity's forearm. "I'm sure the red ribbon will look good with all the others you've won." She turned and strode to the agility field.

Felicity glared after her.

"Wow. She's . . ."

"A bitch. A bitch who's only been doing agility for a year." Felicity huffed out a noisy breath. "Like everyone else, she made lots of mistakes at first. Spent maybe six months coming to meets and NQ-ing. Finally, she got frustrated and told me she was taking a month off to bond with Buster. Sounded strange to me. She and Buster should've already bonded by then. What the dog needed was more training. But when Celeste came back, she couldn't lose. It was like some sort of magical transformation. It still pisses me off."

"She looks athletic. I'm guessing she and her dog run well together."

"Sort of. She still makes a lot of errors, but the dog does the right thing anyway."

"If she's doing well, why's she so . . . snippy?"

"I think she's using agility to make up for her Olympic dreams crashing and burning."

"What do you mean?"

"She was a gymnastics champion in her teens. Blew out her knee, rehabbed, but was never as good. Several years back, she started a gymnastics program for girls—SimNastics. Huge success. She was able to open her own gym—first one, then another. Completely stopped offering her classes through other fitness centers. I'm not sure how many gyms she owns now. But however many it is, it's not enough for her. The woman still needs more victories. Don't get me wrong, I hear she's got an amazing work ethic and inspires the athletes she trains. People in the gymnastics community respect her. But the agility crowd? I don't know a single person who actually likes her."

"I can see why."

A man in a tank top, showing off bony shoulders and several tattoos, approached the ring leading a standard poodle. Apparently at least one guy trained here. But the poodle's arrival meant my turn was coming up. I excused myself and collected Harlow from the crating area. By the time we returned, the poodle was halfway through the course. He flew over the long jump and the last two hurdles. Then he balked at the panel jump. The audience groaned. Tank top man circled back to try again. Success. After a brief consultation with the cowboy, they left the ring.

When we entered, the familiar thrum of excitement ran through me. "You ready, girl?"

Harlow settled onto the ground, eyes focused on me. I unhooked her leash and tossed it aside. While we waited for the trainer's okay, I reviewed the course. Once the cowboy nodded, I took a deep breath and locked eyes with Harlow. We took off.

The Golden flew over the first jump and we raced to the tunnel. She shot inside. Then she launched and landed the next three jumps perfectly. Tight turns, good speed. Next up: the weave poles. Harlow attacked them, smiling all the way. Another tight turn for the second tunnel, then she sailed through the tire like a dart. When she hit the contact point on the A-frame, I knew we had this. My heart soared as we ran the remaining obstacles.

The trainer walked over to me as I played tug-of-war with Harlow at the finish. Her favorite reward.

"Great run. Your first time here, but not your first on a course."

"No."

"Great dog, too."

"Yep. Harlow's amazing. Aren't you, girl?" The Golden wagged her agreement.

"So what are you hoping to get out of this today?"

I let Harlow win our battle and straightened. "I wanted to see how she performs in a new place. Around new people and dogs. And pick up any pointers I can."

The cowboy nodded. "Your footwork is good. So is your anticipation and planning for the obstacles. But"—he held up his index finger—"if you arrive before we start and walk the course, I'm betting you could shave another two seconds off your time."

"Thanks." I hooked on Harlow's leash and led her from the ring.

Felicity and Royal were waiting for us. "Nice run."

"Thanks."

"We're going in for our second run in about five minutes."

"Great. Let me take care of Harlow, then I'll come back and watch."

When I returned to the railing, a deep frown marred Felicity's face. I followed her gaze. Inside the arena, Celeste and Buster were crossing the finish line. Before talking to the trainer, Celeste made a point of smiling and waving at Felicity.

Felicity peeked at the timer on her phone. "Thirty-nine seconds."

"Wow."

"Bitch loves to rub it in." She rolled her shoulders. "Not my problem, right? Karma's going to get her someday. The only thing I can control is myself. And hopefully Royal."

After losing their home during a California wildfire, Peggy Rothschild and her husband moved to the beach community of Los Osos along the central coast. When not at her desk or out walking, you can usually find her in the garden.

Peggy is a member of Sisters in Crime National and Sisters in Crime Los Angeles. *A Deadly Bone to Pick* is her first cozy mystery.

CONNECT ONLINE

PeggyRothschildAuthor.com

📷 PeggyRothschild6

🐦 PegRothschild

Ready to find
your next great read?

Let us help.

Visit prh.com/nextread